Blood, Sweat and Cheers

A Madman's Rise to Fame in Professional Wrestling

Charlotte Mijares

Writers Club Press
San Jose New York Lincoln Shanghai

Blood, Sweat and Cheers
A Madman's Rise to Fame in Professional Wrestling

All Rights Reserved © 1999, 2000 by Charlotte Mijares

No part of this book may be reproduced or transmitted in any form or by any means, graphic, electronic, or mechanical, including photocopying, recording, taping, or by any information storage or retrieval system, without the permission in writing from the publisher.

Published by Writers Club Press
an imprint of iUniverse.com, Inc.

For information address:
iUniverse.com, Inc.
620 North 48th Street
Suite 201
Lincoln, NE 68504-3467
www.iuniverse.com

This book is a work of fiction, and any similarity between person, place or things is purely coincidental

ISBN: 0-595-09808-8

Printed in the United States of America

*To the real Omar Atlas who taught the real
Nancy the meaning of real love.*

Foreword

Keith Daniels got what he wanted. If not, somebody paid. His father Max owned Wild West Wrestling, one of the largest wrestling promotions in America, and ever since Keith could remember, his bible-thumping, womanizing father had bought him out of any trouble he could come up with. And he would see to it that Keith got what he wanted this time. Small and out of shape, Keith was determined to be the World Heavyweight Champion no matter what the price.

When Omar Atlas, the Venezuelan hero came on the scene, Keith knew instinctively that his future as champion was at risk. When his father made Omar the Texas Heavyweight Champion, Keith planned his ruthless, perverted revenge.

Toni, Omar's beautiful, twenty-year old sister arrived from Caracas, full of hope for a bright future in America. Immediately, Keith began his slow seduction of the naive girl. Their wedding took place in the middle of the wrestling ring in Corpus Christi, Texas. In marrying Keith, Toni, for the first time in her life, openly defied Omar, and she lived to regret it.

After the wedding, Omar left Texas in despair at his sister's future with the ruthless Keith. In Chicago, he joined the Hemisphere Championship Promotion where he quickly climbed the ladder to become the Heavyweight Champion. Each step up the ladder of success for Omar meant more torture for Toni. Keith delighted in "punishing" her for her brother's fame. When Keith heard of Omar's championship status, he went too far. In one of his many "punishment sessions" with Tony, he lost control and killed her in the most heinous way imaginable. As usual, Max moved in and cleaned up after his son; the police looked the other way and Keith continued on his quest for world championship.

One thing he hadn't counted on. Facing Omar in the ring. Omar knew. And Keith knew he knew. And he had reason to be deathly afraid. Omar planned to kill Keith in the ring, and he would do it in plain sight of 60,000 fans.

Madison Square Garden would never forget this night.

Acknowledgments

Thanks to Scott Teal, editor of Whatever Happened to ..whtreslr1@aol.com for the cover shot and thanks to Pearl Horace for her reading ability and her vote of confidence.

1

Both bodies were bathed in sweat. You could smell it in the air. They were gasping, trying hard to breathe after thirty minutes of thrashing and rolling. Keith was on top with his opponent's arms held down tightly, his head drooping, and sweat was running into his eyes.

Hell, this was better than all the wrestling lessons he had learned, blood he had shed, and hours spent learning his craft. The climax of victory was sweet. The tired, brown eyes stared up at him, glowing.

"You were great," she said.

"Yeah," he snickered, "You have just been fucked by the future heavy-weight champion of the world."

With no other words of endearment or tenderness, he rolled off her damp body and fell heavily down beside her. His job was done. It was already off his mind. There were plenty more just like her. Nameless, faceless, empty-headed "arena rats" just waiting to be used, abused and discarded. *What the hell was this one's name, anyhow?* How could he get her out of his room fast?

"Could I come to the matches with you tonight, honey?"

"Yeah, yeah, we'll see," he answered, knowing full well that he would never see her again. "Get going now though. I gotta' get cleaned up and over to the office. My old man can't do a damn thing without me."

"Sure, baby." The disheveled young girl was hurriedly dressing so that she could get out of there as she had been told to do. Keith's reputation for temper tantrums and beating women was well known.

"See you tonight at the back gate." The door shut.

Dumb bitch. Like I need her! Let her buy a ticket like the rest of them.

* * *

In the shower, the hot water coursed over Keith's body, washing away her cheap perfume and this afternoon's passion. He leaned back, face up, and hands on hips in his favorite stance.

Why are they all alike? Every night was the same. Women from fifteen to fifty lined up to be chosen like whores on a street corner. It was as routine as brushing his teeth, and by now, just as rewarding.

He thought back to his early wrestling years and his first arena rat. It had been time to televise the Wild West Wrestling television show and he was hurrying into the arena when he first noticed her.

Outside the building he saw a long line of female fans waiting, hoping to be noticed. She was standing quietly, not screaming like the rest and as he passed he gave her one of his long, practiced, sexy looks.

She smiled back, and abruptly he stopped and spoke.

"Hi. How are you?" he asked

"Fine." She giggled. The other girls standing nearby got quiet so they could hear the conversation.

"Would you run and get me a Coke?" he asked, "And bring it to the back door?"

"Why sure, Keith." She eagerly replied.

Two of her friends started off with her. They wanted to be a part of this, even from a distance. They hurried so the Coke would still be cold when they returned. Nothing was too much trouble for their hero.

The girls knocked on the dressing room door wondering who would open it. Much to their disappointment, it was a security officer.

"What do you want?" they were asked.

"We have Keith's Coke."

"O.K., I'll take it." he replied. No money changed hands; none was expected. He was the wrestler; they were "arena rats".

* * *

Next week she was standing there again, awaiting the honor of going on another "Coke run". This time, however, he pulled her out of her place and walked her to the head of the line.

Before they reached there, he said in a low voice, "You want to go some place tonight?"

She couldn't believe her ears. Keith Daniels had asked her out! She knew it was probably for sex, at best, but that is what she had waited weeks for. To be noticed, and by Keith, the promoter's son.

"Great." She answered. Where do you want to meet?

"Be back here when the matches are over and wait in my car. I'll leave it unlocked. Do you know which one it is?"

Of course she did. They all did. And that's why the wrestlers parked in the security parking by the office. It was common practice for the "heels", the dirty wrestlers' cars to get "keyed" or their tires slashed.

"I'll be there," she said, knowing that Keith would tell Security to let her in.

He smiled and left her and went into the arena. The girls in the front didn't mind Keith putting her first in line. After all, she had been chosen.

* * *

After the matches, Keith and the other wrestlers sat around talking and drinking beer. He made no reference to having anyone waiting for him. No hurry, he knew she would wait.

At 1:30 AM, Keith finally went out to the almost empty parking lot. She was still there, sound asleep in the front seat. She barely moved when he started the engine and backed out.

Much later as they pulled into his driveway, she sat up and looked at his beautiful home.

"Is this where you live?" she asked sleepily.

"Yeah." Without another word, he reached across the seat and pulled her over to him, one hand on his fly and the other hand in her hair. She slid toward him willingly, knowing what he wanted.

*   *   *

He sat there with his head back on the seat, eyes closed, gasping for air. She was looking up at him eagerly, waiting for him to speak.

"O.K., now get going. See you next time."

"But Keith, it's late. Can you take me home?"

"Do I look like a fucking taxi? Get out."

As she got out of the car in total darkness in a strange, unfamiliar part of town, he drove on into the garage and shut the door from inside. She watched from the curb.

"Oh damn!" she said, "I forgot to give him my name."

*   *   *

Yeah, he thought, his mind brought back to the present by the hot water pouring over his body, *arena rats are a special breed*. A few guys even married them, but not many. He knew several of the wrestlers who had come into the territory, latched onto one, lived with her, drove her car, then left her when he moved to a new territory; she was lucky if he didn't leave her pregnant.

Keith couldn't remember when he had actually been excited over being with a woman. In fact, he couldn't even remember when he had liked a woman. To him, sex was a form of attack. His anger and frustrations seemed to always come into being when he was dominating a woman, both in bed and out. As the water washed over his face, he closed his eyes, lost in thoughts of his childhood.

Oh yeah, they're all the same. Screw them a couple of times and they think they own you. And my old lady was no different.

He remembered watching his mother and father as Max Daniels, wrestling star, was packing to leave on another tour.

*   *   *

"I didn't think you were working tonight." Said the tall, lanky blonde woman. "You said you'd stay home."

Standing in the bedroom door, the light shining through her sheer nightgown, Frances was watching as Max packed his wrestling bag.

"Why would I want to stay home, for God's sake?" he answered. "Look at you. It's 4PM and you're still in your nightgown and you're half soused already. You've got four kids to take care of and you need a keeper yourself. I can't even take any matches outside the country because you can't be trusted alone with the kids."

"I know you have someone else!" her voice was rising as she sipped her drink. "No one can understand why I put up with your running around. I could have been a model except for you."

In reality, she was right. Absolutely no one understood the marriage of Max and Frances. He was known as one of the most handsome men in wrestling, while she could be called "plain" at best. Her thin skin was quick to wrinkle, and years later she would force it into an unnatural red color from countless skin peels.

Max's normally even disposition erupted into a violent reaction. "For God's sake, Frances, I've heard this a thousand times before. If you want to be a model, go for it."

"Oh sure," she was screaming now, "You know it's too late. You got me pregnant with Keith and ended my dreams. If it weren't for the two of you, I'd be happy today. God, I wish I were free."

"Go get a life!" Max said, as he slammed shut his bag and stomped past Frances, knocking her into the doorframe and spilling her drink down the front of her nightgown.

Neither noticed the small boy standing in the bedroom door, tears running down his face, as he retreated into the silence of his room.

*   *   *

Was that when he had first begun to hate his mother? He stood still as the shower coursed over his body. He realized that the incident between his parents was his first actual memory. It was the first time that he had felt the guilt; he really didn't know when the hate had begun. He knew that screaming and accusations had become a way of life for the family. He'd heard the words, "knocked up" years before he had any idea of what they'd meant. His brother and sisters had all heard the same words, but somehow everyone knew that the blame lay on him—Keith—the oldest. But for him, Mom and Dad would have been happy. There would have been no fights. He'd stopped his mother's hopes and dreams and she never let him forget it.

*   *   *

Keith started high school at sixteen as one of the smallest boys in the class. At 5'4", 130 pounds, he was twenty pounds lighter than his fifteen-year-old brother Greg, who was still back in middle school. Greg was everything Keith was not. Large boned, athletically inclined, he was coordinated and a coach's dream. He made the football team and played quarterback. Keith barely made second string and spent most of his time on the bench. He begged his father for steroids, but Max's stock answer was always, "Don't worry, you're just a late bloomer."

Keith was determined to gain weight and excel at football. By his junior year he had gained thirty pounds by lifting weights, eating protein powder by the scoopful, and food by the pound. Every morning at

6AM he jogged around the neighborhood where they lived, returned to the house, drank protein powder and milk, ate, and went to school. Every night after school he went to football practice and then went home to work out with Greg. Any night Max was not wrestling, he was with his two boys, lifting weights, jogging, and playing touch football. He even installed a weight room complete with Jacuzzi in the basement the year Keith turned seventeen. He added an Olympic-sized pool in the back yard the next year.

Nothing seemed to work. Sixteen-year-old Greg always surpassed Keith in size and ability. Keith's naturally shorter body refused to muscle up. Greg, on the other hand, developed well-defined "pecs", well cut-up legs, and eighteen-inch biceps. He became the star of his football team while Keith continued to sit on the bench.

On the nights when Greg played, the entire family gathered around, including Max, if he was at home, and they all had a fast dinner, rushed out to the car, and enjoyed the evening out at the game. Keith watched his father's face when Greg made a touchdown or ran fifty yards. Max looked like he would explode with pride. He was also aware that his father was comparing him with his younger brother, and that it wasn't favorable.

God, Greg makes it look so easy. I knock my lights out and can't do anything but warm a bench. I work myself to death for Dad and he doesn't appreciate it. If it's the last thing I do, I'll make a 'go' of wrestling. Then he'll see."

*　　　*　　　*

By the time Keith was a senior in high school, Max was keeping a record of his son's daily workouts. No matter how hard Keith worked, Max demanded more.

One February night Max was at home and he decided to watch Keith's workout for himself. He pulled on 'sweats' and made his way downstairs into the basement gym. Keith was standing in the center of the large, carpeted room. Around him were expensive exercise machines, free weights and weight benches. All of the walls were paneled in mirror, and one wall slid back on rollers to reveal a steam room and sauna. The wet bar in the corner was equipped with every kind of fruit juice available, vitamins, and protein powder.

Max stood still at the foot of the stairs. He knew that Keith hadn't heard him coming down. He watched fascinated as Keith walked over to the free weights, selected two one hundred-pound weights and attached them to the barbells.

Still unaware that he was being watched, Keith stood behind the barbells, flexed his fingers, bent his knees, and squatted down, prepared to lift. He wrapped his fingers around the bar, planted his feet firmly, and in one move, quickly lifted the barbell to his chest.

From his vantagepoint, Max strained against his own muscles as he watched, giving his son encouragement under his breath.

Get under it, he thought. Get under it.

But Keith couldn't balance the weight, reposition his hands, and step backwards for balance. Instead, he leaned forward and dropped the weights to the floor.

Suddenly, Max came running into the room.

"My God, man, you're only pressing two hundred pounds", Max screamed. "Greg has been doing 250 pounds for six months now and he's younger than you. Are you a man or a wimp? By God, I can't do anything about your height, but I'm going to build you up if it kills me!"

"It probably will kill me," said Keith, as he hung his head in embarrassment and humiliation. Quickly he recovered, raised his head, and Max could see open frustration on his son's face.

"This is so stupid. I'm working my ass off every day and not bulking up. You told me you'd start me wrestling as soon as I'm out of college. I need to start learning now. If you'd get me some steroids like I asked you, I'd be bulked in my freshman year and I'd show those amateur jocks at school how to wrestle."

"I'll make you a deal," said Max. "You finish your workouts like I've got you going on, and by graduation you can start the steroids. We'll really pick up the weight this summer, and by start of your freshman year, you'll look like a Greek god. Only, you have to promise me one thing."

"What?"

"You don't tell Greg."

"As if he needed steroids." Came the reply. Keith leaned over, picked up a towel from the floor and started across the room towards the showers. Catching sight of himself in a mirror, he slipped into the exaggerated strut of a professional wrestler.

"Lookin' good, huh, Dad?" he grinned at his dad through the mirror.

"Yeah, son, lookin' good." Answered Max's reflection.

You poor pencil-necked geek, Max thought to himself.

*   *   *

Graduation night in Corpus Christi is fun. The weather is balmy and the beach is light all night. The park rangers on duty stay out of the sand dunes and look the other way as the hundreds of cars come to Mustang Island, the small island at the south end of the city just 30 minutes from downtown. Spring break and graduation nights are two wild and exciting events for the local kids. Many a girl has lost her virginity under Bob Hall Pier.

The plan for Keith's graduation was set. Grandparents were coming in from Houston and Tulsa. The whole family would attend the ceremony. After that, Keith would be going to a dance while the family returned home.

At dinner before graduation, Max rose to make a toast.

"To my son Keith. May he be the champion I never was." Said Max.

"Don't worry, I will be."

"We've worked long and hard to get to this point." Said Max. "Now we start concentrating on professional wrestling moves, getting you graduated from college, and into the ring. We start tomorrow morning with your summer routine."

Keith stared quietly into space.

"But enough of this serious stuff now. We've got more important places to go and things to do. First of all, everyone outside!"

Max looked at Frances and smiled. She could see how happy he was tonight. After all, his son would soon be coming into his world. Everyone hurried out of the dining room, through the foyer, and out the front door.

And there at the front curb sat Keith's graduation present. A bright candy-apple red Porsche convertible.

Keith couldn't believe his eyes. He'd always wanted a car like this.

Max walked over, put his arm around his son, and turned around for the small crowd of family to be able to hear his words.

"I insist that Keith and I go on the first ride, then we'd better get to graduation. This young man is on the go!"

He pulled Keith along with him, like two young men with a secret. Their heads were bowed, and the family couldn't hear the conversation, but they could tell by Keith's reaction that he was excited.

"Get behind the wheel," Max said, "drive around the corner and then open the glove box. There's another surprise for you."

The car pulled away from the curb as the family waved and screamed goodbye as if they were seeing two soldiers off to war. Keith pulled around the corner, came to a stop and opened the glove compartment. Inside, lying on a red pillow was a syringe, and he instinctively knew what it held.

"Roll up your sleeve, Graduate, and your old man will welcome you into the world of professional sports."

*   *   *

2

Austin and the University of Texas were eye-openers to Keith. Few people knew who his father was, and he quickly realized that he was 'just one of the new guys on the block, no more, no less. Max had convinced him to live off-campus so that he wouldn't "have to put up with any pencil-necked geeks" if he didn't want to. He had also installed a telephone in his son's apartment so that he could be directly involved in his training program. During the summer, Max had purchased the Wild West Wrestling Promotion Company and had traded in his tights for a briefcase. Because he wasn't traveling, he had ample time to call Keith.

Max called every morning at 5:00 AM to give him today's training schedule. When Keith came in from school, he would check in with Max before starting his afternoon workout. School was an unpleasant task that had to be endured. The one bright spot in the day was his wrestling class. No one else could touch him in the ring. The steroids had added twenty pounds, the extra weights he'd' been lifting over the summer had turned the weight to muscle, and he was fast and strong. By the first week, he was recognized as a leader in his class. For the first time in his life, Keith was judged by his own merits, and wasn't compared to Max.

When the other students had discovered who his father was there had been the usual questions, but most of his friends weren't wrestling fans and couldn't have cared less. In this environment, almost everyone had a father who was either famous or well known in the community. They accepted him for who he was and he began to enjoy a self-confidence that he had never known before.

Keith's routine didn't change much. School during the week, then the 200-mile trip home to Corpus every weekend. By now, Max was moving Keith's workouts up to include "flying techniques" in the ring. He seemed to have a natural flair for it and eagerly worked long and hard. Of course, every weekend also included his steroid shot, "just to help."

One Sunday before Keith went back to UT Max pulled him aside.

"You know, Son, your mother has never been happy. She'd be happier married to an attorney, attending the symphony and vacationing on the Riviera. Well, I'm not that guy, and if I were, I wouldn't like the symphony. I'm just a broken down jock who has been lucky. The business is doing great and I can afford anything she desires. She's found a home she wants. It's on Riverside Drive where all her 'society-bitch' friends live. It has an Olympic-sized pool, tennis courts and maids' quarters. We'll be moving in next week, so by your next rip home, we'll be 'big society snobs.' We're even having a housewarming party on the 23rd. That's weekend after next and she's agreed that you could bring three guys from school for it. You can all sleep in the servants' quarters afterwards. What do you think?"

"My God, Dad, we're really coming up in the world. We'll be there."

*   *   *

On the afternoon of the 23rd, Keith and three of his friends drove to Corpus Christi, ready for the evening's events. Not having been at the new house before, it took them a few minutes to locate it. Keith couldn't believe his eyes. It was a mansion. They had lived in a beautiful home before, but it couldn't hold a candle to this place. Stopping at the security gate, he pressed a button and was impressed when the gate opened to allow them entrance. Once inside, the house loomed before them, a stone fortress. As they drove up the expansive drive toward the front door, he could see the pool and cabanas in the back yard.

"God, what a home." Said Joe, Keith's college wrestling partner. "I thought my parents went all out for our place in Houston, but it's nothing compared to this. Wrestling must be a profitable business."

"Now you know why I'm going into wrestling" said Keith, proud of the opulence of the home and that his friends had noticed. "Let's get undressed and hit the pool."

✵   ✵   ✵

That night at the party, the boys were dressed in their finest, unusual for college jocks. But for the occasion, Frances had insisted that they dress appropriately. To his surprise, Keith didn't even mind wearing a suit. He was, in spite of himself, shocked at the display of wealth. His father and mother had never before indicated that there was this much money in the family. More than ever before, he was determined to become a part of the business. After all, a part of it would be his some day. He stood by the punch bowl surveying the crowd. He watched as servants passed among the guests with heavy trays of drinks. A champagne fountain had been erected in one corner, flowers in large baskets were everywhere, and there was a table of gifts. A string quartet played softly in one corner. Looking closely, he saw no wrestlers present. He knew that these were all his mother's friends. It was she who belonged to the country club, took cruises, went to the opera and symphony. His dad cared for none of these things. Over the years, he had assumed that someone went with Frances, but had never asked whom. He just knew that his parents had lived separate lives for years. He never asked questions. But now, tonight they seemed to be having the times of their lives. They were even dancing together, and Keith had never seen that before. Frances was already 'tipsy', but 'what else is new?"

✵   ✵   ✵

Later, when the first of the guests began to leave, Max found Keith out on the patio with his friends, laughing and reminiscing about high school football games.

"Son," said Max as he approached the group, "I've had about as much of this socializing as I can stand. Let's all meet at the pool at 6AM tomorrow for a few laps to clear our heads. We'll jog before breakfast.

"Sounds great, Dad." he answered

"Great party," said Joe. Thanks for inviting us."

They shook hands all around and Max made his way through the crowd and up the stairs.

Within the hour couples began to leave, stopping to tell Frances what a lovely evening it had been. The boys stayed on the patio, enjoying the breeze, smelling the salt water in the night air, and drinking beer. Light and the sound of music inside spilled out into the night, and around the three young men sitting at the table. Suddenly the music rose. Their heads turned, simultaneously, to the lone couple dancing in the living room. The resonant voice of Barry White was singing about love, and the couple began to move, only slightly, and as the music began a slow beat pattern, they began to undulate, locked in each other's arms. It was a dance performed by two people who knew every inch of their partner intimately. The dance had been performed before. Slowly the man dipped. His partner's tight black dress moved upward slightly over her knees. He pivoted and deftly extended his arm and held her suspended only inches above the floor. Keith was spellbound. He could only see silhouettes on the other side of the drapes, but the woman was magnificent. Every move was perfection. She spun, she turned, and her partner dipped and pulled her into him. The others at Keith's table were mesmerized.

"God, she's something," said Joe.

"Yes, she is."

Abruptly, the music stopped and so did the dancers. The few people left at the party began to applaud. The boys watched as the couple left the dance floor, arm in arm, walking slowly toward them.

"Let's get some air," the woman said as they walked through the drapes, unaware of the small group of boys outside.

"Mother!" said Keith as the couple stepped through the drapes. He was embarrassed both by the dance and by his own feelings. "How could you? I think you've had enough to drink. Look. Some of your guests are waiting at the door."

Frances turned, noticing several departing guests.

"I'll be back when I've said my goodbyes," she said. "Wait here, boys." She tripped slightly and grabbed her dancing partner's arm, stiffened her back, and held onto him as they turned to make their way through the living room.

"Uh, well, I guess I'll call it a night, too." Said Joe as he began moving toward the maids' quarters. "See you at six in the morning."

"Yeah, we have to go, too" said Roy and Dick. They didn't want to get involved and they had seen how embarrassed Keith had been at his mother's unashamed dance.

"Tell you what," Keith said, trying to revive the party, "Let's go to the kitchen and get some bacon and eggs."

"Great," said Roy.

So the three of them went into the kitchen to see if they could find someone.

Later, after large plates of bacon and eggs had been devoured, along with steaming cups of coffee, the boys sat around the kitchen table.

"God, that was the best tasting food I've had in years," said Roy.

"Let's call it a night," said Keith.

So Keith, Roy and Joe headed for the maids' quarters, sober now and ready for bed.

"What a party," thought Keith as they walked around the pool. "What a night; what a life." He was on top of the world.

And then his world collapsed. As they passed one of the cabanas, he saw the door open slightly and two figures emerge and stand, facing each other, at the edge of the pool. The three boys stopped, frozen in time, to watch the abject humiliation of their friend. Immediately they recognized the silhouettes of Frances and her dancing partner as she raised her lips for a final kiss.

"Until tomorrow," she said.

"Until tomorrow."

She turned and staggered toward the house, both shoes in one hand while the other hand clutched her panty hose, one leg dangling behind her as she walked.

* * *

One hot Sunday afternoon the Daniels family sat in the back yard enjoying the sun. Greg finished his tennis game with one of his sisters and strolled leisurely toward the lawn table to have a glass of iced tea and cool off. Max and Frances sat watching the game, each with a tall, frosted highball of bourbon and Seven. Greg and his sister sat down and stretched out. "Whew," said Judy. "What a work out."

"Yeah," replied Greg, panting. "It takes me longer and longer to beat you." He laughed.

Judy drew back her tennis racket in a mock swing at his head. "You know I won. I creamed you."

"But it took you longer," he answered as he playfully covered his head with his arms to ward off her mock blow.

Max and Frances enjoyed this happy exchange between brother and sister. Somehow, they both felt younger, more alive if some of the children were around.

"Greg," Max began slowly. "Why don't you work out with me at the gym and let me pump you up a little. I think you have what it takes for the ring."

"Oh no, you don't!" Frances sat straight up in her chair, eyes ablaze. "He's going into medicine. You've already got Keith. You leave Greg alone. You promised me a long time ago." She slammed her glass down to drive home her point.

"Oh, for God's sake, Frances. I'm not throwing his whole life away. I'm only talking a few matches for the exercise. Besides that, you could use the money, couldn't you, Greg?" he asked his son.

Greg sat looking down the length of his legs, extended straight out in front of him. Slowly he spoke.

"Dad, you know medicine is my life. It's all I ever wanted to do. And it's what I still want to do. But, with school over for the summer, I have three months to kill, so I'll do it until classes begin in the fall. Besides, I do need the money. Don't worry, Mom, I'll be in school come September, I promise."

Frances slowly rose from her chair, looked at her son, then turned toward Max.

"I hate you," she said as she threw the remaining liquid in her glass squarely I the middle of his face. She sat the glass down and quickly crossed the lawn to the big house and slammed the door loudly behind her. No one had spoken or moved. Max looked at both of his children and grinned foolishly as the drink slid slowly down his handsome face.

"Don't worry, she'll get over it," He said.

3

In less than month Greg had his first match. Max had a deep turquoise velvet cape made for him. Greg wore it until he reached the center of the ring where he removed it with a flair. Hundreds of sequins reflected the strong overhead lights and the women went wild as he strutted around the ring, flexing his muscles just as he had been taught by his father. The match lasted less than five minutes, and naturally, Greg won. He hadn't broken a sweat. It wasn't necessary. His opponent knew his business. He had "put Greg over" in a big way. Greg was not only handsome, but because of his excellent physique, he was totally believable as a new gladiator in his father's string of big, tough men.

In the audience, Frances watched with fear. As Greg victoriously circled the ring to thunderous shouts of encouragement, she saw his medical career disappearing into the dust of the dirty ring mat.

* * *

Max watched on the closed screen TV in his office.

"What did I tell you?" he asked Stan, the booker. "That kid's a natural. Just like his old man. We'll build him up awhile and see if we can get him to Japan or Mexico. That's where the big money is."

Keith watched the match from the dressing room door. His little brother had done a great job. He was proud of him. The other men had also watched and they agreed that he was a natural. Keith couldn't help but smile when he remembered how he and Greg had wrestled when they were little boys. Naturally Keith had always won because he was older and stronger. Big brothers always won. As he turned to close the door, someone caught his eye. He looked again at the audience around the ring. Suddenly the smile faded and his eyes hardened as he stared straight into his mother's face. She had never come to see him wrestle in the three years he had been professional. But now, Greg was here and it was a different story. There she was. Sitting there like a number one fan. They stared at each other and as if she could read his mind, she dropped her eyes and wrung her hands in her lap. He stared straight ahead just long enough to compose himself, and slowly closed the door.

*　　　　*　　　　*

Over the next few months, Keith felt himself being pushed back and Greg being pulled ahead. Max was constantly working new "gimmicks" and "finishes" for Greg and he had risen to the semi-final and then final matches in only five months. No mention was made of school now. Frances walked around the house dejectedly, usually with a drink in her hand and a frown on her face.

Keith was tired of begging his father for better matches and more money. He was constantly told, "pace yourself. Your time is coming." But when that would be, he couldn't tell. Max was so involved with Greg that there wasn't room for anything else in his life. Not Frances, not the girls, and for sure, not Keith.

*　　　　*　　　　*

"But Dad, that's just not fair. Damn it all, I've been working longer than Greg and I should go." Keith slammed his fist down on Max's desk. His father had just told him that Japan International Wrestling Promotions wanted a man to be sent over to work for three weeks. The Japanese promotion had a reputation for top pay, and they treated the wrestlers like gods. The pay was in the six figures per week. An apartment was furnished and every wrestler dreamed of going. A six-week stint in Japan meant that a wrestler didn't really have to work for the rest of the year. And now, Greg was to leave for Japan on Monday.

"Get out of my face" his father shouted. "I still run this damn company and I say who goes and who doesn't. He goes and you don't."

Because three other men were sitting in the room watching the whole scene, Keith had only two choices: either sit down and shut up, or leave. He chose to leave.

A strain had been put on the brothers' relationship. They had always been close, even though Frances had always favored Greg in every way. Keith knew that his father tried to make it up to him when they were young, but now he felt abandoned. He still loved Greg, but he was jealous, no doubt about it. Greg had it all; the love of both parents, the admiration of the sisters, and now all the breaks in the business. He had gone farther in his short term than Keith had in almost three years. And now he was going to Japan.

* * *

4

Greg stood in the ring at the Imperial Coliseum in Tokyo. He was waiting for this "second" to separate the ropes for him to leave the ring for the long walk back to the dressing room. As the victor, it was his honor to leave the ring last. Japan had been a huge success. To the small Asian people, Greg was a mountain of a man. He looked over the heads of the ring assistants into the audience. The westernized Japanese women screamed and stomped their approval right along with the men. He noticed that they had exchanged their kimonos for western jeans, and their usual shyness was gone.

Greg had been invited to the promoter's home tonight after the matches for a late dinner. He was looking forward to it because he had not been in a Japanese home. He wanted to see how Japanese families lived. Tonight had been his last match and his last night in Japan. Tomorrow, home to the good old USA.

Tickets for tonight's card had been sold out since the day they had gone on sale. The Japanese had discovered professional wrestling years ago and they loved it. Greg had given his all to the match. He had won, but had left his Japanese opponent with "face." The crowd had loved both men; their countryman for his popularity in his own right, and the "Big American" for his size, good looks, ability and seemingly his sense of fairness.

Making his way to the dressing room between two armed policemen, although Greg was smiling and waving to the cheering, foot-stomping crowd, his mind was elsewhere. He was thinking of the dinner tonight and the flight home tomorrow. Deep in thought, he broke a cardinal rule of professional wrestling. He didn't watch the crowd. Greg didn't notice the lone, gray-haired man separate himself from the others and lunge forward, through the rope barriers. He broke into a run, and as he reached Greg's side, he suddenly stopped, pulled his arm back and made a quick thrust.

Greg's wind was cut off. He couldn't breathe. Oh my God, He thought, I'm cut. He looked down. The handle of an Old World War II Kamikaze sword protruded from his side.

Things were going in slow motion for him. Women screamed. Men ran. There was panic all over the large building. Quickly the police chased the still screaming man, caught him, cuffed him and finally carried him across the floor to a waiting police car.

Greg lay flat on his back. He felt gentle hands touching his side, and an elderly woman cradled his head in her arms. He drifted in and out of consciousness and he heard voices that he couldn't understand. His eyes swam as he turned his head slowly toward the ring. They cleared momentarily, and the last thing he would ever see was the big silver ring bell that signals the end of a round.

5

Frances walked softly into her bedroom. She closed the door silently behind her to shut out the soft, hushed voices of the friends and neighbors who had come to the house after the funeral. She stood with her back to the door and, reaching up to remove her black hat and veil, she looked around the room seeking solace in its familiarity. The huge comfort-covered bed she and Max shared beckoned to her. The heavy mahogany headboard was elaborately carved with the family crest proudly displayed in its center. Signs of opulence were here, from the original oils on the walls to the leaded crystal decanter on the bar in the corner.

She'd stuck it out, spent years locked into this marriage that was a mistake from the start. Now she had money, social status, a beautiful home, and for what? It all seemed so unimportant now.

Frances walked slowly to the bed. She desperately wanted a drink but knew that she couldn't make it to the bar. Her legs grew more tired with each step, and gratefully she reached the comfort of the bed. She lay back, folded her hands across her stomach and stared at the ceiling.

Greg is dead.

She saw again the coffin as it was lowered into the ground. The bronze box that would hold Greg forever. In winter and summer, whatever happened to the rest of the family. When the girls had families of their own, when Keith was away wrestling, when Max was promoting or with another woman, when in years to come the grandchildren arrived,

Greg would still be in that bronze box. Her beautiful child; he would be eternally young, big, strong. He would always be there.

The ringing in her ears started as a barely audible, high-pitched sound as she lay with her eyes closed, remembering the single, red rose she had thrown into the resting-place of her favorite child. The ringing became louder as she remembered how the world came to a stop as she turned and walked away from that rose, away from her child, away from her heart.

And thankfully, at last the blackness and the ringing came together mercifully to take over her consciousness and, for a brief while, stop the pain.

*   *   *

Max was aware of the voices around him. His parents, friends and neighbors were all here. They had all come over after the funeral. They sat and talked in muted voices about unimportant things, hoping that by their presence they could somehow help Max and Frances through their ordeal. They had brought food. As if he would ever eat again. He really couldn't imagine ever getting out of this chair again.

From the corner of his eye, Max saw Frances walk trance-like up the stairs and disappear through their bedroom door. He knew he should go after her, try to console her, but he didn't. He sat.

"It's O.K. Dad, everything will be O.K." The pressure on his shoulder told him that Keith was beside him and had gripped him. Instinctively, Max's head raised, turned and he looked up at his son. Keith involuntarily shuddered as he looked into the blankest eyes he'd ever seen.

Max could hear his daughters sobbing, but he didn't move. The father, the protector for so many years, was now this big, broken man sitting in a chair without the will to move.

Father McCulley appeared in front of him and bent down.

"My son," he began, "God works in mysterious ways. I know you don't think so now, but you will survive. You will never forget, but you will survive. Please take this bible. It will be a comfort to you later." He placed the bible in Max's limp hands as they lay folded in his lap. Unable to move his fingers, Max let the bible slowly slide down his legs and onto the floor.

Hours passed. Someone turned on the lights. Max sat; still in his funeral suit, eyes straight ahead, lost in thought. In his mind he could hear the crowds cheer as Greg ran the 50-yard touchdown. He saw his son's happy face the night he had his first date, and most of all, he heard the roar of the crowd the night he became Heavyweight Wrestling Champion of the World. Max's shining hour. Greg had been what Max had never achieved. He was the champion. And now he was dead.

Max didn't get up when the neighbors left, nor did he tell his daughters goodbye when they left to spend a few days with their grandparents. He watched them all go, well aware that everyone who had been there was secretly glad to be going, glad that their son hadn't died. Their voices faded in the distance and then they were gone.

"I'll be back later tonight, Dad. I'm taking Gran and Grandad and the girls to the airport, but I'll be back." said Keith, going through the door.

Then came the silence. The God-awful, loud, empty silence. Max felt the pressure behind his eyes and his throat began to ache. Then the pressure began in his chest. The band around his lungs began to tighten and he couldn't breather. With an extraordinary effort he sat straight up and willed his lungs to pull in air. And they did. As he began to breathe easier, his mind began to function once again. He hadn't prayed in years, but suddenly the words came to him. Then his mind screamed, *Why me, God? Why my son?* His eyes dropped to the floor and he saw the bible lying at his feet. It lay opened, and as Max bent over to pick it up, the words leaped at him,

"And the sins of the father shall be visited upon his sons."

He reeled backwards, throwing his head back against the chair. *My God, the sins of the fathers! My sins!* He put his hand to his face as the images of the parade of "other women" he'd had appeared in his mind's eye.

I had it all. And I screwed it all up, he thought. *My son is dead because of my sins*. Max pulled himself up and out of the chair and, bible held in both hands, slowly descended the basement steps down into the gym.

First he went to the punching bag. He began to hit. Each time a big fist landed, he'd scream, "Why?" and he'd hit again. "Why? Why? Why?" and he screamed and hit until he had no voice.

Then he made his way to the showers. Standing in the stall, water streaming into his face, his open, silent mouth formed the words, "Why?" But he knew why.

Shuffling, dripping wet across the room, Max walked up to one of the metal lockers, and gripping it in both hands, started hitting his head on the front. Over and over and over. "Why? Why? Why?"

And that's where Keith found his father when he returned. Max lay wet and unconscious on the floor, his bible beneath him, blood streaming from his forehead, knuckles jammed and bleeding, convinced that the sins of his past had killed Greg, his beloved son.

* * *

Keith slowly opened the bedroom door. From the soft glow of the security light on the balcony, he could see his mother's lender form as she lay motionless on the large bed, still in her black dress, eyes closed, hands folded across her stomach.

He walked quietly to her, knelt beside the bed, and lay his head on the pillow next to hers. He looked at her pale, expressionless face as he spoke quietly into her ear.

"Don't worry, Mom, the girls were much better by the time the plane took off. They'll be O.K. Dad is resting in Greg's room. He's asleep."

Gently he turned his mother on her side, and as if she were a child, he held her limp body up with one hand while he unbuttoned her dress with the other. Fortunately it had buttons completely down the back. With no effort, he pulled the dress away from her body and eased her back down onto the bed. She lay in her slip now, deathly still. Gentle, he covered her with a blanket. Through all of his tenderness, she hadn't responded or acknowledged that he was there.

Keith couldn't remember when he'd felt this much tenderness towards her. Suddenly, all the years of inequity washed away. This was his mother and he'd take care of her. And she, in turn, would realize how much he really loved her.

"You rest now, Mom, and I'll take care of everything." His heart filled with compassion for her. She looked so fragile. He didn't know whether she could even hear him or not, but he put his lips next to her ear again and whispered, "I'd give anything to keep you from suffering, Mom. I know how you loved Greg. I wish I could ease your pain. I wish it had been me."

Slowly her blue eyes opened. She looked into the sad eyes of her son, and she said very softly, very deliberately, in words that he would remember the rest of his life.

"I wish it had been you, too."

* * *

Coming back to the present, Keith turned off the water, but continued to stand in the shower, head down, and deep in thought. The pictures were so vivid in his mind that the events could have happened yesterday instead of years ago.

The pain still shot through his chest when he remembered how he had slowly stood up beside his mother's bed and walked out of the bedroom door knowing that he would never feel the same about anything again.

Yes, thought Keith as he stepped out of the shower, *that was the moment I began to look out for Number One—Me! I don't give a shit about anything or anybody. I'm a man with a cause. I'll be champion no matter what it takes!* He remembered that he was to be in his father's office in an hour. *I'm going to get this settled with my dad today.*

Determined more than ever now, Keith stepped back into the room that still smelled of cheap perfume.

*   *   *

6

"Dad, we need to talk about my future here." Keith immediately started on his father as he entered the big man's office. Max looked up from his desk with surprise on his face.

"What do you mean, Son, your future here? This is your business. I've been building it up for years. Just so you can take over."

And there would be much to take over. Max had done a remarkable job of improving a small, one town promotion into a multi-million dollar a year, tri-state wrestling promotion company. He owned one block of valuable beachfront land on Corpus Christ beach and over the years he had built the perfect complex: an arena, business office, and gym with a pool. The three separate buildings had parking lots and afforded easy access for the wrestlers to walk from one building to the other. State-of-the-art equipment, including a remote television van completed the real estate.

The interior of the office building was decorated in shades of blue and huge, heavy leather chairs and couches, along with deep rich mahogany office furniture completed the administrative offices.

"You can't mean you're thinking of quitting, can you?"

Max paled as he looked at his son. Since Greg's death, Keith was his last shot at glory. The girls were O.K., but they were Frances' part of the package they called a marriage. Why couldn't anyone else see Keith the way he did? Others saw temper tantrums and sarcasm. Max saw only impatience and frustration in the way Keith drove himself to live up to his father's expectations. Max knew he had always pushed Keith too hard, but no one pushed harder than the boy himself.

The other wrestlers tolerated him because he was the promoter's kid, and who wanted to risk the wrath of an angry promoter who had the power to make you or break you. Who wouldn't tolerate Keith under those circumstances?

"Dad, I'm 31 years old and the only title I've held so far is the national tag team. And now that's gone. That's the shits!"

"Calm down, we'll work another gimmick for you. Who do you want as your new tag team partner?" his father asked, trying to get his attention diverted to another subject.

"Give me Jesse. He owes you, so he can do jobs and bleed and put me over. I suppose I'll have to teach him how to cut himself."

Keith was settling down some now that the attention was on his problems and he could see that whatever his demands, Max would give in as usual, He threw himself into a massive leather chair across from Max, slumping down, lost in his own plans for his new partner.

Max smiled. "I'll tell Jesse tonight. He won't like it because he really wanted to stay a baby face, but working with you he'll have to wrestle dirty and be a heel.

"Too damn bad about him. Tell him the broads don't like baby faces as well as heels. He should be damn glad to be my partner."

Rising from his chair, Max started around the desk. "It's done then. Come on, let's go do the TV. spots for next month. The cameras are ready and so are the guys. We have women and midgets scheduled for Houston. We've got to get those segments televised quickly. Come on. The midgets are ready to go now."

* * *

7

They made their way down the hall as quickly as possible. Tonight's matches were over and they had places to go and people to do. Tokyo Joe led the way.

Tiny framed, the midget called Tokyo Joe was half-oriental, and half-Mexican. His skin was between tan and brown, and his eyes were almond shaped and dark brown. Wide shoulders and tiny waist, he was perfectly proportioned and a very handsome little man. He wrestled heel.

Cowboy Bob, his opponent and friend, was a dwarf. He had a large head and face, short arms and bowed legs that made walking more of a chore for him. His round face and eyes automatically made him the baby face.

It really didn't matter in this case which one was which, because it was all a comic show anyway. The fans loved the midgets and the children roared with laughter as the little men mimicked the larger wrestlers' actions. The referee played along for everyone's enjoyment. The matches were usually short and no one really cared who won or lost. Their pay was great and so were the fringe benefits. Women couldn't and wouldn't leave them alone!

Tokyo Joe and Cowboy Bob, highly respected grapplers who were known for arriving on time, doing a good job, and not causing trouble, were on tonight's card. They had made dates earlier today with two arena rats, and were eager to get the matches over with and start to party. The girls had run up to their specially built van as the two had arrived and had started talking to the two small men. Before they left to do the television, the four had agreed to meet after tonight's matches for dinner.

Both men dressed hurriedly. They knew what waited for them outside. Cowboy Bob was dressed in western wear; tiny boots and jeans, shirt and vest with a white Stetson hat. Tokyo wore black pants, brightly patterned silk shirt and dress shoes. Both had big smiles on their faces.

Sure enough, the girls were waiting by the van after the matches. Mini skirts and crop tops, ready to go out on the town. Alice, Bob's girl, suggested Diamond Jim's. Her friend Dorothy agreed. They had heard that all the wrestlers went there and the two girls were dying to see all their heroes.

Tokyo and Dorothy got in the front seat of the van. When they arrived at the club, the owner met them personally and arranged the seating so the two men would not be embarrassed. A romantic table had been set at the back of the room in front of a large picture window. There were two regular chairs for the girls and two barstools for the men. No one laughed, and they were treated with respect. One thing that upset the midgets was being talked down to. They were men. All the way. The two girls wanted to find out all about that, and they soon would.

Dinner was excellent. Jim was famous for his steaks and the wine was flowing. After the second bottle of Chablis, Tokyo began his move. Dorothy, being a little "tipsy" was unprepared, but not unwilling.

"I love blondes," said Tokyo. I noticed you right off this afternoon. You stuck out of the crowd," he said. Dorothy giggled at the play on words. She had 44D breasts, which she usually didn't bother to cover very well. A statuesque 5'8", she had a body that would cause any man to look, and midget wrestlers are notorious for always looking for big women. The bigger the better.

Dorothy looked over at Alice, her "running mate". Friends since high school, they had been through many escapades together. They had finally outgrown their groupie days with the rock stars, and they were now making their way through the racetrack and the wrestling scenes. On a dare, they had decided to go out with the two midgets.

"What do you say we go back to the hotel?" said Tokyo, hoping his timing was right. These girls were lucky. Tomorrow the men had the day off; normally, they didn't have time to wine and dine women. It was a fast screw in the van and off to the next town. Tonight they'd spent money, and he hoped it would be worth it. Wrestlers, even the midgets, never had to worry about sex. It was always around.

"Let's go," said Dorothy. "Come on, Alice," she said. He noticed as Alice got to her feet that she was also a little unsteady.

"Jim, let me have a bottle of Dom Perignon for the road," Cowboy said.

Back at the van, it was decided that Tokyo would drive once more, and the other couple got into the back seat again. As she bent low, Alice could feel Bob's small hand slip suddenly up the inside of her thigh. She giggled.

"Why don't you take off the bikinis, Baby?" he asked with a slight slur.

"Sure," she answered, always ready for an adventure. This would be one. The girls had wondered about the midgets, and now they would find out.

Deftly, in one motion, she pulled her panties down around her ankles as she fell, face first, into the back seat.

Cowboy Bob jumped in after her and slammed the door shut. Because his little bowed legs were so short he had no problem standing and removing his pants and shirt. He pulled his belt out of the loops and doubled it over his hand. Clad only in shorts, he straddled the girl's body. Quickly pulling her dress up to expose a tan, firm butt, he cried, "I'm going to have the ride of my life. Giddy up!"

Whap! Went the sound of the leather belt as it hit flesh.

"Owww" wailed Alice.

Tokyo looked back in the mirror. He hoped Bob knew what he was doing. Kinky stuff could be dangerous.

Whap! It came again.

"Owww" To his surprise, he heard a giggle from Dorothy. Maybe she was into this stuff, too.

Pulling over to the curb, Tokyo said, "I guess we might as well watch."

"Fine," said Dorothy.

Whap! Went the leather.

"Ride 'em Cowboy," said Cowboy Bob, as he looked at the red butt which, by this time was twisting and turning. "Lie still, Alice, and I'll let you turn over."

Immediately the churning stopped and as Bob reached under her, Alice obligingly raised up on all fours so he could get his short arms around her to fondle her massive breasts.

"Please let me turn over now" came her muffled voice.

"O.K.," said Bob, standing back, an erection already visible to Tokyo and Dorothy. Tokyo heard Dorothy's intake of breath.

Slowly Alice turned, carefully easing her smarting buttocks onto the car seat. Her thrashing and turning had smeared her makeup and caused her vision to be blurred. Now as her eyes focused, she looked up at this small, dwarf with the large head, small chest, large mid-section, and her eyes riveted on the biggest dick she had ever seen.

"Oh My God!" she screamed as Bob plunged deep inside her.

In the front seat, the couple watched as they drank from the bottle of Dom Perignon.

8

"I'll kill you," the huge man screamed as he kicked his opponent in the head. "You won't live 'til morning."

As he dropped his knee into the throat of the man writhing beneath him, he quickly measured the emotions of the crowd around him. *Now,* he thought.

Standing, Gorilla Lopez looked menacingly around the arena. His knees slightly bent, fists clenched, he slowly circled the ring, staring intently into the gray, smoke-filled space where he knew that thousands of angry, screaming fans had come to watch him get hurt.

His tongue was out, nearly touching the end of his chin; his long hair was braided in rows and the top of his head was shaved clean; sweat poured down his body, running in rivulets down his huge back.

These marks are really buying it, he thought to himself as he looked out over the crowd. Able to see only as far as a few of the front rows, he nevertheless stared directly into the balcony seats for affect. Lolling his tongue out once more, he immediately felt the familiar rush of excitement rise through his entire body as fans screamed and shrieked at him.

He was barely aware of two policemen at ringside, one on either side of a hysterical fan who had tried to climb into the ring. The two policemen, both veterans of many wrestling matches, took no time in dispatching the irate, screaming man out of the arena. Both hands cuffed behind his back, his feet barely touched the floor as he was roughly hauled away between the two policemen past rows of uncaring fans, their eyes riveted to the action in the ring.

Gorilla looked down at Cowboy Jim Nelson, the good looking, mustached hero of every woman in the arena. Clutching his throat, Nelson was writhing and turning, flexing every muscle in his well-tanned body, his 65" chest heaving to give its best effect. Gorilla loomed over Nelson, saliva dripping onto the prone man's blonde hair.

"E-a-zyme gonna' thre-a-zow you into the ce-a-zorner so you can se-a-zee the bre-a-zod," "said Gorilla, as he slipped into " "carney" " a language used by carnival workers and professional wrestlers. He had told Nelson that he would throw him into the corner where he could see the "broad". With that, Gorilla picked him up, held his prone body at arm's length over his head and began to spin around in the middle of the ring.

After four or five spins, he threw Nelson into the corner so he could enjoy looking into the open legs of an excited female fan in the front row.

Cowboy Nelson fell to the mat, face-first, hands down. Gorilla ran over, and with the side of his size 12E boot, expertly drove him through the ropes, and to everyone's shocked surprise except Nelson, into the open lap of the "bre-a-zod" sitting in the front row.

"Meet me at the dressing room door after the matches," whispered Nelson, face down in her lap. Clutching her dress between his teeth, he felt himself being jerked by the tights back into the ring. He finally managed to let go, sniffing one more time the sensual aroma of the woman. His back hit the apron of the ring, and once again Nelson went down; this time to the concrete floor. Lying on his face, his head cradled in his arms, he tried to forget the scent of the woman and get down to business. Gorilla would keep the referee at the other side of the ring and divert the audience's attention long enough for nelson to "get some juice." This was the part, and the ONLY part of the business that Nelson didn't like. "Getting juice." Everyone who was anyone had to do it now. The fans expected it and the promoter demanded it.

Carefully, Cowboy raised his eyes over the level of his arms. All was well. Gorilla had the fans out of their seats while he was beating the hapless referee in the corner. Quickly, Cowboy removed the tiny, tape-wrapped corner of a razor blade from the tape around his fingers. After peeking once again to make sure no one was watching, he very carefully pulled the blade across his forehead.

God, that hurts, he thought as he felt the blood gush out of the wound and into his eyes. *It never quits hurting, no matter how many times you do it.* Tonight he's use New Skin on it to seal it over and tomorrow night his opponent would hit the same spot, breaking it open again.

Cowboy put the blade back in his wristband and raised his blood-soaked head, the signal for Gorilla to come back.

At the sight of blood on their much loved hero, the fans screamed even harder; some came toward the ring, only to be held back by the police. Some women turned away from the blood, while others screamed profanities and threw their paper cups full of beer into the ring.

Gorilla had been milking every emotion he could from the crowd; a master at crowd manipulation, his timing was always perfect. At just the right time he stomped over to Cowboy and reaching through the ropes, pulled him through by the hair of his head. Cowboy grabbed Gorilla's wrist to help him pull the weight of his body through the ropes without scalping the handsome wrestler. Gorilla knew what to do now. Bending Nelson backward over the top rope, he began noisily sucking the forehead where Cowboy had cut himself. The crowd was uncontrollable. Eight policemen were now standing with their backs against the ring, ready to call out the riot squad if they needed them.

"We'd better 'go home' now," Gorilla said to Cowboy, "before some brave son-of-a-bitch proves he's a man and jumps in here and stabs me like they did Black Mauler in Toronto last week."

"I'm ready," said Cowboy. "I'm lined up for tonight." His voice was just barely audible coming from the side headlock he was being held in.

Flipping Cowboy to his back, Gorilla picked up his legs, expertly twisting them between his own, and fell backward into the famous submission hold, the Figure Four Leg Lock. The referee came running from the corner and threw himself to the floor beside the two grapplers and counted.

"One—Two—Three"

As he held Gorilla's hand over his head to signify him the winner, the referee whispered under his breath to the two men, "Max wants us in his office right after the matches. Be there."

*　　　*　　　*

"What a waste of time," said Cowboy Nelson as he entered the office of promoter Max Daniels.

"I've got my night all lined up. The gal in the front row is waiting outside and we're stuck in here listening to Max blow and go."

"Man, we go through this once a week and sit here like a bunch of idiots while Max testifies," answered Gorilla, "What shit."

As they walked into the inner office, they were greeted by the subdued voices of every man who had been on the wrestling card that night. They were all sitting around the large office, some with wet towels over their heads, hair still damp from their recent showers. A couple of them were drinking quietly from half filled bottles of beer. Behind the large desk sat Max, and from the beatific look on his face, they knew they were in for either a lecture or a sermon from the "born again" religious-fanatic.

"Let's get the show on the road, Max" said Cochise. "I want to get to Diamond Jim's before the crowd gets down there. I'm dry as a bone, and Marilyn is waiting in the car."

"Wait for the rest of the boys," said Max.

"Aw, come on, man, we've had a hard week and we want to relax. We've worked every night for six weeks and we're tired." the Indian argued.

"I've asked you men here tonight," said Max, "to tell you what we're planning and to warn you about something. Roger the Wrestling Bear is coming and I don't want any problems. The last time he was here, some son-of-a-bitch put honey on Greg May's tights before the matches and Roger chased him around the ring four times. He finally caught him, sat down on him, and it took eight guys to pull the damn thing off poor Greg. The audiences laughed their asses off at us. I don't want any practical jokes this time."

"Remember last time he was here, Max?" asked Gorilla. "The stupid thing is crazy about Cokes. Sits on his back feet and holds a Coke bottle in his front seat and chug-a-lugs like an old sot. Well, the last time, his trainer had him in the dressing room and the bear was sitting there like a gentleman, drinking his Coke when the janitor comes around the corner. Bumps right into Roger his eyeballs were just about even with the bear's Coke bottle. Man, that guy started screaming and his mop and pail both hit the ceiling at the same time. He started running and we chased that poor schmuck clear out of the building before we could stop him. I thought he was gonna' have a heart attack." They all laughed, remembering the poor janitor and the look o his face.

"Don't forget," said Max, "this is the same bear who killed his trainer's wife last year."

"Oh yeah," said Gorilla, "I had forgotten that."

"She had raised him since he was a baby," continued Max. "He loved the hell out of her. One day the family was gone and she went out to feed him. The son-of-a-bitch took one whiff of her and mauled her to death."

The atmosphere changed as each man pondered the scene.

"Where can I borrow that bear?" the Indian said, breaking the stillness and bringing back the usual good spirits of the group.

"O.K., guys, back to business," said Max. "You know our business is going great, but I'm planning a big change. My son Keith is going to run things from now on. He's our new booker."

A shocked silence fell, as each man tried to absorb the enormity of the announcement. They knew Keith Daniels, the spoiled, egocentric son of the promoter. Known throughout the wrestling world as a tantrum-throwing, foul-mouthed bully with a father who saw none of his faults, he was probably the poorest candidate anyone could imagine for the position of booker for this successful company.

The booker is responsible for creating the serial-type television program each week, creating situations so fans will want to watch next week to see what happens. This also brings the armchair fan out of his home and down to the arena when wrestling comes to town.

He also decides who will wrestle whom, what will happen in the ring, and who will win the match. Since Keith had never worked any place other than his father's promotion and had absolutely no booking experience to rely on, this also seemed like a bad business decision on Max's part.

"Max," ventured Cochise, giving voice to the question that was on the mind of every man in the room. "Can I ask you why you made this decision?"

"Because he's my kid and I want him to do it," boomed Max. "Some day this will be all his. He's got the best interest of the business at heart. Besides, the Lord told me to."

"But don't you think he's kind of inexperienced?" he ventured further.

"I don't give a shit," said Max. "That's my decision. He takes over tomorrow."

You could almost hear each man groan to himself as he left the room.

"Thanks, Max." the Indian said, barely audible as he walked out the door.

"You're all welcome" he replied.

*   *   *

Goddamn, thought Cochise as he left Max's office, *We're in for a hard time now. That little bastard has never been away from home and has only been wrestling for three years. It scares the hell out of me what's going to happen to this company. He'll be putting himself over in every match. The rest of us won't stand a chance in hell. What a mess.*

Cochise, the 260-lb. Choctaw Indian from Lawton, Oklahoma, was one of the "old timers", the "over-40" wrestlers who had come into the sport after playing professional football for years. He'd been let go from the New York Mariners after the coach's wife caught crabs from him.

Cochise picked up his eel skin wrestling bag in one hand and his Haliburton attaché case in the other as he started across the parking lot. Two uniformed police fell in step with him; one on each side, to escort him to the new white Cadillac Seville parked in the area reserved for wrestlers.

Even though it was two hours after the matches were over, eager die-hard fans were still hanging around, hoping to get a glimpse of their favorite heroes or throw something at the heels.

The heady scent of Royal Secret hit him as soon as he opened the driver's side car door.

"Hi, Baby," he said as he wedged his thick body under the steering wheel.

"How did the meeting go, Cochise?" asked Marilyn Jackson, his current love, and Texas Women's Wrestling Champion of the World.

"You can't believe it, Baby, Max is going to make Keith our new booker."

"My God, you can't be serious," came the reply from the dumbfounded woman. *Here go the girls. Everyone knows he doesn't like girl wrestlers. I guess I'd better start calling other territories and see if they have any openings.*

Marilyn hoped she was wrong. She desperately wanted to stay here. This company had worked with her, bringing her up from opening events to the championship in two years' time. She was doing well, working every night, and making the big bucks. She also knew that it wouldn't be easy to find another place for her. Although she was beautiful with her bleached blonde hair and almost perfect figure, she had a bad temper and had a reputation for violence outside the ring. A veteran of 15 years, she had wrestled every city from New York to Corpus Christi and had been asked to leave most of them due to her violent nature. Her battles with Cochise were legendary.

"Don't do anything yet, Baby, maybe Max will change his mind. You know how he is; tomorrow he may see things differently."

"You know better than that. He is a push over where Keith is concerned. If he can figure a way to work this whole territory around and make a star out of that spoiled brat, so be it. So what if he screws everyone over meanwhile. Keith hates all girl wrestlers, women in general, and his mother in particular. Everyone knows that. I personally think he is a closet fag."

"You're not alone there," agreed Cochise. "Some f the guys are sure of it. They don't think Keith knows it yet; some day he'll probably wake up in some drag queen's bed and discover he liked it."

They both had a laugh in spite of the otherwise somber mood.

"Forget it, let's go to Diamond Jim's."

9

Cowboy Jim Nelson left the office and headed to the dressing room. He had forgotten the woman in the arena after Max's bombshell announcement. But sure enough, she was waiting for him. He walked straight up to her. She smiled at him and said, "Well, here I am, Cowboy."

He gave her his dazzling, toothy smile that could melt a glacier and answered, "Great, I'll shower and change and meet you in my car."

He pointed out his car and ran into the dressing room. He was one man who delivered what he advertised.

She had touched up her hair and makeup by the time he came out. His cologne reached the car before he did, and it paved his way. He smelled good, he was gorgeous, and he was a gentleman.

"First of all, what is your name?" he asked her, looking directly into her eyes.

"Georgia," she said shyly.

"O.K., Georgia, how about some breakfast?" And off they went to find an all night restaurant.

They ate and talked and the time flew. Cowboy lowered his voice and took her hands in his.

"Georgia, usually when a man meets a woman, they take their time and get to know each other and fall in love over a period of time. I can't afford that luxury. When I saw you tonight, I knew you were for me. And since we've been talking, I'm more and more convinced. Surely you feel it too? I'm at a disadvantage. I never know how much time I'll have at any place. I'd like to take weeks or months to get to know you. But we may not get to do that. I want you and you want me. Can you trust me enough to believe me? You're not just one more woman to me. I want you to be my woman. What do you say?"

"Anything you say, Jim. I feel all of those feelings myself. I have to believe you. I want you, too. Any place, any time. Now."

He squeezed her hand. "It has to be special the first time. Come with me."

They got up from the table and left, arm in arm. He put her in the car and they drove off, happy in their new-found relationship. They drove to his apartment and he told her to wait in the living room, kissed her and went alone into the bedroom.

Ten minutes later he opened the door again and stood, resplendent in white silk pajama bottoms that accentuated his golden tan and big, muscled chest. The ever-present smile made her head spin.

He walked over to her, kissed her deeply, and picking her up, carried her over the bedroom threshold.

The bed was turned down, two dozen candles were the only light in the room, and beside the bed on the night stand was a bottle of champagne and two crystal, stemmed glasses.

Jim sat on the bed and stood Georgia between his legs, facing him. He tenderly took off her blouse and brassiere. He kissed each nipple and under each breast. He slid her skirt and slip to the floor. As he slipped her panties off, he kissed her navel and buried his face in her soft flesh.

As he stood, his pajamas fell to the floor. His erection was as magnificent as the rest of his body.

Gently, he lay her in the center of the big bed, and walking around to the table, he filled the two glasses with champagne. Turning, he handed one to the waiting woman. Sipping slowly, he looked down at her. She was medium build, blonde hair and pretty face; and tonight he would make her feel like the most beautiful woman ever born.

As their eyes met, he extended the glass over her body and slowly poured the champagne over her breasts and onto her stomach. She could feel it run between her legs. Taking another drink, he lowered his head to her stomach and followed the stream of champagne.

Kissing and licking, soon the champagne disappeared from her body. He did this three times, until neither of them could stand it any longer.

"Please, please," she moaned, over and over, until finally, the Cowboy was on top of her and, with total abandonment, each gave and took what they both wanted.

* * *

10

Twice a week, Max would venture from the colorful, slightly seedy world of wrestling to the highly touted, much desired world of muscles, pain and sweat; the local public gym where muscle building and staying tan are the ultimate goal.

His body was too abused from years of both football and wrestling to further submit it to too strenuous a routine, so he was running track, albeit very slowly in his attempt at keeping intact what athletic build he had left.

Across the room, he saw a new face. Black hair, large brown eyes, and wide smile with perfect white teeth, the young man lifting weights could have been off the cover of "Muscle UP" magazine. He was surrounded by several young men who were watching him lift the large, heavy free weights.

"Who is that man, Bob?" Max asked the trainer standing next to him.

"That's Omar Atlas from Caracas, Venezuela. He's here with a Latin American wrestling promotion. The Valdez brothers just brought him in. He works out here every day and woman and youngsters are really crazy about him."

"Max's interest was immediately aroused. This guy could be a real heartthrob with that kind of charisma. All Max had to do was convince him to forget the other promotion and join his. He would convince Omar that he would make more money and fame with Wild West Wrestling than he ever could with the Valdez brothers.

"Hey, kid, come on over when you finish up," Max yelled across to Omar as he continued running around the gym.

"O.K.," he replied.

Later, Omar sat down next to Max in the locker room. The older man was just about dressed.

"Did you want to see me?" Omar asked with a puzzled look on his handsome face.

Motioning for Omar to sit beside him on the dressing bench, Max explained who he was and named some of the men who worked for him. Omar had heard many of the names before.

"How would you like to make some big money?" Max asked.

"Yes sir, the younger man eagerly replied. I have a mother and two sisters back in Venezuela who depend on me. This chance that the Valdez brothers have given me means a lot to the four of us. What do you have in mind?"

"I don't have time to discuss it now, but come to the office tomorrow," Max said. He couldn't wait to see this young Adonis in the ring. "I have a deal that will make you forget the Valdez brothers. Come by and we'll discuss it." Max rose from the bench, handed Omar his business card and left the gym.

* * *

"Tell me about yourself, Omar," Max said as he leaned back in his chair and propped his huge feet on the desk top in his usual position.

"Well," said Omar, "I'm 26, not married, have two sisters and a mother to support. My father died years ago. My mother won't leave Venezuela, but I want to make enough money to bring my sister Toni over here as soon as I can. She's got to have a better life. She's a god Catholic girl and I promised my mother I'd take care of her. The Valdez promotion was a way out for me and I'm very grateful to them."

"Forget that," said Max. "Come to work for me and in one year you'll have all the money and fame you can handle. If you draw well, you'll get a good percentage. My wrestlers make a percentage of the gate every night and the more the fans come out to see you personally, the more you'll make. The more I believe you add to the card, the more money you'll make. I'll take care of you personally and within two years, you'll be the heavyweight champion of the world; Madison Square Garden, you'll have it all. What do you say?"

Omar's heart was pounding. To be able to work for a big promotion like Wild West Wrestling was like a dream come true for him, but he had dealt with promoters before. He had learned not to jump at every opportunity they offered. Let them wait. Because in professional wrestling, the promoter holds all the cards. Omar knew that in America, as in Venezuela, the wrestlers are paid as "self-employed", meaning "no benefits." Get hurt or killed in the ring, the promoter is not held responsible. If he feels like it, sometimes he will pay the wrestler's hospital bill if a fan stabs, shoots, or maims him, but not always. Some promoters are so unscrupulous that the wrestlers are paid just enough money to get by, and even have to pay their own transportation. He hadn't been in this country long enough to trust this man, and it was a big gamble. At least he knew the Valdez brothers. Max's offer was tempting, however.

"I'd like to think about it."

"Sure," Max said, "Let me hear in one week."

As Omar stood to leave and extended his hand to shake the big promoter's hand, the door was suddenly pushed open and shoved back against the wall with a resounding "thud". Keith stood squarely in the middle of the doorframe glaring at his father through bloodshot eyes set in a haggard face with two days' growth of beard.

"Who the Hell is this Mexican? I didn't send for one." He raised his voice and arm simultaneously, as if to strike out at Omar.

In a fraction of a second, Omar jumped sideways, squatted, and raised both fists in the age-old boxer stance of self-defense. His face was no longer handsome. His lips were drawn back from his teeth and his eyes were squinted in a warning that even Keith in his hung over condition could read.

"Hey, whoa, wait a minute," Keith now dropped his arm and started backing out of the room, almost whimpering. "What's your problem, man? I didn't mean anything".

"Don't ever threaten me unless you mean to follow through," Omar said through clenched teeth. Slowly, still face to face with Keith, Omar straightened, squared his shoulders and turned toward Max.

"Thank you, Max, I'll let you know." Saying nothing more, he stepped in front of Keith and walked through the door as if he were not standing there.

"Hell, I could have taken him. He just caught me off guard," Keith crossed the room with his usual swagger, still caught up in his tough guy image.

Max had watched the whole scene being played out without saying one single word. The difference between the two young men was startling. Nearly the same age, Omar was hard-bodied and healthy looking, while Keith was getting soft and flabby from too little exercise and too much liquor. Max had been hearing rumors lately about drugs, but didn't really believe it. He knew his son wouldn't do anything that stupid.

"I said, 'who in the Hell is that Mexican?" repeated Keith from where he sprawled in a chair.

Max explained how he had met Omar, liked his looks, and was trying to sign the Venezuelan to a contract. He carefully avoided saying anything about making him a star or how popular he thought Omar would be with the women and younger men. With Keith as jealous as he was and because he was also the booker Max feared it would never happen. Keith would see to that.

"He'll be popular with the Hispanic fans. We can make up a title and give it to him."

"Well, I don't like him. He's just one more, dumb son-of-a-bitch as far as I'm concerned. I don't want to use him except to do jobs for the other guys."

"We'll see," Max said, "Go get cleaned up and let's work on this week's schedule."

His son rose, lumbering across the room like a spoiled child and slammed the door without another word to his father.

Fifteen minutes later, Max was on the phone telling the Louisiana promoter about his new "future star." Leaning back in his chair and looking out the window as he spoke, he saw Keith's latest arena rat drive up and Keith get in the car. The two drove off into the distance.

*   *   *

The next morning Omar appeared at Max's door.

"I'd like to talk. I need to know what you really have in mind for me. How long do you want me to work, and how much money will I make?

Max looked up and smiled. He knew he had his man. Money talks and everyone has his price. He lived by this motto.

"Come on in—we've got a lot to talk about. I've got lots of plans for you. We'll start off by having a few boys do jobs for you; letting you beat them, putting you over and making you look good. Then we'll build you up with a tag team partner and then you'll be off on your own. I'll guarantee you that within two years you'll have the heavyweight championship title. You'll make a million bucks a year. How does that sound?"

"Too easy," was the reply. "What do I have to do to get there?"

"Anything we tell you to do. You may have to bleed a little, but these are the prices we pay. Do you trust me or not? Nothing will happen to you."

"What about Keith? He's your son and I could tell yesterday that we'll never get along. He's the booker and pulls all the strings. Also, he has quite a reputation.

"Leave Keith to me. He may pull the strings, but I still tell him which ones. How about it, man, you in or not? It's your choice. You want glory or cash? That's what we deal in here, green cash and lots of it."

"Count me in," said Omar. "Sounds good to me."

"It's done then. Be here tonight at 6:30. We'll start you out in the second match and you'll win. You'll be a baby face. What do you say?" asked Max.

"I start tonight."

11

The phone was ringing as Max hurried across the room, reached his desk and bellowed,

"Yeah? What?" Silence. Long silence. "You don't say. The hell you say. Sure, send him on down." A huge smile covered his face as he turned and called Stanley, the referee into his office.

"Stanley, you're not going to believe this. The Canadian promoter is sending us a 'gibroni' who is seven feet eight inches tall and weighs 350 pounds. He's only twenty years old, and green as a gourd. A real 'gibroni.'"

Stanley sat down across from Max, giving him his full attention. Middle-aged and of small build, he was one of those people whom everyone likes. Even tempered, but no pushover, he held his own with the big men he worked with. They respected him so much and liked him so much that he as not subjected to the roughhousing that usually went on between the giant men.

He had just walked in off the street one day, asked for a job, and had fast become an indispensable part of the team that put on the productions night after night, week after week, year after year. He was part of the planning, he refereed some matches, delivered the 'finishes' to the dressing rooms and was one of the few people Max ever listened to.

"Let's make him a mystery man," Max said. "Give him amnesia and he can't remember where he came from and always looking for his home."

"Great," Stanley said. "But he doesn't really need much of a gimmick, he is one. When do you expect him? Is he coming in alone?"

"He has a special van and he'll drive. I didn't want him to fly and allow the press to get a look before we introduce him from the ring. He really isn't someone we can hide. We've got to train this guy and find out what he can do. I think he should be here in a few days, but we need to hurry.

The crowds are down because of school starting. We could use some more women here. Call Princess and see who she has on hand."

"Sure, Max, I'll take care of it. She still gets 10% booking fee for every gal we use who is under contract to her." Stanley was already headed for the door to carry out Max's orders.

"How the Hell are you, Stan?" Keith called as he passed Stanley on his way into his father's office. Stanley stepped up his pace and pretended he didn't hear him. *What a disgusting human being*, thought Stanley. Max didn't deserve having a son like him. Max thought his son had real potential. Thought he could be champ some day. Yeah, right. Keith could wrestle when he wanted to and could work the crowd into a frenzy. But the idiot was getting flabby and burning himself out on booze and broads. Half the time he had a hang over. But it probably didn't matter. Max would push him clear to the top, no matter who he had to use. *Oh well, it's not my problem.*

* * *

"O.K., Dad, let's get the show on the road. I haven't got all day. I'm taking the 2:20 plane to Minneapolis to work there for three days."

"Yeah, I hadn't forgotten. But we've got this big giant of a man coming in and I've got great hopes for him. Our ticket sales are down and we can use a new angle." Max was trying to explain everything to Keith so they could figure angles, finishes and shows for the coming month. It was not often he and his son had enough time to go through everything.

"I don't care about all that shit. You handle it. I gotta' make up the cards for next month. Have you done the publicity?"

The phone rang. The secretary announced, "There is a delegation of people out here who want to speak to you."

"Ask them to wait just a few minutes," Max told her. Turning to Keith he asked, "Do you know anything about a delegation of people due here?"

Keith looked puzzled and shrugged his shoulders. Max hurried around the office picking up anything that the "Marks" shouldn't see. He waited until Keith had left by the back door before signaling for the delegation to be let in. He stood behind his desk, hands folded behind his back, and beaming with his warmest, most sincere pontifical smile.

Four middle-aged women clutching their handbags came eagerly into the room.

"Hello, I'm Max Daniels." The woman closest to him accepted his extended handshake.

"Hello. We are here today representing "Mothers of America," an organization which acknowledges outstanding role models for teenagers. Cowboy Nelson has done many things for us in the past and we have found out that his birthday is in two weeks. We just love him. He is so good looking and such a clean wrestler and role model, we were wondering if it would be possible to present him with a birthday cake on television that night?" she gushed.

Max's antenna went up. This was great! They could make the presentation at the beginning of the main event. Cowboy was in a two-out-of-three with Keith. They would get it all on film. Great! It would be good public relations for wrestling.

"Well, ladies, we don't usually do anything like this, but since it is for such a worthy cause, and we strive to be good role models, and we think the world of Cowboy, we can make an exception. How big will this cake be?"

"It would be large enough to feed five hundred people. There are thirty of us and we all intend to make some of it. But don't you worry, we'll get it down here. It's our pleasure."

"I'll tell you what. We'll have our announcer tell the people when you are to bring it into the ring. We'll tell everyone it's Cowboy's birthday and everyone can sing 'Happy Birthday' to him. After the matches, we can have you cut it into little pieces and everyone can have a little bite. How does that sound? I'm sure Cowboy will be happy."

"Oh, Mr. Daniels, that is wonderful! We'll bring napkins. You don't have to worry about a thing." They were happy and excited as they left the office.

*   *   *

Rumors and stories flew around the arena. By the night of the show there wasn't anyone this side of Dallas who didn't know what was going to happen. Much money had been spent publicizing the "birthday party."

The ladies called and received permission to hide the cake in the office until the final match. They had also received permission to take a knife into the arena to cut it, but only if they used a plastic one, since Wrestling Commission rules forbid weapons in an arena during matches.

The big night finally arrived, interviews had been taped and the first match was being filmed.

The secretary heard a noise outside and looking up, she saw the largest cake she had ever seen being carried into the office by three men on a 4' x 8' piece of paper-covered plywood.

This thing is a work of art, she thought. In the center was a scaled down wrestling ring with two candy wrestlers and a referee. The wrestlers were placed on a mat and the referee had his little icing arm in the air, as if counting "one-two-three". Around the ring were icing chairs and fans, some sitting, some standing and you could almost hear them screaming.

She was amazed. These people must have taken days to complete this little mini-miracle.

At five minutes until ten, the three men returned, picked up the cake, and went in the back door of the arena, the purse-clutching women following them eagerly toward the ring.

They waited for their cue. The referee announced into the microphone, "Ladies and gentlemen, in this corner we have Texas' own 245 lb. Cowboy Nelson."

Applause and screams as the cowboy circled the ring and flashed his smile as he settled into one corner.

"And in this corner, we give you the well known 240 lb. Keith Daniels." Cat calls, boos, and smattering of applause followed Keith as he preened and finally sat on the top rope of the turnbuckle in his corner, waiting.

"Before we begin tonight's matches," Stanley the announcer began, "We have a rather unusual announcement. Tonight is Cowboy Nelson's birthday." Applause and whistles filled the arena.

"And the Mothers of America have asked, and have been given permission to present him with a cake."

At that time, the three men struggled valiantly to get the huge, heavy cake up the three steps and between the ropes for their hero's approval. He looked properly astonished and pleased, and the audience went wild.

Keith smirked from his position above the ring, looking down on the cake.

The four women fluttered around the inside of the ring and Cowboy was kissing each of them demurely and properly on their cheeks. While the confusion was going on, Stanley once again announced that everyone would receive a piece of cake on his or her way out. That did it. They stomped and whistled, and the referee decided that the 'marks' must leave the ring for the match to proceed.

The ladies were the first to leave. Cowboy escorted them to the ropes, sat down on the middle one, and raised the top rope for the ladies to duck under. He gallantly handed each lady down to the security officer waiting at the foot of the ring steps.

As he turned to help the men, Cowboy heard a scream begin to roll through the fans, which got louder and louder as it reached the ring. Looking up, something caught his eye.

He looked at Keith's corner of the ring, to the turnbuckle where he had been sitting, just in time to see him do a forward flip and land squarely in the middle of the cake!

A tidal wave of cake and icing hit the front row fans on all four sides of the ring. No one escaped. Not the wrestlers, the three men, the referee, the announcer, nor four little ladies standing, horror-stricken, unable to believe what they had just seen. The piece of wood was in splinters. The three men ran from the ring in total fear as the Cowboy ran across the ring to get Keith.

You could see the rage in his beautiful, icing-covered face. His big party had been ruined. His fans had been disappointed. His anger gave him strength and he grabbed Keith and pinned him to the mat in less than two minutes.

After the pin, he rubbed his hands together in a gesture of dismissal and walked away, not claiming the victory of the match. He felt vindicated. The fans roared their approval. He was still their hero.

Later, as the crowd hurried for the exits, each wanting to get home and clean up, they all felt they had seen something unscheduled and spontaneous

In the dressing room, standing next to each other in the shower, Keith and Cowboy were busy scrubbing icing off their bodies. They laughed. "Man, we sold it tonight."

12

The following week, everyone was in the office discussing the matches they were having that night. The arena rats were lined up outside behind the building, waiting to see their favorite man show up. The baby faces would drive up together and the heels either together or each in his separate car. The masked wrestlers never had anyone with them.

As they arrived, the men hurriedly left their cars carrying their seemingly weightless suitcases, smiling, waving, and looking over the fans, as they disappeared behind the office door. No fan was ever allowed inside.

Once inside, no longer on display, they would drop their cases, groan and moan, complain of their aches and pains, and flop into the nearest chair.

They had a right to complain; they wrestled six or seven nights a week, sometimes twice a day. Then they jumped into cars for the long drive or catch a plane to the next town to do it all over again. The public never sees this side of their lives, nor do they care.

The men were sitting around, killing time, and waiting to go to the dressing rooms to change for tonight's matches when all hell broke loose in the parking lot. Screams, horns blowing, and running feet could be heard. Max and Stanley reached the window first.

"What the hell is going on? Some damn fan going nuts?"

Standing beside and above a black van was the largest living human they had ever seen. A leonine head with shoulder-length hair and piercing green eyes were the first things you saw. Big, well-shaped lips smiled under a long, slim nose. The man had shoulders that looked like football shoulder pads with long arms ending in hands that could easily hold a basketball in each one. The giant's torso was well muscled, and his waist tapered down so much that he had the overall appearance of a statue of a Greek god. The legs were immense and his feet looked like snowshoes. He was slowly making his way to the door, happily smiling and friendly. When he arrived at last, he quietly opened it and said, "Hi, I'm Pierre." His voice came from the bottom of his feet and the tone was about the same as a foghorn on a dark night. The volume was awesome.

There was a stunned silence. To a man, everyone was looking up with fascination. Max and Stanley came running.

"Come on in. We've been waiting for you." The giant came into the office. A couple of the men jumped up from the couch so that he would have some place to sit.

After introducing Pierre to the wrestlers, Max asked them to leave so that he could discuss future plans with the man. They left the office to file across the parking lot to the main arena building.

The guard at the back door was a regular who knew each man; he smiled and jumped to hold the door open for them as they entered. Inside, the fans lunged forward against the ropes that formed a walkway for the men.

As the wrestlers walked down the walkway, they scanned the crowd. The fans were being held back by uniformed policemen, whom they always believed were there to protect them from the "heel" wrestlers. In reality, the police were there to protect the wrestlers from the fans. They, like boxers, cannot hit a person outside the ring; if a fan enters the ring, however, he does so at his own expense. There have been many wrestlers seriously injured by fans. They have been stabbed with ice picks, knives, and scissors. They have had staples shot into them from staple guns, and battery acid shot at them from water guns. Most wrestling promotions have lawsuits going on almost constantly due to the ridiculous cruelty of the fans to the wrestlers.

*   *   *

The semi-final match was a tag team between the Rebels and the Vanderbilt brothers.

The Rebels wore yankee pants and came out with a rebel flag. Dirty, big, with heads shaved bare, the fans loved to hate them. They were well established as heels and were notorious for their dirty moves in the ring. Blood usually flowed during their matches.

The Vanderbilt brothers were crowd-pleasers. Their blonde good looks and tanned, muscled bodies belied their heavy coke habits. Women went crazy over them, jumping on their chair seats to see better, screaming and making lewd sounds as they passed, and when they could get close enough, they were not above slipping papers into the grapplers' hands with phone numbers on them.

The big blonde brothers stood center ring with one arm across each other's shoulders, waiting and enjoying the effect they were having on their audience.

The spotlight hit the dressing room entrance and down the walkway came the Rebels, gesturing and waving to the shrill calls and boos from the fans. Here and there, an odd man would applaud and then quickly put his hands down, as people around him turned to gaze at him.

As soon as the referee had introduced the four, they all ran, head on into the center of the ring. The referee hadn't yet given instructions or told them to begin. Bedlam broke loose and the referee tried to get one man from each team to leave the ring. Arms and legs were locked together, men were bouncing against the ropes, people were screaming. The referee waded into the confusion in the middle of the ring, and began to speak to all four in carney.

"Keep up the confusion. They're running in the big guy in two minutes." He ran around the human mass of bodies looking helpless and stupid.

Suddenly, a spotlight shone once again on the dressing room door. Tension mounted as the crowd waited, eyes riveted on the door for what seemed like an eternity. Then the door opened and out stepped Pierre. Looking up into the crowd, eyes adjusting to the glare of the spotlight, his handsome face turned slowly for all to see.

Pierre was a sight to behold. His hair had been brushed to stand out from his head in all directions. A large, red cape hung off his shoulders. The briefest of wrestling trunks barely concealed his manhood, but the huge bulge was there for all to see. His body was shaved and oiled down for maximum appreciation of his huge muscles.

Pierre stood dead still for only 30 seconds. Then he took off toward the ring in long strides, pausing only slightly to take the three ring steps at once, stand on the apron of the ring and step over the top rope.

The fans went wild. Never had they seen anything like this before. He calmly reached down, picked up the Rebels one at a time and threw them into a heap in one corner of the ring. They lay motionless.

The giant walked over and lifted the Vanderbilts to their feet, dusted them off, and as the audience exploded with laughter and applause, he again calmly stepped back over the top ring and once again, strode down the walkway and into the dressing room. He never looked back.

The four men now stood in the middle of the ring, pretending they didn't know who he was or where he had come from.

From the table beside the ring, Stanley was saying into the microphone, "Ladies and gentlemen, you have just met the Mountain Man." The crowds cheered, he was on his way.

A legend had begun.

13

Paulie Swan, the HCW booker was in town to see Max about some upcoming "shows." They were in the office when Paulie asked, "Who do you have that looks good? I'm tired of sending our champion Lance Lawrence against the same old names."

"I've got a new guy coming up, but I'm working him up slowly. Omar Atlas. He had his eye on the Olympics at one time, and the Mexican promotion brought him in. I stole him from them."

"Oh, for God's Sake," said Paulie, "Not another muscled up empty head. Between the body builders and the Kung Fu experts, what's next, Rodeo Riders?"

"No, not this guy. You know how the Hispanic wrestlers "fly" in the ring? He does it real well. I watched him yesterday and he looked damn good. We've also got this big guy, Mountain Man, but you know how that goes. Everyone has to lie down for him and he's too big to really do many holds. But the fans really love him."

"Maybe we can use him later on. Omar, too. If he's as good as you say he is, maybe we can pass the title on to him for awhile. Lance could use the rest." Paulie said.

"How about Keith, Paulie? He's been around a long time and he really works the crowd. What do you say?"

"Well, Max, maybe if he'd beef up a little and calm down a little. We'll see. Where is he? I thought we could party tonight. There's a club here I'd like to go to."

Max noticed Paulie had changed the subject, but decided to let it go for now. Reaching for the phone, he said, "Let me find him for you, Paulie. I'm sure he'll go out with you tonight." Under his breath, he whispered, "You bet your sweet ass he will."

*   *   *

Diamond Jim's was one of the few places the boys could go without being bothered by the public. Close to the arena, sitting out on a pier over the water, the club and its manager offered great meals and relative privacy. Offering the best in food and drinks, it was where they always congregated. Jim's allowed the wrestlers a place to relax and be themselves, and the club was handsomely rewarded for the effort. If and when the men caused trouble, or occasionally broke up the place, Max was quick to compensate generously for damages done.

When Paulie and Keith came in, there were a few hands raised and a couple of greetings, but mostly, they went unnoticed. As they stood at the bar waiting for their eyes to adjust to the darkness and hopefully, their ears to the deafening beat of the music, Paulie said to Keith, "O.K., we're here, where are the women?"

"See those two across the room, sitting alone and looking this way? The redhead is mine. Look at her. Real class. The blonde is yours."

"O.K.," Paulie replied. Makes me no difference. They're all alike in the morning gone. Both men laughed, nodding their heads as they shouldered their way across the dance floor to the two women.

"Hi, Gals," smiled Keith, turning on the charm. "This will be a night you won't forget." Targeting the beautiful redhead, he turned to her and quipped, "Your place or mine?" He laughed and threw his head back as if he had just said the wittiest thing in the world.

She looked straight into his face, slowly bringing the glass to her mouth and drinking. Still looking, she sat the drink down and said, "No, this is going to be a night you'll never forget. Get Lost." With that, she picked up her purse, said goodnight to her girlfriend and walked toward the door.

Keith stood as if he was frozen in cement. Frozen in time. He could feel his face burning. His ears were ringing. Paulie had just witnessed the worst humiliation he had ever received, and was laughing until he saw the look on Keith's face.

"Come back here, you bitch," he shouted. He turned and ran through the crowd to catch up with her. When he did, he grabbed her arm, jerked her around to face him, and started yelling at her. "Do you know who I am? Who do you think you are, bitch?" His voice had risen to a high-pitched shriek that carried to every person in the restaurant. The place became silent. Two bouncers started instinctively toward him, knowing all too well how this would end.

Before the bouncers could reach them, however, a large hand reached out of the darkness and a low, calm voice said, "Take your hands off the lady." Keith stopped yelling and looked beyond the redhead into the face of Omar Atlas.

"Stay the hell out of this, Mexican." But as he said it, he lowered his arm. By that time the bouncers had reached the fracas.

"Come on, boys, not in here. You know the rules," the manager said. One man on each side of Keith, they walked him back across the room to where Paulie was now sitting with the blond. As he walked along quietly now, Keith muttered to himself, "I'll get that S.O.B. if it's the last thing I do."

Reaching the table and sitting down, he couldn't resist one last look. He saw Omar and the beautiful redhead leaving the club as the heavy door shut behind them.

*   *   *

As Omar unpacked his wrestling bag he could smell the redhead's perfume. It was everywhere; on his jacket, his tights, even his towels. She had insisted on helping him pack his bag before the matches tonight.

He still couldn't believe how she had asked to leave Diamond Jim's with him last night after her confrontation with Keith. She was the most beautiful, classiest woman he'd ever been with. He'd been so proud when he walked into the arena tonight with her. His name was on the marquee: Tonight, Omar Atlas. And this woman, she was so beautiful.

*   *   *

"Good luck tonight, Omar," said Brown Velvet, his partner. "Just relax and we'll let the heels lead the match. I'll start the match and as soon as we can, I'll tag you. Then, I'll come back in and finish and you can watch and see how it goes. We're gonna' go one fall, they'll get disqualified when they throw me over the ropes, and we'll get the win. Let's go."

The sounds of "La Conga" blared over the loud speaker as Omar and Brown Velvet stepped out the door of the dressing room, ready to make the trip to the ring. He saw a line of fans a hundred feet long, standing behind metal stanchions, straining against the ropes, hoping to get a closer view, maybe even a touch. No one knew Omar, but everyone knew Brown Velvet, the popular black grappler.

"Let's go, Man," whispered Velvet as he stepped out ahead of Omar, falling into place between two security guards who would make the trip to the ring with him. Elbows bent, big smile on his handsome face, Velvet began to trot, causing both guards to trot alongside him to keep up.

Omar fell in behind, noticing that two other guards took their places beside him, so now there were six men trotting to the strains of the music, making their way to the ring. A rush hit his chest, spreading all through his body. He'd never experienced anything like this in all the events he'd ever been in. Just the size of the arena was enough to scare you.

The house lights dimmed and the spotlights hit him, but not before he'd seen Helen, the redhead, stand up in front of her seat and wave. He thought he'd explode. He was sure it couldn't get better than this.

As Omar approached the ring, he opted not to go up the steps. Adrenaline surging, he vaulted up onto the apron and over the top rope. Landing on two feet, he rolled over into a somersault and sprang to the top rope on the opposite side of the ring. The crowd loved it; Brown Velvet broke into a grin.

"Man," he said after the introduction, "it didn't take you long to get with the program. That looked great."

"In this corner from Caracas, Venezuela, weighing 265 pounds Omar Atlas. And his tag team partner from Atlanta, Georgia, weighing 257 pounds, Brown Velvet."

Now the fans knew who he was. They loved Velvet and so they loved Omar, and since he'd made such a dramatic entrance, they were waiting for more to come.

"And in this corner from Houston, Texas, weighing 249 pounds, The Texan and his tag team partner from New York City weighing 257 pounds, Black Bart."

"Boo" came the thunderous response from the audience as the "heel" tag team was announced.

The four men moved to the center of the ring, glaring at each other as the referee went through all the motions of the perfunctory checking for concealed weapons, sliding his hands down each man's body, carefully avoiding the razor blade pieces each man carried. One by one, they lifted their feet for him to touch the underside of their ring boots.

"Here we go, Omar," said Velvet as he walked back to the "red corner". Omar climbed through the ropes to stand on the outside of the ring.

"Remember, men, you have to be touching the ring post when you get tagged to come into the ring." were the referee's instructions. Watch yourselves.

Omar stood within arm's reach of the ring post as Velvet turned to face his opponent, Black Bart, who had chosen to go first.

As they circled each other, glaring at each other, fingers flexing in the age-old show of anticipation, Black Bart as the heel, would lead the match. He would determine which hold would come next and how the team would get into position to execute the "finish", or the end of the match. He had already been told who would win. It was his job to make it look good, make it look real, and make it exciting.

Quickly, Bart grabbed Velvet's hands and bent his fingers backwards until the black man was forced to his knees, arms straight out in front. Without warning, Omar vaulted over the top rope, landed in a football lineup crouch and sprang forward over Velvet's head, landing a forearm chop to Black Bart's chest area.

The fans went wild; Bart went flying through the air, and Velvet slapped Omar's hand, signifying that he was passing the match to the Venezuelan. No one seemed to notice that Omar wasn't holding onto the ring post.

As Brown Velvet retreated to the corner, Omar jumped up and down in place over the prone form of Black Bart.

"Come on, get up," he screamed. The crowd was on its feet. Black Bart got up on all fours, glaring at the newcomer. From behind Omar, out of his line of vision, came the Texan. Sneaking through the ropes, he suddenly dashed up behind the jumping man and making a wedge out of his two hands, came down hard on the back of Omar's neck.

Red flashes of light tore across Oma's eyes. The din of the crowd became a whisper. Everyone moved in slow motion. This was not supposed to happen, but it had.

Suddenly seized in a full Nelson, Omar heard only the words of The Texan in his ear.

"Glory Hound. Prima Donna. Think you're the star, don't you? I'll teach you to try to hog the spotlight." The pressure on the back of his neck was unbearable.

Omar looked around for Brown Velvet, but could see Black Bart block him from entering the ring. As he felt himself beginning to black out, Omar made, with the last of his strength, the final effort. He raised both arms straight up in the air and dropped to the floor out of The Texan's grip. As The Texan bent over to pick up his victim, Omar was miraculously able to quickly lie down on his back, bring his feet up over his head, and kick his opponent squarely in the face. He heard the two front teeth crack upon impact. The Texan's head flew back, blood flew all over the front row spectators, and the referee came running.

"One—Two—Three" The bell rang, and Omar was an "overnight success."

Brown Velvet came over and hoisted Omar to his shoulders.

"You were fantastic, Man, a Natural" said Velvet. "You worked like we've been a tag team all our lives". he said.

The sounds of "La Conga" came to his ears again and he knew it was time to leave the ring. The exhilaration was so intense that he couldn't catch his breath. It took all four security guards to keep back the crowd as he made his way back to the dressing room. On both sides of the aisle, he could see fans, mostly women and girls, who'd come down from the bleachers to get a closer look at the Latin dynamo. This time he trotted in front of Brown Velvet. He'd arrived!

*   *   *

As he entered the door to the dressing room, the wrestlers were standing where they'd been watching the match.

"Great job, Omar," said Cochise.

"You did great," came Mauler Savage.

"God Damn Glory Hound" muttered Keith.

14

As she stepped off the plane and onto the ramp, Toni felt a mixture of emotion; anxiety, fear and exhilaration. She was happy to be joining her brother Omar in this exciting country, afraid because it was her first time out of Venezuela, and a sense of freedom because she was on her own for the first time in her 20 years.

For her graduation from finishing school, Omar had promised to send her a ticket to the United States, and he hadn't failed her. She had never doubted for one minute that the ticket would come. Since Omar had left Caracas to wrestle, he had not forgotten his family back home. Over the years the checks had come regularly, first to their mother, and after her death last year, they had been coming to Toni and her older sister Maria whom she lived with. He had paid her way to the American school, where she learned to speak English perfectly.

Now her dreams had come true. She was landing in Corpus Christ, Texas, her wishes fulfilled, her life ahead of her.

She would find a job and contribute toward her upkeep; until then, she would live in an apartment Omar would find for them.

Toni scanned the crowd in the airport. Suddenly there was a surge toward the front door. People screamed and waved their arms and ran toward the door where she could see the tops of two heads above the crowd. The men were slowly making their way towards her. She recognized Omar, but who was the blonde gringo with him? She knew by the screams that he, also was a wrestler.

"Omarsito," she screamed, "Omarsito, over here."

Omar broke away from the crowd and came running.

"Toni," he yelled, waving his arms and grinning from ear to ear. Quickly he came to her, threw his arms around her, and wrapped her in a gigantic bear hug, which immediately squeezed the wind from her lungs. She was crying with joy, hugging him back, and trying to talk, all at the same time.

"The country it is so beautiful" she said to him in Spanish. "It is even more beautiful than I had expected. I've seen Dallas and Miami and it is beautiful."

"So this is Toni," came a voice at her side. She turned and looked into blue eyes framed with jet-black eyelashes so long that they looked like the curled lashes Tony had seen on famous models.

"I've heard so much about you, but your brother didn't tell me you were such a knock out. I'm Keith."

"He's beautiful," she thought. Keith had dressed 'to the T' to come with Omar to the airport. Normally, shorts and tee shirt were about as dressed as he ever got, but he had seen pictures of Toni, and had decided to see for himself. He had a rule. Never pass up a beautiful woman, no matter who she is.

As they left the Customs office, Keith took one arm and Omar took the other as they walked quickly through the airport lobby, fans pushing and shoving to get closer to the two grapplers.

"I have a couple of apartments for you to look at, Toni," said Omar. "You need to like the place, because I won't be there much and you'll be all alone. You can't go with me from town to town, so we need to find some place safe for you to stay."

"Let's go to the house for lunch first," said Keith. "Mom knows you're here and she's fixed lunch for Dad, so let's go by and at least drink a beer with the old man. How about it?"

"Thanks, Keith," Omar said. He couldn't understand why he was being so nice to Toni; this was totally unlike him. He wouldn't offer lunch to any woman without wanting anything in return.

As they came to the car, Keith quickly ran to the other side, opened the door, and looked down the front of Toni's dress as she slid across the seat.

"Scoot over and sit in the middle, Toni," Keith said. He got quickly behind the wheel and watched her skirt slip higher and higher, exposing long, firm brown legs.

As the big Lincoln pulled away from the curb, Keith really turned on the charm. He pointed out places of interest, talking to Toni, and answering all of her questions about America.

As they pulled up to Max's house, a huge gate automatically opened to allow entrance to the big car. Toni's eyes opened in shock and wonder. Never before had she seen such luxury. In Caracas, only the governor's palace equaled the splendor of this mansion. Keith knew what an impression this was making on the young woman.

"Mi casa su casa," he said to her, slightly above a whisper. "My house is your house." He could feel the heat of her body pressing against him as she stretched to look at the magnificent home.

As the car pulled in front of the large stairway in front of the house, he saw his mother standing in the door, drink in one hand, cigarette in the other. Tall, elegant, and dressed as usual in the latest Halston fashion.

He hoped she would manage to stay sober through lunch.

God damn her, anyway.

    ✷   ✷   ✷

Max was down by the pool, his bible in his lap, dog at his side, and religious music rolling over the expansive countryside. He looked up when he saw them coming. *Here they come, the sublime and the ridiculous, he thought.* Too bad Keith had to be the ridiculous. He raised his tanned arm, motioning the men to him.

"Come on down, guys, let me read to you out of the bible," he screamed to them over the sounds of 'Nearer My God to Thee' blaring out of the 20 speakers placed in shrubbery in strategic places all over the acreage. No one in this house had any choice of what to listen to.

"No, Dad, come on up. Mom says lunch is ready." Screamed Keith.

"Hell!" said Max as he dragged his crippled body out of the chair. "I wanted to read to you out of the bible."

All through lunch, Frances was animated and sweet to Toni. "Where did you learn such beautiful English?" she asked the girl.

"In the American school. It was required, and I knew I would be coming to America. I was an eager student."

"You must come back tomorrow," Frances said. "We'll go shopping. I know all the little boutiques downtown where my daughters and I shop."

"I would love to, Mrs. Daniels," said Toni, "but we don't have our apartment picked out yet and Omar has to leave town soon."

"Nonsense," said Frances. "Don't even worry about all that. The clothes will be my treat." Keith wasn't surprised. Since Jeannie and Judy had been at college, his mother had been very depressed. She had been drinking more and more lately, and this would keep her occupied for awhile, anyway, until the new wore off for her.

Drinking was one of her escapes, buying clothes was another. She probably bought $2,000 to $4,000 worth of clothes a month and didn't wear half of them.

The poor bitch thinks that will help. She needs to get another boyfriend. She had one last year and she was less trouble than he could ever remember her being. She can't even do that right. I don't think the guy is even around now, he thought.

"Please, Omar, please let me go shopping. It would be so much fun. I've dreamed of shopping in America, buying American clothes, please let me. We can find an apartment later."

"We can take her to church on Sunday, too," Max interrupted. Before he could answer, Frances stood up, leaned across the table, and said, "I know what we'll do. I want to show Toni around Corpus Christi, buy her some clothes and introduce her to some of my friends. They are going to love her with her darling accent and beauty. I'll even take her to Reggie, my hairdresser. You go on, Omar, and bring your things here and you two can stay with for awhile until she knows her way around. If she were my daughter, I wouldn't want her to be alone in an apartment for a month or two while you go on the road. We have 23 rooms and nine bathrooms, I believe we have the room. What do you say?"

The last thing Omar wanted as his sister under the same roof as Keith Daniels' parents, but before he could open his mouth, Toni had thrown her arms around him, tears of joy were streaming down her cheeks, and she was laughing and crying all at the same time.

"Por favor, mi amor, por favor." He understood that she would be happier here than in an apartment alone, but he vowed to himself never to leave town with Keith in the house with Toni.

"That is wonderful of you, Frances. I can't begin to thank you enough."

"Nonsense, I'll enjoy it," came the answer. "You two can have the suite upstairs next to ours. It has its own stairway down the back of the house, and you will be free to come and go at all hours and won't wake 'us girls' when you come in late at night. It's agreed then. Keith, as soon as we finish dinner, go get Toni's bags out of your car. We'll unpack while you and Omar go get his things. Tomorrow you two have to leave for Waco, and Toni and I will begin our shopping spree."

She hugged Toni as they started up the stairs. "This is the way to your suite, dear."

Omar watched them climb the stairs, a sense of foreboding edging its way into his consciousness. Keith also watched, smiling slightly.

I couldn't have planned this any better if I had tried.

* * *

Toni came downstairs for breakfast, wearing only her gown and robe, because Max and Omar were always gone by this time and she ate with Frances. It was a routine which had quickly been established in the household.

As she reached the bottom step, she looked into the large, sunny breakfast room.

Keith was sitting at the round glass table talking to his mother. He looked wonderful. Tanned, rested and handsome.

Surprised to see him, Toni smiled sweetly and asked, "What are you doing here so early? I thought you were out of town with Omar."

"No, I'm leaving early tomorrow morning. I changed my plans. Omar and the boys left today." His gaze started at her head and ended at her toes. "You look beautiful this morning."

"Are you hungry, dear?" Frances was already slurring her words, as she was on her third bloody Mary. She looked at her son. He had been here more since Toni and Omar had moved in than in the last two years. Something was up. She didn't like this at all.

"How about some eggs? I'll call Maria."

"No thank you, I'll just have coffee and juice."

"Well, girls, what are the plans for today? More shopping?" He smiled and leaned back in his chair, the frail china coffee cup seemingly out of place in his large hand.

"I have tennis today from four to six and your father and I are going to the country club for dinner tonight," Frances answered. *Unless, of course, he backs out one more time to stay home and read the bible all night*, she thought.

Keith was immediately interested. He sat up in his chair. "How about you, gorgeous? What are your plans?" He looked at Toni's face but hoping her robe might slip down a little, since she was leaning forward to sugar her coffee.

"I really don't have any plans. Since Omar is out of town, I'll probably stay in and write a few letters." She didn't want to tell Keith that

Omar had forbidden her to leave the house with him under any circumstances.

"Fine! I'll pick you up at 7:30, and we can go for dinner and dancing on the beach at Diamond Jim's and I'll introduce you to some of the boys. Omar seems to have kept you hidden out here with Mother. No one has met you yet. Then we'll drive around and you can see some of the town other than the stores. What do you say?"

Toni really had no reason not to go. She was afraid of what Omar would say, but what could she do? She looked at Frances' face, but couldn't read anything there. After all, he was her son. And she and Max had been so good to Omar and her.

"Well, I guess it'll be O.K. Yes, I'd really love to go. I haven't been out dancing or for an evening out in such a long time."

Keith rose, hugged Toni gently, kissed the top of Frances' head and winked at her.

"See 'ya tonight," he said as he walked to the front door, quickly, before Toni changed her mind.

Frances watched him suspiciously as he left. No, she really didn't know what he was up to. To kiss her was out of character enough, but to come on to Toni; she certainly wasn't his type. No painted dolly or stewardess-type. She must really watch this. Something was wrong.

* * *

That night when Keith came to pick her up, Toni couldn't help the excitement she felt. He had always been so nice to her and it had been so long since she had dressed up and gone out with a good-looking man. And was he good looking!

She planned her entrance t the last detail. She wanted him to be pleased with her.

And he was! She stood at the head of the stairs, looking down at him. Her long, curly hair fell on dark skinned, smooth shoulders. And laughing brown eyes looked into his. A large, full mouth and gorgeous teeth with a big smile greeted him. She wore a form-fitting, short white beaded dress that Frances had talked her into buying. She was magnificent!

"Do I look all right? " she asked, knowing full well the answer.

"All right?" he almost choked. "You are absolutely beautiful!" He held out his hand as she slowly descended the stairs.

At the bottom, he took her hand, kissed her lightly and said, "Let's go, our reservations are made."

The handsome couple left the house and began chapter one of their future.

*   *   *

The club was packed. Their table was one of the best; Keith had seen to that. Jim greeted them, slapping Keith on the back and looking Toni over from head to feet.

"Welcome, welcome, your table is ready. Right by the dance floor, as you requested."

While they were being seated, Toni looked at her plate. Two white boxes were lying side by side. Her eyes shone brightly as she looked expectantly at Keith.

"What is this?" she asked.

"Just a little token from me to you," he smiled back at her, softly patting her hand.

She chose the larger box first. Lifting the lid, she saw the most beautiful gold cross she had ever seen. It was gold filigree and had one-quarter carat diamond in the center.

"It's so beautiful. Oh, thank you, thank you." She put it softly to her lips and then her cheek. "I've never had real gold before," she told him.

"Look at the other box," he said. She carefully lifted the lid of the second box.

"Ooh," she said. Her eyes looked at him for an explanation. In her hand lay a delicate gold bracelet with tiny diamonds surrounding a dangling letter "T". "It is so beautiful, but I cannot accept it. Omar would kill me."

"Don't worry, I'll handle Omar," Keith said. "Do you like them?"

"You have given me my first gold and my first diamonds. Thank you so much."

He gently put the bracelet around her wrist as she watched with emotion-filled eyes. "I want to be the first everything in your life from now on," he said.

*   *   *

Back at the Daniels' mansion, the lights were out except for the master bedroom.

Max was propped up in the huge bed, quilts and pillows thrown in disarray, reading his bible and Frances sat in front of her makeup table. This was a nightly ritual for both of them and they usually didn't talk much. But tonight Frances had something on her mind.

"Max, Keith and Toni are seeing each other a lot. Did you know that?"

"Yeah, the boys told me. It sure isn't making it any easier in the business. Keith and Omar hate each other. What difference does it make to you? She's just one more dame in his life.

"I don't think so," Frances said, brushing her blonde hair. "She is a wonderful young girl and I think she is in love with him. But I don't know if he can love anyone."

"If the Lord intends them to be together, they will be. She may be just what he needs. Young, innocent and so naive. He keeps her pretty much away from the boys."

"I'm not questioning whether she will be good for him. I think she will, but what about him being good for her? I've come to care a good deal for her. The girls love her, too. She fits right into the family." I wouldn't want to see her get hurt.

"Don't worry, it'll pass. How many have we seen come and go in Keith's life?"

She sighed and put the brush down. She didn't want Toni to "go" like the other ones. Oh well, what could she do?

She rose, walked around to her side of the bed and lay down beside the already snoring Max.

15

Cochise and Marilyn entered Diamond Jim's the same way they usually did arguing.

"Damn it, Marilyn, I told you not to worry about something that hasn't happened yet. Don't get so excited. Maybe things will be O.K. and you won't have to leave."

"Maybe I'll become a movie star, too," was the reply. "You know he can't stand me. I've called all over the country and nobody is using girls now. It's almost like I've been blackballed in every territory."

As they straddled two bar stools, Cochise said to the bartender, "Give me a Chivas and soda, and a Screw Driver for the lady."

"Just cool it, Baby, and play it by ear. You've been doing a great job here, the crowds love you, and I see no reason for Keith to make you leave. Have you tried to talk with him, or are you just building this all up in your mind? You know how you are, Marilyn."

"Hell yes, I've tried to talk with him. He won't return my calls, and the only time I see him is in the dressing room at the matches or while we are doing t.v. He uses that as an excuse not to deal with me." Her voice was rising now, and Cochise recognized the signs of unreasonable wrath forming.

"Is everything O.K?" said the bartender.

"Sure is," said Cochise. "The lady here is PMSing; otherwise, we're fine. Give me another Chivas, please."

"Would you look who's coming through the door?" she suddenly asked.

"He was surprised she hadn't picked up on the PMS thing, so he knew this must be something spectacular. He turned his head and saw Keith coming into the club with the most beautiful brunette he had ever seen. Not like the made up "show girl" types who Keith usually had attached to his arm.

Cochise couldn't help but wonder how old she was. He had a daughter who was 17, and this girl looked in that age group to him. Looks like he's robbing the cradle, he thought to himself. He watched with utter disbelief as Keith, impeccably dressed for once, pulled the chair out for the girl, handed her a menu, and was seemingly hanging onto every word she said.

He saw the girl open two small, white boxes, saw the smile on her face, and couldn't help but feel sorry for her. She was so out of her league.

"What are you looking at, Indian? Something interest you?" came the voice of Marilyn, the ScrewDrivers starting to work on her brain.

"You know I like blondes," he joked.

"And brunettes and redheads and anything else you can find. You're not too particular, if you ask me."

His first reaction, because of his uncontrollable temper was to slap the crap out of this half drunk, disheveled woman who was starting to sound like a fishwife. Instead, he mumbled, "Damn straight I'm not particular. Look who I'm here with tonight."

"You son-of-a-bitch," she screeched, "you doped up, over the hill, fat Indian. I'm not the one who puts black shoe polish on the back of my head to hide my bald spot in the ring. I'm not the one who looks so much like Buddy Hackett that the fans think they are getting his autograph. You old fart!"

He didn't even look up. Slouched behind his Scotch, he was still thinking about the brunette and Keith. He didn't see Marilyn's handbag coming. With two hands she gripped the Dooney bag, pulled her arm back as far as it would go and swung like Arnold Palmer. Whap! The bag hit Cochise on the right temple, temporarily blinding him and knocking him completely off his barstool.

People ran all directions as he crashed to the floor, tearing loose the right sleeve of his $1,000, custom-made silk suit. Cochise lay there for thirty seconds, and then jumped up, face black with rage, and fists clenched.

"You bitch! Look what you did. Whatever you do, don't stop running 'til you hear glass and smell shit, because if I catch you, I'll kill you!" He lunged.

Using her years of acrobatic wrestling skills, Marilyn jumped completely over the bar, landing on the backside, and headed for the kitchen door and out into the alley.

Jim, used to this fighting duo, was standing in the kitchen, patiently holding the door open so that she could make her retreat. He knew that whatever damage would take place, the wrestling company or Cochise himself would cover the cost; however, the inconvenience was bad. He had learned over the years that one reason for the phenomenal success of his nightclub was that patrons never knew what to expect from the local wrestlers, but they were eager to watch. As long as the wrestlers didn't draw any of his customers into their melee, he was happy. Making more money than he knew what to do with, Jim always saw to it that the doors, front and back, were always open to the wrestlers.

Marilyn sped past him, shoes off, skirt pulled up so high that the crotch of her white panties was visible.

"Shut the door behind me," she screamed as she tore out the back and into the alley.

"Hold that door," came a bellow as Jim looked up in time to see Cochise vault over the bar.

Pretending not to hear, and buying Marilyn some time, Jim closed the door and walked away.

16

Keith was in his father's office.

"I don't give a God damn! I've carried Jesse as far as I'm going to. I don't care how we do it. I don't want to be a tag team any more. The fans want to see me, not him. I want to go out on my own. You promised me when we started," he whined like a small, petulant boy.

"I want a chance at Paulie's champion. You know I'm good enough, Dad." He always reverted to Dad when trying to soften Max up for one reason or another.

Remembering his last conversation with Paulie, Max couldn't see much chance of that happening. But he couldn't bring himself to tell this to his son.

"Take it easy, Keith. If it's that important to you, we'll work it. Tonight, we'll have you turn against Jesse and you and the other team will beat him up. As the other two work him over, you run out of the ring and we'll send the stretcher in. That will get the crowd on their feet. You know how they react to a stretcher."

Looking pleased, Keith had once more gotten his way. He could feel the weight of the championship belt right now. Look out Omar Atlas, look out everyone, he thought to himself.

That night his match went as they had planned. Jesse resented having to do a "job" for Keith and being let go. The fans would be told that he was badly injured and in the hospital. They would even stage an "interview with a doctor" from his hospital room before he left town.

And then Jesse would begin the phone calls and pictures mailed out all over the United States to other promoters.

*   *   *

After the matches, father and son were discussing the following weeks' activities.

"Look, Dad, now that I've gotten rid of Jesse as my tag team partner, I want to build myself up as a single. Next week in Dallas, I'm going to wrestle Omar and hurt him. We'll use the Alka Seltzer bit. I'll hit him in the throat, he'll foam at the mouth, and the marks will buy it. We can say he's in the hospital. Give him some time off so he can go back to Venezuela for a visit." And leave Toni here with me, he thought. "He's getting too popular. I want Cochise on top so eventually we can meet each other and sell the joint out."

"That's fine, Son, but let's don't put Omar out of commission. He's good in the ring and we need all the action we can get. I've heard from Lorenzo Petri in Chicago that he's interested in a merger. I talked with him last week and he's been watching our t.v. shows, so I want all the action we can have on the shows. As owner of HCW, he's strong. He could put us in the big time."

Max didn't want to tell Keith that it was largely because of Omar that Lorenzo was interested in their territory. According to some of the boys, Lorenzo had already approached Omar to quit Wild West Wrestling and come to HCW, the biggest and best territory in the United States. The money was great, the travel international, and the fame was unexcelled. A wrestler could easily make a million dollars a year, plus another $50—$60,000 as his percentage of the souvenirs which used his name or face. Omar, however, had turned him down. Because of his loyalty to Max for giving him an opportunity in his large promotion, and because Toni seemed to have found a second mother in Frances, Omar had decided to stay where he was.

So, in Lorenzo's usual style, if he couldn't persuade you, he'd buy you. He called Max and suggested a merger. Now Keith wanted to get rid of Omar.

"No, Son, get someone else to do the Alka Seltzer routine. Omar's not doing any jobs. We're pushing him to the top."

Keith rose from his desk, came over to this father's chair, leaned over him and screamed, "What do you mean you talked to Lorenzo? I'm the booker, or have you forgotten, old man?"

"No, Son, but he called me. I didn't call him."

"Did you tell him to talk to me from now on?"

"No, Son, but next time he calls, I will." Max hoped that Keith wouldn't let his jealous nature ruin this deal. A merger with Lorenzo Petri would make Keith rich and Max richer. He was afraid that when Keith found out who Lorenzo was really interested in, he would blow the deal for everyone. Booker he was, but not a good one. Max rued the day he had decided to let Keith book. Every promoter who had ever been successful had a non-wrestling booker. That way, matches could be created with a purpose without letting his ego and his own reputation get in the way. But not his son Keith.

The door opened, and Mad Dog McGuirk stood there, wearing only the brief jockey shorts worn under wrestling tights. "I just found out I'm working with Black Panther tonight. Do you have anything planned for me?" asked the heel.

"Yes," said Keith. "You're gonna' start tonight with him and beat him. Then for the next few weeks, as long as we can milk it, you'll "go over" in every match. Then, finally you're gonna' meet Cochise. It will be feathers against dog food. You win, you chop up his headdress; he wins, you eat a can of dog food, since you're Mad Dog. We'll do the corned beef hash switch like they did with you in Canada. We'll buy a can of dog food and a can of corned beef hash. We'll switch the labels, and then when you lose the match, we'll open the corned beef that has the dog food label, and we'll force feed you the meat."

"That sounds good, boss," said Mad Dog. As he turned and started back to the gym next door, he turned with a smile on his face and said, "Oh yeah, next time get an Alpo label. Maybe they'll call and make a deal for a commercial."

* * *

17

Max called the men together. "Boys, we've got a real big talent coming in from the West Coast. You've all heard of him. Rooster Red. Now you know his gimmick, his rooster rides into the arena on his shoulder and sits on the top rope during the matches. As soon as Red pins his opponent, the rooster flaps his wings and crows. It's the damnedest thing I've ever seen. It took three years to train the chicken, and Red is crazy about that bird, so absolutely no tricks. I'm serious about this. No one hurts the damn bird. Understood?"

"Sure, sure." They understood the unwritten law of wrestling. No one intentionally injures anyone and no one messes with another man's gimmick. Whatever happens in the ring can look deadly, but in reality no one intentionally gets hurt.

No one wants to wrestler a "crowbar", someone who is stiff and will hurt you, and no one wants to work months perfecting a gimmick, only to have someone senselessly ruin it in one match.

In fact, before a match, there is a saying, "I give you my body, you give me yours." That is a simple way of saying, "I won't put you out of commission so that you can't work, and you won't put me out of commission so I can't work." If someone gets hurt, it is either an accident, the promoter has said to, or someone gets mad.

"Max," asked Cowboy, "Who is wrestling Red tomorrow night?"

"Manny Ho," Max replied, nodding toward the wrestler.

Manny Ho, at 220 pounds, was not as large as some of the men and they really didn't like to work with him because he was just a little crazy. In his youth, his gimmick had been breaking wooden blocks with his head, and some thought he had broken a few too many along the way. Also, sometimes for no reason, he would arbitrarily decide to win a match even if he had been told not to.

Max explained, "Remember, Manny, leave the rooster on the top rope and let him do his thing. This is not something that can be replaced if you tear it up, and you can't pay for it and make it right. Leave the thing alone."

"Sure, boss, no problem."

* * *

That night the match started with a fanfare and the introduction of Big Red.

A red spotlight hit the man and followed him toward the ring as the announcer said, "And now, ladies and gentlemen, new to this area coming from Ontario, Canada, Big Red Robinson and his rooster, Rojo."

Big Red came down the walkway, six feet six inches tall with a bushy, red beard and a head full of wild red hair. His small, black eyes darted around the arena, while on his massive shoulder sat a large, red rooster.

Going through the ropes, Red stomped around the ring three or four times with Rojo held high above his head. Wings flapping, feathers flying, the rooster crowed as if it were sun up and he was in his own hen house surrounded by his harem.

The crowd laughed and clapped as Red put Rojo on top of the ring post in his corner. The bird knew what was expected of him. He fluffed his feathers and squatted and waited for his part of the show to begin.

To the beat of native-sounding drums, Manny Ho made his way down the aisle to the ring and into the spotlight.

Manny was scary looking under normal conditions, but tonight he was awesome. He wore a wide Afro with feathers sticking out, painted face, loin cloth over his tights, and carried a seven foot spear, with what appeared to be scalps dangling from it.

As he neared the ring, drums began to beat louder. Big Red paced back and forth, strutting and making faces, and egging him on.

The ring announcer was about to announce Manny Ho as Big Red's opponent for the evening. Manny circled outside the ring slowly. Once, twice, then, quick as a flash, he rolled into the ring, stopping right in front of Big Red. But he didn't stop there. He continued to roll until he was directly in front of Rojo. He jumped straight up, grabbed the rooster by the neck, swung it twice around the top of his head, and threw it to the mat, breaking Rojo's head completely off his neck as deftly as any butcher ever had.

There was absolute stunned silence. As the headless rooster thrashed around, the only sound in the building was the sound of his wings flapping. Twenty thousand people were gripped by what they had just witnessed, and wondered what Red would do now.

Both wrestlers' eyes were riveted on the now still, dead bird.

All at once, an agonized scream sounded!

Big Red was sitting in the center of the ring, the broken body of Rojo cradled in his arms, and sobbing as though his heart would break.

*   *   *

18

"We need to talk," said Frances as she came into the expansive den. Max looked up from the t.v.

Oh shit, here we go again, he thought. He reluctantly turned down the volume on the remote, losing the last of a religious sermon.

"What do you want now?" he asked, not wanting to be bothered with anything she could possibly have to say. It was probably another invitation to the club, where she loved holding court with the rest of her hard-drinking, under-loved, overweight, tennis-playing female friends.

"I'm concerned about Keith and Toni," she said. "They seem to be getting more deeply involved with each other. I don't like the way Keith is coming on to her. She is naive and inexperienced. She told me the other day that she is waiting for 'Mr. Right', and you and I both know that Keith isn't 'Mr. Right' for a girl like that. We've offered her the sanctuary of our home, and we can't let anything bad happen to her. I'm thinking of talking to Omar about the situation," she said as she walked to the bar to fix herself a drink.

"Look, just stay out of it. I'm sure when the new wears off. He'll look some place else. You know he doesn't stick to any one girl for long. He'll get tired." Said Max.

"You make me sick," she answered as she whirled around from the bar. "You don't care what he does, or to whom. It's been that way since he was a child. Whatever it takes to get Keith what he wants. And that's what's wrong with him today. You and I both know that he's into drugs, and you stick your head in the sand and pretend you don't know. How is this young girl going to cope with him? Please tell me that."

The fierceness of her attack startled Max, but not for long. And all that stuff about drugs was pure crap.

"Reverend Goodwin told me to pray for him, and that's what I'm doing. God will take care of Keith. He always has."

"No, stupid, he hasn't taken care of him, you have. And you aren't always going to be around to do it. Open your eyes and look what you've created. A dirty, foul-mouthed hothead who enjoys inflicting pain on others to get what he wants, because he knows damn well that you'll jump in and pay for whatever he does.

And now you're allowing him to lose money in a business that took us 20 years of work to build."

"Us? Us?" he screamed. "Who in the hell told you it was US? Do you remember when Keith was two and you deserted us in California and took every cent with you? It took me years to get that back together after you came crawling back home broke. Then do you remember all those trips you took to Vegas? I was borrowing money to make the business go and you were gambling your ass away, humping whoever you felt like? What the hell do you mean US? I've worked my balls off for years while you sat your ass on a barstool at the country club.

Do you think that just because I've found God that I've forgotten all that? Not on your life I haven't. Now don't you dare try to interfere with my business at this point, or you'll be sorry. You understand?"

"Yes, I understand," she replied, hurt that he would throw their past at her like that, "But I love Toni, and I'm not going to let anything happen to her, either."

"Butt your ass out of that situation, too. You make Omar mad and cause him to leave this territory and go to HCW, and I'll personally pack your bags for you to leave this house."

He pulled himself up from his recliner, and walked over to Frances at the bar.

"I said, 'do you understand?' he said as he slowly twisted her arm around behind her back.

"Yes, I won't say anything," she said, grimacing in pain, her drink crashing to the marble floor.

"Good. Then we understand each other. Now sit down here with me and watch Brother Robinson." He leaned over, retrieved the remote, just in time to hear the final notes of 'Old Rugged Cross' coming from the TV.

"Amen," he said.

*   *   *

His back against the cushions, Evangelist James Robinson's voice droning on, Max wondered when he had first begun to hate Frances. And when she had first begun to hate him.

Hell, it hadn't even started out O.K. He'd been wrestling that night they met in Tulsa. He'd won over Crusher Wolaski. Another match in another town; no more, no less.

Later, in the dressing room, Nick Novak, one of his best friends in the business, had said, "Hey, I can't believe it. I just looked at my booking sheet and it says you and I are both off tomorrow. What say we stay over here and party tonight? There is a 'kicker" joint named the Cimarron Ballroom where we could go. It's huge, and those red necks won't recognize us. If they're dancing on Wednesday nights, they won't be wrestling fans, or they would be at the arena on Wednesday night. What do you say?"

"God, a 'kicker' joint?" he had answered. "I hate kicker joints."

"Yeah, but think of all those nice, tight butts in blue jeans. And they have girls there, too." Nick laughed at his own joke. A huge, good-looking man, 6'6 "of rippling muscle, he had the same appeal to women as Max did. They were known as the "lover boys" of professional wrestling.

"O.K." Max finally said as he buttoned his shirt. "Am I O.K. this way, or do I need a rope and chaps?" he grinned.

"You look great. You have your boots, blue jeans and shirt, that's dressed up at the Cimarron. That's about what I'm wearing. Come on, let's get a bottle and take it with us. This dump is a dry state."

*   *   *

The Cimarron Ballroom. According to the marquee out front, "former home of Bob Wills and His Texas playboys, now featuring Leon McAuliff", playing the meanest steel guitar that everyone who was anyone in Tulsa, Oklahoma went to the Cimarron.

The two wrestlers, each one carrying a fifth of Jack Daniels wrapped in a brown paper sack under his arm, walked through the lobby of the building, and on into the ballroom itself.

"Great place to hold a wrestling match," said Max, looking around the huge building. High 20' ceilings, excellent sound system, and a room that could easily hold two thousand people slanted for a better view of the huge stage. A great place.

On stage, Leon was belting out "Oklahoma Hills"; the two-steppers were going like whirling dervishes, boots stomping, skirts whirling, dancers laughing.

Nick said, "God, sometimes I wish we didn't work at night"

"Yeah, but these poor schmucks are working tomorrow while you and I are at the gym and in the pool."

"Yeah, and on the road," Nick answered.

"I'm not sure I could handle this smoke every night," said Max

"That's the one drawback. But did you ever see so many long-legged gals with tight butts? They must check butts on girls as they come in here. Not tight, you can't come in." Again, the laugh at his own joke. Max joined him.

As the two wrestlers stood in the doorway surveying the situation, they were unaware that they too, were being watched.

"My God, Frances, would you look at what just came in?" said Suzette, her best friend. "Look at the doorway. My God, they must be body builders."

Frances slowly swung her head around to look at the two men. "You're right, Suzette, they look like something off of Muscle Up Magazine. They're even tall enough for us." She laughed.

Height had always been a problem for Frances and Suzette. Both of the girls were tall, Frances was 5'9", and Suzette even taller at 5'10". All through school the boys had been shorter and even in the insurance firm where they both worked they were the tallest of the 120 women who worked there.

That was what first brought them together and they had formed a friendship six years ago in school. Now they were as tight as sisters.

"Tell you what," said Frances, "I'll take the one on this side and you take the taller, blonde one. He must be 6'6". Now, our only problem is how do we meet them?"

She could see past the men, where several unattached women sitting at the bar had already turned around with their backs to the bar, and were unashamedly "eyeing" the handsome men.

This is the chance of a lifetime. These two hunks were definitely out of their class, but it was worth a try. Suzette called the waitress over.

From years of hard experience, the two wrestlers had learned one really good lesson. Don't sit at the bar. Some four-foot-tall, rowdy redneck was going to get drunk and challenge you some time before the evening was over. It never failed. Thus, professional athletes seldom go to public bars, but prefer private clubs where usually, not always, but usually no one had anything to prove, and you only had to clean out the place once in awhile. John Q. Public is unaware of the fact that as long as a professional wrestler holds a current license, it is automatically a felony for him to hit anyone outside the ring. Cowboy Redneck doesn't give a shit, and most wrestlers don't either. Challenge one and he will break your bones on the spot and go to court later. What the hell! The promoter will pick up the bills!

So, Nick and Max sat at a table not too far away from Suzette and Frances. Because it was a dry state, the procedure was to take your bottle in, wrapped in a paper sack, and keep it under the table. You paid for your mixers and ice. They had just "stashed" their bottles under the table when the waitress appeared with two cokes and a bucket of ice.

"Compliments of the two ladies to your right."

Max and Nick swung around to their right. There sat the two women, pretending to be in conversation, well aware that they had the attention of the two gorgeous men.

"What do you think, Max?" asked Nick. I want the brunette and you can have the blonde." Suzette, tall and sultry with green eyes and large breasts, was watching while pretending to be so interested in what Frances was saying.

"Shit, the blonde has no tits." He answered. She's plain, her hair is brown, and she has no tits."

"Come on, Man," said Nick. "Remember, you owe me one from Dallas. Remember the dog I dated so you could be with Stella?"

"Man, there must be 400 women in here, Nick, let's try for two more."

"No, God damn it, you owe me, and this is a knock out woman and it's only a one night stand, so what difference does it make? You can close your eyes. I'm going over. Come on."

Nick picked up his drink, tipped it to Suzette, and raised his eyebrows at her in the age-old question; "May we join you?"

She nodded her head ever so slightly, and the two men stood up, collected their bottles and drinks, and walked the short distance to the table.

Nick and Suzette hit it off immediately. Of course. Max wished they hadn't. From the first waltz when Nick had asked her to dance and had shown off like a fool on the dance floor, Suzette was hooked. Nick had gone with a ballroom teacher for a few months, and now you couldn't stop the asshole when they got in public. It was all Max could do to put two feet together and dance. And of course, Frances wanted to dance. They danced once and that took care of that.

Sitting at the table watching Nick and Suzette wasn't the highlight of his life, either. Then the fact that Frances smoked like a stovepipe in January didn't impress him, either. She did seem to have a good sense of humor, and by the end of the evening he was actually enjoying himself.

The booze was kicking in, he was pretty much used to the smoke blowing in his face, and he sat in a kind of contented glow, listening to her dream to become a model. *Not without plastic surgery*, he thought.

Finally, the dancing duo came back to the table. By this time, Max had pulled Frances' chair around next to his, and he was sitting with his arm around her. Her voice was going in and out of his brain on waves of Jack Daniels.

Nick and Suzette were wrapped around each other like two old friends at a high school reunion, laughing and talking, all at once. Max noticed that Nick wasn't even drunk. Guess the dancing did it.

"What say we leave here now, girls? Let's go back to our hotel room where we can be alone and get out of this smoke. Max looks like he needs a little sobering up." He looked at Frances and, looking at her smeared mascara and sprayed hair, decided they'd better go before the lights went up and Max went down for the count.

"Fine, let's go," agreed Suzette. The dancing had curled her hair tighter with perspiration, her cheeks were flushed, and a slight film of perspiration on her breast mounding out of her low cut blouse made her just about the sexiest woman Max had ever seen. Her attitude didn't hurt either.

"Oh, I don't know," said Frances, "I'm feeling pretty tipsy."

"Oh, come on, girl," said Suzette, eager for action, "Where's your sense of adventure?"

Without waiting for an answer, Max bent under the table to retrieve what little was left of the Jack Daniels in his sack. He found it, picked it up, and before he straightened up, he glanced across just in time to see

Suzette's long, thin fingers running up Nick's leg. She scraped her fingernails along the inside of his thigh.

"We'd better leave now before we all get embarrassed," said Nick, as Max's face appeared above the tabletop.

*   *   *

The foursome made it to the Ritz Hotel, where the grapplers were staying that night. As they staggered across the lobby, the desk clerk, used to wrestlers and women, never looked up from the t.v. set.

They got into the elevator, where Nick immediately had Suzette's blouse unbuttoned and was busy working his hand inside.

Max looked at Frances. She was leaning up against the handrail, legs buckling, head thrown back, trying to stay awake.

The elevator stopped with a sudden jolt, throwing the four drunken passengers to the floor in a heap. Max felt a breast under his hand and knew whose it was. He gave it a squeeze before it moved out from under his hand.

Nick was helping Suzette to her feet. Arms around each other, they weaved their way down the hall to the room.

Max started to get up, then a wave of dizziness hit him and he fell back down. One more time. He made it this time, and noticed that Frances hadn't stirred. She was down and out.

Better get her out of this elevator before someone comes and pushes the button.

He reached down and picked her up. She was surprisingly light for so tall a girl. That's because she has no tits.

Max carried Frances down to the room the two men shared. *Just my luck. Tonight of all nights the hotel had to be booked and we had to share a room. Just swell.* Because of the Indian Nation Tribal meeting celebration in town they had been lucky to get even one room. The Ritz was where they always stayed after the matches, so they always had a block of rooms, but tonight he had been forced to double up. He hadn't cared, because he and Nick always got along.

At the room, he gently kicked the partially open door. It opened all the way and he entered, carrying Frances in his arms. On the king-sized bed, naked and half-drunk, lay Suzette and Nick. They neither one noticed that he had come in.

Quickly, he turned out the light and sat Frances on the chair. Her head immediately fell back and she was dead weight.

Shit, he thought, *My luck. I might as well get some sleep. No action here.*

He took off all of his clothes and stood there in the dark, listening to the increasing sounds coming from the bed.

"My God, you're a stallion."

"What a great body."

Boy, do you owe me, Nick, you bastard, he thought, the Jack Daniels starting to work on him again.

Leaning down, he took off Frances' blouse. He could see in the dim light of the room that she wore no brassiere. Her breasts were small, but firm, pink and virginal looking.

Then he took off her blue jeans and was surprised that she wore no underwear. He lifted her and gently carried her across the dark room to the far side of the bed. Praying that the two "screwing minks" weren't in the center of the bed, he put her down.

He eased himself onto the bed between her and the wall and was clinging there, trying not to fall off as the bed began to bounce.

Frances' eyes suddenly flew open.

"I have to pee." She said, as she suddenly sat bolt upright, put one hand on Max's stomach, and bolted over him and onto the floor. She hit the floor running to the bathroom.

As the door opened and she switched on the light, Max turned to catch the action on the bed. Suzette looked over at Max's tan face, blue eyes and long eyelashes. She reached down, grabbed his head, and pulled his mouth over to her.

Frances turned the light out before she opened the bathroom door. Stepping out of the light into the darkness, her eyes didn't focus, and then when they did, she saw her friend Suzette with Nick and Max. But only for an instant. She blanked out and hit the floor.

*   *   *

The next morning, Frances woke up in the king-sized bed, naked and alone. She could hear the shower running in the bathroom. *I guess they left us*, she thought.

"Suzette!" she called

"Come on in," Suzette answered.

Opening the bathroom door, she realized that Suzette and both men were in the shower, lathering each other with soap, groping each other, and having a good time.

"Come on in, Girl," said Suzette. She pulled back the shower curtain and Frances saw her friend naked for the first time.

Thick black hair hung almost to her waist. Eyes smiled at her behind long black eyelashes with beads of water sticking to them, making them glitter. She had huge, firm breasts with dark nipples, and long, slender legs completed the picture.

Frances looked down at her own naked body, so white that it was almost luminous. Her hair was the color of a wren bird, she knew she had no visible eyelashes to speak of, and her eyes were so small you could hardly see them. Her breasts were smaller than the pectorals on either of the men with Suzette. She realized that she couldn't compete, and rather than try, she would give up.

"I'm going back to bed until you three are finished," she said. Closing the door behind her, she went back to bed, pulled the covers over her head, and cried.

In the bathroom, Max stepped out of the shower, and on his way out the door, turned and said, "I'm gonna' go give Frances a sympathy screw."

✶   ✶   ✶

Four weeks later, Max wrestled in Tulsa again. Nick wasn't on the card.

Guess I'll go to the Cimarron Ballroom and see if Suzette is there, he thought to himself as he stood in the showers after the matches. There was a knock on the dressing room door.

"It's for you, Daniels."

Stepping out of the shower, wrapping a towel around his waist, he hurried to the door. Maybe Suzette saw I was on the card and came down, he hoped.

He opened the door, and there stood Frances. But she wasn't alone.

"Max, this is my mother and father. I have to talk with you. I'm only 17 and I'm pregnant."

Yeah, that was the day he began to hate Frances.

✶   ✶   ✶

19

"Omar, it's for you," said Frances, as she handed him the poolside telephone. It was Sunday, and after church everyone was outside in the pool. Keith and Omar would leave in two hours for the trip to Austin for tonight's matches. Although most people are resting on Sunday, it was just another workday for the wrestlers, like athletes of all kinds.

"Hello," he said into the phone. "Yes, yes, I understand, and I will be happy to do it." He returned the telephone to its cradle.

"What was that all about?" Keith raised his head from his towel.

"That was the office calling. I need to leave a little early today. There is a young boy in Austin who wants to meet me in person. He is a cancer victim and is scheduled to be operated on tomorrow morning, and before he goes into surgery, he wants to come to the matches and be introduced to me."

"When are you supposed to meet him? We can get some press coverage," said Keith, sleepy now from the fierce rays of the sun. Call the office back and have a photographer available."

"No, I prefer to meet him alone. I want to give him some souvenirs from the company, a picture and a small gift from me. This is too serious for us to turn it into a photo opportunity. His mother says he is very weak and he faces an operation tomorrow that the doctors are only giving him a 50-50 chance of recovering from. I'd rather meet him alone, dedicate my match to him, and talk to him when he comes out of surgery."

"Whatever," answered Keith because Toni was there. He was thinking, What a stupid shit to miss this opportunity. We could even send a crew to the cancer ward, but this bleeding heart Omar doesn't want to take advantage of an opportunity. *What a fucking idiot.*

That night in Austin, Omar spotted the little boy and his mother the second he entered the arena. The office had arranged special seating for them on the front row.

Hurrying to dress, Omar went down to the little boy in the wheel chair, bent down, shook his hand and said, "Hello, I'm Omar Atlas. What's your name?"

"Jimmy Wilson" replied the small, pale child.

"How old are you, Jimmy?" the grappler asked.

"I'm eight, Omar, and I watch you on t.v. every Saturday night and I've come down here to see you every time the doctor said it would be O.K. when I'm not too sick from my chemotherapy. I have cancer, you know."

Choking, Omar looked deeply into the little boy's eyes and was startled at how sick he looked.

"I've made arrangements with the promotion," the big man said, "for you and your mommy to come as my guests every time we are here. You just get well and present this card at the ticket booth, and you can both come in at any time. You have to promise me one thing, though," said Omar.

"What?" asked Jimmy.

"You have to promise me that you will have your mommy call me tomorrow after your surgery and let me know how you are. I have to go to San Antonio to wrestle tomorrow night, but I'll be home tomorrow morning. Please let me know."

He handed Jimmy's mother the card and his home telephone number so that she could get right through.

Jimmy's mother was crying, but her tears were tears of joy, because her little boy had been granted his fervent wish to meet Omar Atlas.

And how well it had turned out. He had been so kind to Jimmy, she was so thankful.

"Thank you, you don't know what you've done for my son," she said.

"You're so welcome," answered Omar as he stood up, turned around, and faced the fans, who were ready to swarm around him for autographs. The security guards had kept them back until Omar could speak with Jimmy, but now they were surrounding him, thrusting pieces of paper at him, begging for autographs.

Then an idea hit him. Stepping back, Omar picked Jimmy up from his wheel chair and sat him on the ring apron. He vaulted up into the ring, picked Jimmy up, and motioned for the microphone to be lowered so that he could speak.

"Ladies and gentlemen," he said. Immediate silence, as everyone who saw the huge man holding the small child listened to find out what was going on.

"Ladies and gentlemen," he repeated, "Let me introduce you to Jimmy Wilson, a friend of mine, and a young man to whom I will dedicate my match tonight."

Pandemonium rang as people stomped and cheered. They loved this big man, and they realized that this was a sick child he held in his arms. Jimmy was grins from ear to ear, and within seconds, his small arm was raised in the universal sign of victory.

Omar walked to every side of the ring. He held the boy up for everyone to see, and each time he did so, the cheers grew louder. Finally, afraid of tiring Jimmy, Omar took him back to his chair, put him down, tucked his blanket around him, and bolted back up the aisle to the dressing room.

All through the matches, Omar watched from the back of the arena as Jimmy had the time of his life. He ate popcorn, he drank cold drinks; he cheered for his heroes and booed the villains.

The other wrestlers got into the spirit, and before the night was over, all of the action was taking place in front of Jimmy.

Finally it was Omar's match. Stopping on the way into the ring to pat Jimmy's head, Omar chose the corner on his side of the ring to stand in. Jimmy called encouragement all through the match, and when Omar won he clapped and screamed.

As Omar left the ring, he winked at Jimmy and said, "I'll be seeing you, Jim."

Jimmy Wilson died at 10:32 a.m. the following day.

✶ ✶ ✶

20

The boys had gathered for a birthday party for Mountain Man. They decided to have it at Max's house because it was big enough for everyone and private with no "marks" around.

Surprisingly, Frances had said O.K. She usually didn't mix with the wrestlers, but even she liked Pierre. He was like a big puppy; always wanting to please and be liked, and everyone did like him.

However, Pierre didn't seem to be able to have a serious relationship with a woman. Several arena rats claimed to have slept with him, but there was no one serious person in his life.

As the men and their wives came in, they were ushered out to the patio and pool area.

The pool was an Olympic sized spectacular, with cedar decks all around it, and everyone was sitting around enjoying the cool of the evening. The bar-b-Q pit was smoking and laughter was everywhere.

Pierre was standing beside one of the tables as a short houseboy started past him carrying a tray. With one sweep of his gigantic arm, Pierre scooped the man up. He stood there with the startled man sitting on his arm, tray still in his hand.

"Hall-O, little man, my name is Pierre."

"Hello," answered the poor fellow, "My name is Tom." Everyone laughed and watched as Pierre carefully set the man down where he had picked him up.

It was hard to believe this mountain of flesh and bone was so gentle. He looked like he could break you in two with one of his huge hands, and he could. His hands were so large that his "pinkie ring" fit over a hen's egg. Yet he was the kindest, most gentle of men.

Around eleven o'clock, two house boys came in with a large birthday cake on wheels.

Everyone started singing "Happy Birthday" and when they got to "dear Pierre, happy birthday," the top popped off, and out stepped a gorgeous, long legged, tan woman in a thong bathing suit. Long black hair cascaded over her large breasts. She broke into a shimmy and stepped out of the cake and shimmied straight toward Pierre. His face shone and he smiled from ear to ear.

She took his big hands in hers and said, "Happy Birthday from the Boys." The two walked off together toward the parked cars and a room, which had been reserved at the Hilton in Pierre's name and paid for by the boys. It was quite a sight. He was 7'6" tall, and she was 6'2".

As soon as they had gone, Max broke up the party. The boys and their wives and girlfriends were disappointed. Everyone was having a good time. Everyone, that is, except Max.

"Drunks, that's what they are," he mumbled as he sat, finally alone. Where in the hell is Frances, he wondered. "Frances, where are you? Frances!" he called as he raised himself, slowly and with difficulty from the lawn chair. He started for the house. "Screw her," he said.

In the quiet of the night there was a small "click" as the nearby cabana door shut carefully.

* * *

Frances had heard Max call her name. She stood in the cool darkness of the cabana, her back against the smooth wooden door, lost in thought.

Another gathering; his friends, his people, his life. No one had even noticed when she left the party. She might as well be one of the chairs.

She had tried to mingle with these people, but they were all so crude, so vulgar. Can you imagine, a girl coming out of the top of a cake? That was movie stuff. Real people don't do things like that.

Suddenly she was so tired that she didn't think she could make it to a chair. Luckily she was thoroughly familiar with the inside of the cabana, because it was as dark as midnight in the small room. There were lights around the makeup mirrors along one wall, but Frances chose not to turn them on. She wanted to be alone. Trying to picture in her mind's eye where the rattan chaise lounge sat, she inched her way across the room, juggling her Scotch and soda in one hand as she went. Her long "sarong" bathing suit cover up was wrapped around her legs, and quickly she reached down with her free hand and unbuttoned the waist. Deftly, she unwrapped the garment from her body and threw it where she believed a chair to be. She heard the sarong hit the floor and said, "Oh shit!" Oh well, Maria can pick it up tomorrow.

Reaching the safety of the chaise lounge, she sat down and, once again juggling her drink eased her body back until her feet were straight out in front of her and she was sitting in an upright position. She sipped her drink and, listening to the sounds of laughter and music outside, wondered how her life could have turned out so differently than she had planned.

*   *   *

21

From the time that she met Max at the Cimarron Ballroom, her well planned, carefully thought out life had ceased to be in her control. She had a plan when she left school. She would work for two years, save all of her money, and then get into an accredited school. She wanted to be a model; hadn't everyone always told her that she should become one? By the age of 12 she was 5'6" and when she finally stopped growing she was 5'9". Her size five body would have been perfect. Frances knew that she was not beautiful. God, Max had pointed that out often enough. But she also knew that raw beauty was not always necessary for a model. She had class. At least she tried to have class. Max had never understood that, even from the start.

When her parents had found out that she was pregnant, they were disappointed in her. When she told them he was a professional wrestler, they were fit to be tied. She'd tried to tell them that she hadn't told him how old she was, but they wouldn't believe her. So, they had insisted on a confrontation with him. The following week she had seen Max's name in the newspaper. She and her parents went to the matches and afterward had met with him in the dressing room. She could remember it like it was yesterday. The humiliation of it all.

The four of them had gone to a restaurant, sat in a booth, and shattered her dreams for the rest of her life.

At first Max had been shocked, then he denied, and after her father had explained that in Oklahoma you don't "knock up our children," he became more logical. Especially when he found out that her father was the Chief of Police in Tulsa. She sat there in a daze, not believing what was happening to her while her parents and this stranger determined her life for her. Abortion was not considered or discussed by any part.

The next morning at 10:00 AM, Frances and her parents met Max at the County Court House. Her father had made all of the arrangements. Blood tests were waived, the license was purchased, and the wedding was performed.

Frances stood in front of the justice of the peace in her white suit which she had bought at J.C. Penney's six months ago for her first job interview and wondered how all of this could have happened. Her mother stood there looking at her only daughter wondering where she had gone wrong and what fate had in store for her, married to this huge, handsome man who she instinctively knew was a womanizer. Frances' father stood, not hearing the justice of the peace. He was telling himself what all he would do to this stranger if he ever laid one hairy paw on Frances. And Max stood there, numb, mad, and fighting the urge to bolt and run. He wondered how long this wedding would take, and when they could get on the road to Oklahoma City for the matches that night. He had always made it a firm, fast rule not to travel with a woman, and now he had this one anchored to his ass!

By the time Keith was born, Frances was sick of the life of a wrestler's wife. Her idea of a home was not an Airstream trailer pulled behind a car. However, Max saw nothing wrong with it, and was happy to leave her with the baby while he drove off to other towns to the matches. By the time she was eighteen years old she was alone with a new baby, depressed, and lonely. And then it started.

"God, what a week," Max said as he came through the door of the trailer. Stooping low because he was so large, he saw Keith lying on a blanket on the floor. A big grin lit up his handsome face, his blue eyes shone through thick, black eyelashes, and he literally came alive when he saw his son.

"Come to Daddy," he said as he came on in and reached down to scoop the baby up in his arms. "Can't believe you're six months old," he said, still talking to Keith. "Let's go outside and sit under the trees. Dad doesn't have to wrestle tonight."

Without saying a word to Frances, he carried the baby outside, blanket and all, and spread the blanket on the ground.

"Bring me a beer, please," he called over his shoulder in the direction of the trailer.

When she brought the cold bottle of beer, Frances sat down on the blanket beside her husband. "Why don't we go dancing or to a movie tonight?" she asked. "Mongol's wife said she would take care of Keith."

"Look, I only see my son one night a week. I'm not about to leave him while I sit in some stupid movie watching some shit on a screen for three hours."

"Please, Max, don't cuss so much," she said. "Do you want Keith to grow up cursing and swearing, or do you want him to grow up with some manners?"

"I just don't want him to grow up a pussy!"

Before Frances could bring up the subject of the movie, The Mongol came over from his trailer next door.

He sat on the blanket and Max told Frances to bring Mongol a beer, "and bring me another one, too."

The rest of the evening, the two wrestlers sat and talked about business while Max fed, diapered, burped and put to sleep his contribution to the future, his son Keith. Frances went inside and read another romance novel.

* * *

The next evening, Frances told Max that she wanted to go to the matches with him. She hadn't been since Keith had been born, and she was so bored that she would go any place. Again, Patsy, Mongol's wife, had offered to baby sit and Max thought that was O.K. since he didn't want Keith to breathe the smoke at the arena.

They pulled into the reserved parking space at the arena. Frances walked next to Max as they went inside. Once inside, she quickly found herself a seat in the section reserved for families of the wrestlers. Several other wives who she knew were also there. One of them was Tiger Ramirez' wife, Sylvia, the gossip columnist of the wrestling world. Childless, she had made a practice of traveling with her husband for the ten years they had been married. She prided herself on the fact that, "My husband doesn't screw around on me, I travel with him." What she didn't know was the fact that when they traveled, he always paid for two rooms, side by side, and while she slept at night, he met arena rats in the room next door. That was the excitement for Tiger.

"Hello, Frances."

"Hello, Sylvia."

"You haven't been here in months, Frances. Where have you been, at home with the new baby?"

"Yes, but he's six months old now and I can leave him long enough to come to the matches from time to time."

"You shouldn't have stopped coming," said Sylvia, rolling her eyes at Frances.

"Why? What do you mean?" A bad feeling was starting in the pit of Frances' stomach.

"Nothing, I'm just telling you that if I were you, I'd be traveling with Max."

This was something new. This was something she hadn't thought about or worried about. Was this woman trying to tell her something? No matter how hard she tried, Sylvia would not tell her anything more. They sat, side by side, watching the matches.

After the matches were over, Frances went to the car to wait. She watched the arena rats, wondering if one of them might be after Max. The wrestlers filed out, bags in hand, some carrying damp towels, and sometimes one of the arena rats would fall in beside one of the men, in a prearranged agreement.

Finally, there were no more arena rats, the lights were out, and the cleaning crew was picking up paper cups and rubbish. Becoming alarmed, she decided to try and find Max inside the arena. She had no idea where the dressing rooms were.

Frances walked into the building and down the stairs towards where she hoped the dressing rooms would be found. Every step she took became harder. She knew that Max would be mad if the other wrestlers saw her looking for him. He didn't want them to think he was "pussy-whipped." Finally, she came to a door. She gingerly reached out, opened the door and stepped inside.

The lights were on, the showers were off, and her husband and a bleached blonde, makeup crusted, big breasted arena rat were locked together on the massage table.

Frances gasped and turned to run. The door had closed part way behind her and she slammed into it and was knocked down onto the floor.

"What the hell?" screamed Max. He looked up and saw her in the floor and immediately jumped off of the woman and came running to her side.

"Are you O.K.?" he asked as he squatted down beside her.

As her vision cleared she could see her naked husband, and standing behind him, a naked blonde woman looking down at her, and she instinctively knew that she would never feel anything but disgust for this man and regret for herself. She was trapped in a marriage that wasn't a marriage, held together by a baby that she had never wanted.

*   *   *

In the cabana, lost in thought, Frances took another sip of her drink. The music and laughter had died down and she knew that the birthday party was over. Not thinking now, she listened to the trailing sound of people leaving, cars starting, and finally, quiet.

She lay back, embraced the darkness, and remembered.

* * *

They had four children by the time Frances was 28. Max had not been with her for any of the births. They had bought a home in Corpus Christi and she stayed there with the children. He was on the road, wrestling every night, and they had fallen into a dull routine in which neither of them had to think much. They had their children and Max was an excellent father, especially to Keith. She realized that was partly because of his schedule. Wrestlers, because they work at night, are able to spend quality time with their children if they so desire. Max had. She couldn't fault him as a father. He attended all the games, plays and ceremonies. He gave of himself. If she could wish for one thing, it would be that he be a little less devoted to Keith. She believed he doted on his son far too much.

To her, he gave nothing. She enjoyed dancing; after they married, Max never danced with her again. She enjoyed the symphony, the ballet and the theater. All of those things take place at night and even when he was home, he wasn't interested. It was Max and his kids. And then there was Frances.

When they had been married for fifteen years, she joined a bridge club. Suddenly she was interested in something. She enjoyed the game and liked the women immensely. They shared her love of the arts, and the women attended events together.

One Saturday night it was Frances' turn to host the bridge game. She bought exciting gifts for the prizes, prepared dessert and coffee, and looked forward to a lovely evening. That morning, Max came into the kitchen and told her that he wouldn't be wrestling that night because his opponent had been injured and he was given the night off.

"Don't worry," he said when he found out about the bridge club. "I'll stay out of your way. We're playing touch football at Tiger's house this afternoon and we'll drink beer afterwards. By the time I get home, your bridge game will probably be over."

The women came and had a wonderful evening. The coffee and dessert were delicious and the gifts appreciated. The women were all standing at the back door by the pool entrance, ready to leave, when Max showed up, followed by three of his "weekend touch football team" members.

Drunk and laughing, they made their way to the pool area. The women watched.

"Last one in is a chicken shit," screamed Max. "Get naked and be somebody." The women stood at the back door, mouths open, unable to speak, and watched as the athletes quickly disrobed, ran up to the diving board, and one by one, dived in. The bridge club was disbanded within two weeks, each of the members finding that she had important business elsewhere.

Frances was distraught. She cried for days. Her only friends and now they were gone. One of the women told her that the woman's husband didn't want her "in danger from those drunken wrestlers."

Frances didn't speak to Max for one week. After that, he left town for a week and the following weekend he returned, dejected and ashamed.

He came in the house with flowers, the first since she'd had the children, and a bottle of champagne. He found her sitting in the living room, still not speaking.

"Please, Frances, he said, "I know I've been a bastard, but let's don't drag this out. We have our kids and we need to get on with our lives. I'm sorry I embarrassed you in front of your friends. Can't you forgive me?"

He had been nice to her since then, and God knows she had forgiven him for worse. There was always the blonde in the dressing room to remember. And what were her options? She couldn't support the four children and they needed a father. Maybe she should forgive and forget.

Frances stood up and walked into his waiting arms. She felt desire for him rise up in her for the first time in years.

He took her face in his hands and kissed her lightly on the lips. She turned her head, took one of his huge hands off of her face and kissed one finger, and then the next. Now she stood there with his fingers over her mouth and nose. What was that? Her head jerked back as she recognized the odor.

Her husband had just come home from being on the road for a week and he had the smell of sex on his hands.

*　　　　　*　　　　　*

Ah, but that was a lifetime ago, thought Frances as she lay in the cool cabana. When she still had dreams. Now she settled. She took whatever kindness she could find from whomever she could find it. She heard the cabana door open, someone slip in, and the door closed again. She turned her head toward the sound and said,

"Come in, Cowboy."

22

Omar stood outside the door of Toni's bedroom. "Open this door now!" he shouted.

Inside the room, Toni jumped out of bed and ran to the door, her robe clutched around her.

"What is it?" she asked. As the door opened, her brother stood glaring at her, eyes red with anger, and fists clinched tightly at his sides. "I told you that you were not to go out with Keith. He is a dog who treats women with no respect. And the first time I leave you alone, you disobey me and go out with him!" His voice was low, and he was fighting to keep calm.

"He hurts everyone who loves him. Do you want to be next? I forbid you to see him again!"

"My brother, this is not Venezuela. I love you and owe you everything. But, last night was the most wonderful night of my life. He was a gentleman and gave me lovely gifts. He gave me a gold cross and a beautiful bracelet. We danced and ate and I felt so special."

"Gifts! Do you want to be a puta?" he shouted. "Give them to me. I will throw them in his face. The boys saw you there last night and told me. I'm warning you. Stay away from him."

Omar stormed out of the room and went to confront Keith.

Toni lay on the bed crying. "I am a woman, not a child. I will decide whom I see. This is America."

Just then the phone rang and Frances called to Toni. "It's Keith. He wants to speak to you, dear."

Drying her eyes, she picked up the receiver. "Yes," she answered, holding back the tears.

"Toni, is something wrong?" Keith asked. "Are you crying? What happened?"

Toni told him about the scene between Omar and her, leaving out some of the details he had said about Keith.

"Don't worry, baby, Nobody's gonna' stop us from seeing each other. Last night was special. You're what I've been needing for a long time." He paused to give her time to think. "Do you want to see me again?" he whispered.

"Oh, Keith, you know I do. Last night was special for me, too. You were wonderful. How could you ask such a question."

"I just wanted to be sure," he replied, "I have to work tonight, but I could pick you up after the matches. If the damn boys are going to squeal every time they see us together, we'll have to go where they can't see us."

"I can't tonight, Omar is too upset. But he will be out of town Saturday. We can spend the whole day together if you want," she said.

"Saturday it is, then. I'll call you later tonight, after the show. Bye-bye."

Her tears were dry by now and she smiled as she put the phone down. He wanted to see her again as much as she wanted to see him.

Keith also put the phone down and smiled. But it was a different smile. *So Omar is unhappy. Big fucking deal!*

* * *

Without knocking, Omar entered Max's office where Keith was seated behind the desk.

"You son-of-a-bitch," Omar shouted. "Stay away from my sister! I swear to God that if you hurt her, I'll kill you!" Keith didn't even get up from the desk. His eyes narrowed, and a smile spread his lips.

"Slow down, Mexican, and take it easy. I haven't done anything to Toni. We had dinner. That's all. Fuck with me and you'll be without a job and she'll be outa' this country. Is that what you want? I'll see Toni until she tells me to stay away, not you. You understand? Now, get outa' here. Now!"

Omar stood riveted to the floor. His first impression was to jump the desk and strangle Keith. Then his mind jumped in all directions; sending Toni home, losing his job, and probably having to go back to Venezuela himself. No money, hunger. All these things ran through his head at once. The only thing that was crystal clear was his fury. He would get out of this company as quickly as possible and take his sister with him. Until then, he was trapped.

"What I said still stands. You hurt my sister and I will kill you!" He walked slowly toward the desk, looked Keith straight in the eye, and turning, walked toward the door, unconsciously breaking into the wrestler's strut. The door slammed shut behind him.

"Mexican son-of-a-bitch" Keith muttered to himself.

*   *   *

23

As he stepped out of the back door of his father's house, Keith could hear the sounds of church music coming from the pool area. He knew where Max was. He only came to the office in the afternoons, now. He proclaimed that he was "retired", but bookers and promoters still called him rather than deal with Keith, much to the son's concern. This was something he needed to get straight with the old man today.

"Dad," he said, "Omar tells me he is going to Chicago for a shot at the big time."

"Yes, Son, Lorenzo called yesterday and asked if we could send him up for a couple of weeks."

"Why didn't you send me if they wanted someone from this territory?"

Max didn't want to tell Keith that he had asked Lorenzo to take Keith, and had been told, flatly, "No."

"I think they needed a Hispanic wrestler. They are having a tournament and wanted to see how he would get over with the Chicago fans. He will be there a couple of weeks, and this could speed up our merger with HCW. That will mean a lot more money to both you and me." Keith could be bought, but he still wanted the best bookings for himself, and Omar would probably make $20,000 for the two weeks' work with HCW. Keith wasn't stupid. He knew that.

"God damn it, Dad, I want to talk to you about that. You know I make all the business deals. I'm in control now. How do you expect me to keep the boys in line if you go behind my back and send gibronis to Chicago instead of me?"

Now Max was beginning to get mad. "Look, Omar isn't a gibroni, he's a seasoned wrestler. He's paid his dues, he's a good worker, Lorenzo likes him, and this may help us to go into business with him. I've already committed him, and he is going. You need to take him off the card at the Boys' Club at Beeville next week. Lorenzo is sending one of his new boys, Wild Man Monahan. He's only had two matches and he wants us to "break him in." Book him in Beeville next week and we'll see what he can do. He dresses in African Native costumes and has his hair fried so that it stands out all over his head like he's been electrocuted. His pictures look good. He's a heel, so let him ride to Beeville with a carload of heels.

"Big fucking deal. Are you sure you will let me handle the boys club at Beeville? Sure I can be trusted? Something great like Chicago comes along and you handle it. I get the fund raiser at the Boys' Club in Beeville."

"Keith, for Christ Sake, shut the fuck up. I said he's going, and he's going. Don't act like such a dick head. Look at you. If you'd quit chasing pussy all the time and work out, you'd look like Omar and maybe get a little action yourself. Now get out of here. Hand me my bible."

"Bee-fuckin-ville," said Keith as he made his way back to the house.

* * *

24

The Boys' Club was buzzing with activity. Boys from six to 16 had been selling Wild West Wrestling tickets to make money to build a swimming pool. And tonight was the night. The main event was Keith Daniels versus Glen Massey. Good versus bad. The boys had been waiting since after school, and the matches didn't start until much later.

8:30PM was the magic hour. For two wild, exciting hours, these kids from underprivileged homes would forget their troubles and dream the dreams of thousands of boys all over the United Sates. They would watch and pretend. They were the Glen Masseys, or if they were of the bully persuasion, they would dream that they were Keith.

Because some of the older boys had been told they could help the ring crew and earn some money, they had arrived at six o'clock and were waiting for the big truck to arrive which would be carrying the ring.

They all stood around, excited, playing "big shot" to the smaller boys, impressing them with how they would be a part of tonight's show. Suddenly a cheer rang out from the boys who were waiting in the back lot of the building. They had spotted the big 18-wheeler truck with "Wild West Wrestling" painted on it, with silhouettes of two wrestlers in the ring.

"Stand back," said Manuel the ring boss, as he jumped out of the now-backing van and proceeded to instruct Jose, the driver, up to the back loading doors of the building.

Thank God this place has double doors, thought Manuel, and plenty of willing help, too. That's one of the good things about playing these small towns for charity. We always have lots of help. The kids are eager to be a part of the show, and we can get out of here in half the time it normally takes us.

Man, we can be on the road by 11:PM tonight. Great, he was thinking as he made his way through the young boys surrounding him and begging to help.

"O.K., O.K." he said. "Open those double doors and keep them open. There is a certain way we have to carry this sucker in. The ring weighs 1,200 pounds, so don't try to lift the corner posts unless you are over fifteen years old, and there are two of you to carry them."

This was the same speech he gave in every town; otherwise, you have six-year-olds trying to lift the 200-lb. corner posts. He didn't want to be responsible for any injuries. These kids were too eager.

The boys formed a line and each was given something to carry. The ring is twenty feet square, the inside area is eighteen feet square, and there is a particular way in which every piece must fit for maximum strength and noise.

First, the side rails were carried in and put in place. Next, the corner posts were carried in and the side rails snapped into place. Then chains were criss-crossed on the bottom of the corner posts. After that, specially slotted 2 x 8 x 20 boards were placed vertically into notches in the sides of the side rails. Then 2 x 6 x 20 boards were laid down horizontally on the top of the vertical boards. They would make the noise when a man hit the mat. Horizontal boards lying on the vertical boards. It would also give the wrestler a very small spring action, which lessens impact and injuries.

After all the wooden boards were in place, a foam pad was used, two inches thick, twenty feet by twenty feet, such as gyms use for exercising.

On top of all that came the canvas mat cover, which was tied down to the frame by rope being pulled through eyelets in the cover.

An excellent ring crew accomplished all of this with precision timing, aided by and their helpers as they went town to town. Three ropes, which are actually chains inside a plastic tubing, completed the ring set up.

When the ring was together, Manuel handed out the free tickets and instructed his "volunteer crew" to be sure and meet him here after the matches. Those brave ones who did would be paid cash.

7:30 and there came the cars. The Cadillacs and Lincolns began to arrive. First came the big, white Town Car of Max Daniels, the promoter. Then came the red Mercedes convertible, which they soon learned held Cochise Whitedove, the beautiful, blonde Marilyn Jackson by his side. She will wrestle Lorraine Black tonight, and she will win. Although Lorraine was by far the better wrestler, Marilyn was beautiful, feminine looking, and drew large crowds.

A baby face in the ring, everyone in the business knew that she was a pistol-carrying, foul mouthed, mean bitch.

As the cars pulled up and disgorged their occupants, the grapplers made their way through the crowds; the baby faces stopping to sign autographs, the heels pushing their way to their respective dressing rooms.

"Whew, thank God we at least have dressing rooms and showers here," said Marilyn to Lorraine as she walked in. "Some of these small towns don't, and I hate to wait until we can get to a motel to clean up."

"Yeah, I hate that, too," said Lorraine, easing her 6'2" well-muscled body into a small chair in front of a temporary makeup table. "The best deal is when we play the coliseum, where they have actual honest-to-God dressing rooms with showers and makeup tables, the works," said Marilyn.

"I heard about your fight with Cochise," said Lorraine. "I heard you got him drunk and slapped him off a bar stool. Good for you." She laughed.

Lorraine, like Marilyn, was a contrast to "what you see is what you get." In the ring, she stalked her opponent, taking giant steps with her long, muscular legs. She screamed, shrieked, and pulled hair.

However, outside the ring she was actually shy, retiring, and passive. Because of this, Lorraine had been taken advantage of by almost every promoter she had ever worked for. She and Maxine, another girl wrestler had been "married" for many years, and Lorraine was known throughout the wrestling world as a "straight shooter" who kept her word, arrived on time, did her job, and didn't bitch about a damn thing.

"I'm going downstairs and talk to Maxine for awhile," said Lorraine. Maxine was usually in the dressing room with her, helping her dress, but tonight she had eaten something on the trip into town that had made her sick, and she was lying in the car.

"O.K., gal, I'm going to take my shower. I'll leave some hot water for you."

She laid everything out. Bathing suit, panties, wrestling boots, long tube socks, and the necessary falsies for protection against breast injuries. Although generously endowed in the breast area, Marilyn wore them to protect her nipples should she be thrown face first onto the mat, or hit in the breast by her opponent. Of course, some of the skinnier girls cheat and wear two pairs, if nature hasn't been too kind.

She laid out the spray deodorant, which was a necessity. Marilyn always took great care to prevent body odor. Over the years she had learned that although no fan will complain of sweat odor from one of the men, he will be very vocal if one of the girls smells bad.

If there is any doubt about the arrival of a menstrual period, tampons are used, "just in case." Sometimes if a period was due soon, the exertion of the match would bring one on. She remembered well the time she started her period right in the middle of the ring, and if the referee hadn't noticed on her white bathing suit, she would have been mortified. Instead, he whispered in her ear to end the match and she disqualified herself and ran out of the ring. Only when she got back to the dressing room did she discover the problem. Even today she could remember how embarrassed she had been.

As she stepped into the shower, Marilyn closed her eyes and began to ponder about her relationship with Cochise. Maybe it wasn't too good for the two of them. She had such a bad temper, and he was an insane man when he got going. She was getting tired of all the fighting and drinking and drugs. He could do more coke than anyone she had ever seen. She knew that if she started trying to keep up with him it would be the end of her, her looks, and her reputation. She didn't know how he kept going.

Suddenly, Marilyn knew that she wasn't along. Quickly she stepped back and, rubbing her hand over her face to wipe the water away, she forced her eyes open and stood looking right into the eyes of Glen Massey.

"What do you want?" she asked. No answer. He just stood there, looking stupid, with a half-smile on his face.

"I said, what do you want?" she repeated.

"Nothing," came the answer. "I'm in the wrong dressing room." Still he stood there, in wrestling gear, water running over him now, and smiling.

"Then get the fuck out," she screamed as she pulled the shower curtain out of his hand and put it around her body.

"Sorry," he said as he turned and left.

Downstairs, behind the building, Lorraine was leaning into the window of a new Chrysler New Yorker. Maxine sat inside, her head back on the headrest, a cold cloth on her forehead.

"You sure you don't feel like coming inside, Maxine?" asked Lorraine. "I worry about you out here alone in the car. You know how these fans are. They'll hurt you if they know you are with a heel; or at least tear up the car. Maybe I can get someone to stay with you until my match is over and then we can leave."

"Don't worry about me, it's dark back here." Maxine had just started to argue when they both saw Glen Massey coming toward the car.

"Hey, Glen," said Lorraine. "Since your match isn't until the main event, how about staying back here with Maxine for me until I'm finished?"

"Be glad to," he answered. "I'll stand here with you, Maxie."

Just then, the light coming from the back door was blocked as someone came racing through it out into the parking lot. They all recognized Marilyn, barefoot, her bathing suit pulled on over a wet body, hair dripping; she was running toward the car with a high heel boot raised over her head.

"I'll teach you to stare at a naked lady," she said as she brought the heel of the boot down onto the back of Glen's head.

"Oh my God," said Maxine from the car as Glen went down and Marily straddled his prone body.

"No you don't," said Lorraine as she grabbed the arm that was about to deliver another blow. "For God's sake, Marilyn, Glen has to wrestle in the main event." They all three looked down at Glen, out cold on the parking lot, a fallen warrior. "Get inside, Marilyn, and I'll have Maxine drive Glen to a doctor and get him sewn up before the main event."

Marilyn went, struggling against the larger woman all the way back into the building.

* * *

"Marilyn, you bitch!" screamed Cochise. "You put six stitches in Glenn's head before the matches. Thanks a lot. Do you know, or do you care what you did to the main event? He couldn't stand any side head-locks, he couldn't be thrown into the turnbuckle, and he couldn't get his hair pulled. Thanks a lot for ruining the match, and I'll bet Keith breaks your damn neck for you."

"I know, Cochise, but I just lost it when I looked up and he was standing there watching me shower."

"Well, God-damn, woman, it isn't like you haven't been seen by men before. Give me a break. You're one of the wildest broads I know."

"You are absolutely right, Cochise. I must have lost my mind. Keith is trying to get rid of the girls in the territory now. I'm lucky to be here and now I've jeopardized that. I promise to watch this temper."

"That's better," said Cochise. Glen wants to apologize to you. I'm going to get him. If you have one ounce of brains, you will accept his apology and go on. Your career may depend on it."

"O.K." she said.

"He's showering now, you go downstairs and play a game of pool and wait. I'll bring him to you," the Indian said.

"Alright."

Marilyn was just putting the six ball into the side pocket when Cochise and Glen came down from the dressing room. Glenn had that same half-smile on his handsome face. Blonde and light skinned, the blood in the back of his bleached hair had turned it pink.

Marilyn stood up as they approached. Glen checked her out. She now had on the high heel boots. No danger there. She looked calm. She was standing watching them approach, her pool cue at her side.

"Marilyn, I'm sorry", he said. Suddenly, the pool cue made an arch in the air, Glen went down, and the doctor later put six stitches in the front of his head to match the six he had in the back.

* * *

"Come on, men, let's get out of this place," said Max as he stuck his head into the dressing room. Thanks to Marilyn, we've caused enough commotion for tonight. Everyone get in their cars and get out of here as fast as possible so we can leave with a little dignity." The men were showering after the matches. Glenn had been taken back to the doctor and the Boys Club Director had suggested that they leave before they show the young boys how to murder each other.

Wild Man Monahan had driven from Corpus Christi to Beeville with Mike Young and Rory Maine, the other two heels on tonight's card. On the way to the matches he had been kidded unmercifully about his huge head covered with springy, dry black hair. It stuck up so high over his head that if he held his fingertips together over his head, his hair reached the fingers. Now that the hair was wet, it was kinky and stiff.

"Man, why don't you comb that stuff so you don't have to wear it twelve inches high when you're out of the ring? It goes great with your native costume, but you look like shit with shorts and tennis shoes on," said Mike.

"I can't help it, my sister put a permanent in it to make it frizz, and she cooked it too long. It's kinky from the scalp and won't lie down."

"Never mind now," Rory said, "Max wants us to hit the highway. Come on, don't bother to comb it, it'll dry in the car. Besides, we need to stop and get some beer for the long ride home."

* * *

25

"How long have you been wrestling?" quizzed Mike.

"Only for about two months."

"Have you traveled from town to town in a car, or has all your travel been done through airplanes?" Mike asked again as the car sped down the highway headed home.

"I haven't done much automobile travel yet," was the reply.

A knowing glance passed between Rory and Mike. Mike looked into the rear view mirror. All he could see was a silhouette against the back window. The electric hair of Wild Man Monahan gave the appearance, in the dark, of a monster sitting in the back seat with a head three feet wide and three feet tall.

"Say, Kid," said Mike as he watched Wild Man through the mirror. "Ever hear of the 'streaking game' that wrestlers play on the highway?"

"Sure. The guys spend so much of their time in cars traveling from town to town that they play games to amuse themselves. Everyone knows that."

"Well, are you into doing wild things?"

"I, I guess so. How wild?"

"Well, here's what we do," said Mike. "We go one at a time, take all our clothes off, and as we drive through one of these small towns, the naked one jumps out of the car, runs up to a restaurant, looks in the window, and stands there for as long as he can without getting caught. The others wait in the car, motor running, ready to go. At the precise last minute, the "streaker" runs back to the car, jumps in, and we all drive off. The one who stands in front of the window the longest wins fifty bucks. Are you game?"

"Well, I don't know. How do you know when to bolt and run for the car?" he asked.

"When someone is about to grab you. Believe me, you'll know. Want to try? Are you a man or a wimp?"

Wanting to be accepted by these rugged men, but not able to visualize himself in this roll, Monahan hesitated.

"Oh shit, man, come on. We'll both go first and show you how to do it."

"You can't beat that deal," said Rory. "I'll even go first." With that, he began to take off his shirt and pants.

"O.K., but only if you guys go first," was the reply from the back seat.

"We're just about to Flaksville," said Rory, "Watch this action."

Without another word, Rory began the very difficult task of removing his clothes in the front seat of the car. Finally, buck naked, he uncapped another beer, sat back and waited.

Denny's was up ahead. Big picture window. Saturday night, full house. Mike slowed the Lincoln down to a crawl and double-parked next to the front door.

"Here's my watch. It has a second hand. You keep the time, Monahan."

With that, Rory jumped out of the passenger side of the car, and went running as fast as he could the twenty feet to the window. He slammed into the window, all 255 lbs. of him, stuck his tongue out, and plastered himself to the glass pressing his nose, tongue, and stomach hard against the window.

Four booths filled with people were against the window on the inside. Twelve people looked up in time to see this monster pasted to the outside, watching them. Forks stopped in mid air. Mouths were frozen open and eyes were bulging from their sockets. And then, all at once, pandemonium broke out. From the car, the wrestlers could hear the screams from the inside. People were knocking into other people to get away from the window. Mothers covered children's eyes. And then Rory ran. Fast.

Mike leaned over, opened the door, and Rory hit the car running. The three drove out of the parking lot, laughing until the tears rolled down their faces.

"O.K., we're fifteen miles to the next town. Who goes next?" said Mike. "Since you're in the back seat, Monahan, why don't you go ahead and take your clothes off and you can be next. While you're at the window, Rory can get behind the wheel and drive away when you get back. I can be undressing to go next."

"That's fine," answered Monahan. Anything to be "one of the guys."

As the big car entered Eversville, all eyes were scanning the restaurants for nice, large front windows. Finally, they saw it. Jack's Pancake House. By now it was after Midnight, all of the late night bar patrons were getting ready for breakfast, and there was a full house.

Mike, once again crawled to a silent stop next to the large picture window. This restaurant had no booths, but tables were pushed up to the window, and the patrons behind the first row of tables got to look outside.

"You ready, Monahan?" asked Rory. "Remember, you have to beat my time of two minutes fifteen seconds. You have to stay at the window longer than that."

"Sure," said Monahan. With shaking knees, Monahan slid across the back seat and out into the night air. Looking both ways and seeing no one, he quickly ran up to the window as he had seen Rory do. Hitting the window with his 250 pounds, he slapped his palms flat, making a "bang" on the pane, he stuck his tongue out, and pressed his stomach against the window. Monahan had forgotten that in the hurry to leave Beeville, he still had his African makeup on. What the patrons saw from the inside was a huge, naked man plastered against the window with big black eyes circled with white paint, and red and green stripes on his cheeks. His hair stood out three feet on all sides of his head, and he was sweating profusely, despite the cool weather.

Two women fainted. An African American woman ran to the restroom screaming something about "voodoo", and three men jumped out of their chairs and ran over their wives while trying to get away.

In the middle of all this, the Japanese cook ran out of the kitchen, machete in hand, screaming something about what he would cut off when he got outside.

Although it felt like Monahan had been pressed against the glass for an hour, he was certain that it was more like three or four minutes. When he saw the machete, though, h e decided he had been there long enough.

Jumping backward, he ran full speed to his left toward the car just in time to see the Lincoln pull out of the parking lot and out onto the highway. He would always remember the sound of those two ass holes laughing as they drove off down the road.

26

Toni and Keith had been seeing each other for three months now. He had remained the loving, tender man who had started taking her out. But how much can a man stand? He decided tonight was the end of his patience.

The two lovers were parked in front of Max and Frances' home. They had just had another wonderful night. Food, wine, laughter, and dancing. Now they were sitting in the car, his arms around her, and he was kissing her neck. Eyes closed, she was totally relaxed. His hands moved up and cupped her breasts.

Toni's eyes flew open and she sat straight upright. He tightened his arms and pulled her back to his chest.

"Honey, I need you now. I love you. You know that." Keith whispered hoarsely into her hair.

Struggling, finally breaking free, Toni said. Everything everyone says about you is true. You don't love me, this is just a game you play to amuse you and entertain your friends." She was facing him now, tears running down her cheeks. She opened the car door and ran into the big house.

Keith didn't move. He had no desire to meet either his drunken mother or his bible-thumping father now, so he stayed in the car.

The lights went on in Toni's room. He sat and watched the window until finally it was dark.

"Damn!" he thought, "why did I do that? Like some horny teenager." He pulled away from the curb and drove towards his apartment.

"I wonder what Brenda is up to tonight."

At eight o'clock the next morning, the phone rang. It was Keith. Toni answered with a cold, "Yes?"

"Baby, I'm so sorry. I don't know what happened. It's just that I love you too much. What do you expect? Hell, I'm only human. And you know since we've been going together, I haven't been with anyone, don't you? A man has needs."

A small smile began to format the corner of her mouth. She was beginning to thaw like he knew she would.

"Well, yes," she replied, "but you said you loved me and then you made me feel so dirty."

"I know, Baby, I'm nuts! But I do love you. Can you ever forgive me? Is it really too late? Could we have dinner tonight and start over? Please, Baby, I adore you!"

"Oh yes, yes, yes! I love you, too. You know that. I can't wait to see you tonight." Toni was smiling and laughing and crying with all the emotion only a twenty-year old girl can have.

"I'll leave the matches early, have Stanley finish the payoffs for me, and pick you up at ten o'clock. Oh, and Baby, can you watch for me and come outside so I don't have to deal with my folks?"

"Yes, Mi Amor, I'll be there." Her heart raced. How could she kill time until ten o'clock?

She ran to the phone and called the beauty shop. Everything had to be perfect for tonight. Ten o'clock couldn't come soon enough.

*   *   *

At ten on the nose, Keith's car pulled up and Toni ran out of the house and into his open arms.

Surely, make-up kisses must be the sweetest kisses in the world, she thought. He pulled her close and suddenly slacked off. He sure wasn't going to mess this up again tonight.

*   *   *

The club was crowded as usual, but they had their regular table. A candle separated them and added extra glow to their happy faces. They had talked it through and made up as both hoped, each, however, for different reasons.

The dance floor was alive with bodies swaying to soft, sensual music. Her head was on his shoulder and her eyes were closed as they danced the night away. Finally, the band took a break and the two returned to their table.

At Toni's place lay a long stemmed, white rose with a red bow.
"Oh, Keith, you think of everything," she said, picking up the flower.
"Toni, wait!" Keith spoke quickly.
"What, Mi Amor?" Toni asked.
"Before you pick up your rose, would you look at me?" As she did, he said, "I need you, I want you, and I love you. If I can't have you any other way, I'll marry you. What do you say?"

Without even hesitating, she looked at him and said, almost in a whisper, "Yes."

He kissed her, long and hard. In fact, a little too hard. Her lip hurt where he had pushed it against her teeth.

"Now look at your rose," he said.

Picking it up, she looked at the bow. Right in the middle was an engagement ring with a large, perfect pear-shaped diamond.

"Oh, Keith," she exclaimed. "This is so beautiful. And so big! I love it I love you!" She jumped up, ran around the table and sat down on his lap. She threw here arms around his neck and they were both laughing.

She was still saying, "I love you, I love you." Suddenly aware of what was going on, the club grew quiet for a brief moment, and then, as if on cue, the patrons began laughing and clapping, enjoying sharing the moment with this beautiful couple.

* * *

The next evening, Max, Frances, Keith and Toni sat around the pool talking. For once, Frances was not drinking at all. She and Toni sat across from each other, as did Max and Keith.

"I'm so excited," Frances said, "The first wedding in the family. And we all love you so much, Toni," Frances gushed. "What kind of wedding do you want?"

"I want a small wedding in a small church, beautiful white gown, my sister and brother, and Keith's family there. It will be so beautiful. Christmas is a good time. What do you think?"

"Max would love that. I'm sure he would like to perform the ceremony, but since that's impossible, this will be the next best thing." Frances laughed and smiled at her soon to be daughter-in-law.

Max and Keith were now by the bar-b-q pit cremating their hamburgers. Max was as happy with the news of the coming nuptials as Frances was, but for more pressing reasons. The publicity would be a great draw. Keith Daniels was marrying Omar Atlas' sister. How much better could it get?

"Son, we'll have the gardener fix up the back yard and Toni can come down the stairs and on out onto the patio. The grotto will be great for the ceremony and I can read from the bible. We can fit three or four hundred people in here. Maybe we'll have a prayer meeting afterward. What do you think?"

"Fuck the yard wedding! This is no picnic. Hell, man, we'll rent the coliseum and do advance publicity, get married in the ring, and charge twenty-five bucks a pop. If they wanna' come to the reception, that's one hundred bucks. We'll make a killing.

"But Keith, it'll be a damn circus. This is your wedding day. What will Toni say?"

"Listen, I don't give a fuck if you run midgets chasing elephants around us while we tie the knot! If it brings in the dough, that's all I care about. And don't worry about Toni. I'll handle her," answered Keith, who was busy fishing his burger out of the coals where it had dropped during his outburst.

"Well, it's your wedding. The coliseum is big enough. We'll have a blow out like this town has never seen before. Do you know what month it'll be in?"

"Yeah, December. She has it in her head to be married then. Says it will be her Christmas present."

"I'd better get Stanley on the publicity," said Max. Two months isn't very long to get this show going. Let's go all out. December is always low attendance because of Christmas and no money. Do you know what date yet? A weekend would be best."

"Any Saturday is O.K. with me. Take your pick."

The four people spent the rest of the night discussing the coming event. Tony finally gave in to the coliseum wedding after Keith convinced her that if they did the public ceremony, everyone would know he was a married man and the arena rats would back off. Max thought this was a "great touch." By the time the young couple said good night to the parents, Toni was calling them Mom and Dad. She would soon have the family that she had longed for.

October passed quickly. The excitement at the house was almost equal to the frenzy at the office. Frances and Toni went to fittings, florists and caterers, and getting closer every day. They were almost like mother and daughter.

The director of the local Little Theater was choreographing the arena show. Nothing could be too flamboyant for this big event. He and his merry band of men were running around town getting everything together.

Keith was scheduled to wrestle every town possible to "hype" the big wedding day. He made announcements on television that he was tying the knot in Corpus Christi in December. He and Toni hardly saw each other the whole month.

In Tyler the following week as Keith was entering the arena, he saw a familiar face in the crowd.

"Hey, Keith, I hear you're getting' hitched," yelled Brenda as he passed her. She had driven two hundred and fifty miles to follow him from town to town. She and two other arena rats came together, hoping to snag one wrestler or another; it really didn't matter whom.

"Yeah, you hear right. December eighteenth at the Coliseum. Are you gonna' be there? They're having a big reception after."

She thought a minute and said, "See ya' there. How about tonight. One last fling?"

"Maybe. We'll see," he replied, walking faster. "Where are you gonna' be?" he asked.

"Marty's" was the answer. Keith knew where this was. The boys usually picked out one place in each town and claimed it until someone tried to show off and challenge one of the big men. Then, like Arabs, they would all pick another spot and move. Keith waved as he reached the door.

At least now he knew where the action was tonight unless something better came along. He could make his "duty call" to Toni from any phone. Then he would be free for the night.

* * *

27

The publicity had been out for two months. Everything was in place and ready to roll.

At ten o'clock in the morning of the big day, large trucks pulled up to the huge Corpus Christ coliseum on the water's edge. Men spilled out, almost at a run.

Large, green Scotch Pine Christmas trees were carried in and lined up the aisles from the dressing room to the ring. Flower vans arrived with large urns of white flowers of every kind. A wedding arch had been set in the center of the ring on a turntable that would rotate throughout the entire ceremony.

No one would miss a gesture or a word. The microphones would be concealed in the flowers and twinkle lights on the arch as well as in their clothing. Clouds of white net hung above the center of the ring and fake doves hung on thin wire, giving the illusion of flying birds and white, puffy clouds.

Long banquet tables had been set up in the room next door. It was usually a conference room for businessmen. But this night, it was an English garden. White flowers and green grass and plants were everywhere.

White linen covered the tables and waiters scurried everywhere, putting out the food and drink for the festivities. Ice sculptures of wrestlers in different holds were on each table.

And in the center, standing alone, was a seven-foot wedding cake decorated with lovebirds, doves and flowers. White was the only color in the room and there were candles everywhere. The wrestling company wanted to make sure everyone got their money's worth. The food would be plentiful and the champagne would flow.

That evening, shortly before eight, Frances looked at Toni sitting at the mirror in one of the dressing rooms having her face made up by the television station makeup artist. Her six bridesmaids (all wrestler's wives) and matron of honor, her sister Maria from Venezuela were gathered around her. Laughing and happy, they were like young girls at a slumber party.

Frances smiled, remembering her own wedding day. So much happiness, she thought, look at her face. So many expectations. So much faith in her man and their future. Where does it all go?

Years ago, she, too had all the hopes and expectations for her own marriage. Here she was, thirty-two years later and what did she have? A husband who bored her with all his religious fervor that made him weak instead of strong, and a son who hated her. Why, she didn't know. But not a day went by that she didn't think bout it.

The only ray of hope in her stupid, dull life were her daughters. So far, they still loved her. But they had their own lives to live. Almost grown, they kept in touch, but weren't around much.

And then came Toni. She gave Frances new life. Someone close by to love, who loved her back. If Keith hurt her-

While Frances was with Toni, Max was with Keith in the other dressing room, watching him get ready. He and his best man were combing their hair and joking around about the wedding night, as men have done since time began.

All the other men were standing around in various stages of dress listening to Keith try and convince everyone that Tony and he had not been together yet.

There was a lot of laughter until Omar came through the door. Suddenly, it was quiet.

Max couldn't help but wonder how his son would handle marriage. He still didn't know why Keith wanted to get married. If Toni was a virgin as he kept insisting, she couldn't be pregnant. Thank God! Max knew all too well how those marriages turned out. Hadn't he and Frances had that kind? He really didn't regret Keith's birth. After all, Keith was his whole life. But what a price to pay.

Stuck with a woman who hates you for the rest of your eternal life.

Omar hadn't said a word to anyone. He continued dressing, as if he were alone in the room. The tension was thick and the men stole glances at him from the corners of their eyes. Everyone knew how Omar felt about the marriage. Keith ignored him as if he were not in the room and finished dressing. When Omar had finished putting on his tuxedo, as quietly as he had entered he left the room.

* * *

At last, Toni was dressed and ready to join Keith and become his wife. She held her glittering crown headpiece out to Frances.

"Mamma, please?"

Frances had tears in her eyes as she adjusted the crown and pulled the veil down over Toni's face. She stepped back a few paces to observe her handiwork.

She had made sure Toni had the gown of her dreams. The white bodice was covered with pearls and glittering cut crystals. It was low-cut and fitted to show off her slim body.

The full, billowing skirt and long, beaded train accentuated her tiny waist. The long, hanging gardenia bouquet came almost to the floor. She was a vision worthy of being on the cover of any bridal magazine. Frances was well pleased. She hugged Toni and left the room to join Max in the packed arena.

Everything was ready. The entire coliseum was sold out. Some fans were even standing along the back wall. Security had been tripled for tonight. The sound system was playing soft music and thousands of tiny, white twinkle lights were everywhere. Each Christmas tree was decorated with the lights and small white doves.

The main lights went out. Except for the trees, the arch and ring, there was total darkness. The first strands of the Wedding March began. A pinpoint spotlight shined on the door of the dressing room.

White carpet had been rolled out and as the spotlight's glare got bigger, the attendants started down the long walk, slowly, carefully in the centuries-old processional.

As all of this was happening, Keith and his best man entered the ring on the far side. The last young woman had reached the halfway point.

The organist came down hard on the keys, announcing the bride. Toni appeared on Omar's arm. There was a gasp from the fans. She was so beautiful and he was so handsome. Her gown and train swept the floor and the long, glittering veil brought back memories of fairy tale princesses and their princes.

Cinderella on her way to the ball, every woman in the audience could imagine herself being the bride and every man envied the groom.

From the corner of the darkened arena, someone lit a cigarette lighter. Then one more, then two, then three, and in less time than it took to reach the ring, everyone was standing and holding flaming cigarette lighters over their heads. They were clicked off as quickly as they had been lit and it was dark once again.

The ropes had been taken off the ring for this occasion and Omar helped Toni up the stairs, her long train swirling around her.

Keith stepped up beside her, smiling down, looking into her eyes. He gently lifted the veil from her face so none of the fans would miss the drama. Everyone else took their places and the ring began its slow turning, and the wedding began.

When the ceremony was over, there wasn't a dry eye in the audience. "Ladies and Gentlemen, I give you Mr. and Mrs. Keith Daniels," the "minister" announced as Keith kissed Toni and the two turned to face the crowd.

A loud roar went up. The screaming and shouting all but drowned out the Wedding March, once again playing as the bride and groom took bows and waved to the people who thought they had just witnessed the wedding of Keith Daniels and Toni Morales, lovely sister of "Omar Atlas" Morales.

The actual wedding had been performed at four o'clock that afternoon. The "minister" here had been a paid actor. Such is wrestling. Such is show business.

The reception was as wild and as much fun as money could buy. No one went away feeling cheated. The band was great; the wrestlers were dressed in their finery, along with their wives or girlfriends. The arena rats were there to look over the wives, and it was one of the very few times that the wrestlers mixed socially with the "marks."

Everyone was happy. Almost.

In the confusion and noise, no one noticed the big, sad man quietly pick up his suitcase and head for the waiting taxi.

Omar had done his duty.

But he could stand no more.

* * *

28

Toni gazed out the window of the plane. The flight to Vegas was mostly uneventful, but she didn't mind. Keith was sleeping in the seat next to her, and she was thinking back about the beautiful wedding. Toni had cried a couple of times. When Keith had asked her why, she had told him that she was disappointed that Omar hadn't stayed for the reception.

They both knew that this was the only time in her life that Toni had openly defied Omar. He hadn't wanted her to date Keith, and now this.

She couldn't even believe that she had been strong enough to defy him; ever since childhood he had been the dominant force in her life. Since Papa had died, he had been the only father, brother, male family member that she had, and now she had lost him. But God, how she loved this man beside here. He had been so kind and understanding, he had been right beside her all the way. She had never been "wined and dined" in her entire life, and he was so attentive. And when they went places and the fans swarmed over them, he always looked out for her and saw to it that she was not crushed in the melee.

And now she was his wife. Mrs. Keith Daniels. Toni had heard the stories about how the wrestlers had girlfriends in every town. She remembered Frances telling her about The Turk's wife. She leaned back into the cushions of the plane and remembered how Frances had told her the story.

* * *

Annie Nashavian, The Turk's wife of ten years, had heard that he was seeing an arena rat in Dallas. She decided to go to the matches and see for herself. That week, she told him that she would travel with him, and she did. She made the complete loop, starting in San Antonio, going through Corpus Christ, and ending in Dallas.

The trip went well, until Annie developed a migraine just as they were coming into Dallas. Turk wanted her to go on to the hotel, but she declined.

"I'll be fine, the matches don't last that long, and I'll wait for you by the dressing room door afterward." She didn't want to give him the chance to talk to any girl and warn her.

During the matches, Annie felt worse and worse. She decided she would lie down in the car until t he matches were over, and then meet Turk by the back door. She climbed in the front seat, lay down, and promptly fell asleep.

"Oh, my God—Oh, my God," she heard as she tried to force her eyes open. The headache was still there, but she could at least focus her eyes. She looked out the window to see where the sounds were coming from at the same time she felt the car shaking.

"Oh, my God," it came again.

"What the hell?" She opened the door and the car light came on. Annie looked in the back seat. There, toes up, lay a young girl, thrashing and moaning. Her legs were wrapped around a very startled, very scared Turk.

Toni knew that this would never hapspen to her. Keith had been so attentive; he had never even looked at another woman when they were out together.

Frances had tried several times to approach her, to give her an idea of what lay ahead, but Toni knew that her fears were unfounded. They loved each other; they didn't need anyone else in their lives. Hadn't Keith told her that enough times?

*   *   *

Toni couldn't believe Las Vegas. From the time they left the airport, for the entire drive through town, out to the strip to Caesar's Palace where they had the bridal suite, she couldn't believe her eyes. Although it was midnight, the downtown area was like daytime.

Toni looked out the taxi, her beautiful eyes wide with wonder. Keith laughed at her. He'd been here many times, and was obviously enjoying her excitement.

When they arrived at Caesar's Palace, she read the marquee: Welcome Mr. and Mrs. Keith Daniels. She grabbed her camera and took a picture. Then Keith had to get in the picture. Then she asked a passer-by to take both of their pictures. She was like a child in a toy store. With every passing moment, she became more enchanted with her new surroundings, her new life.

"Please follow me, Mr. and Mrs. Daniels," said the bell captain as he unlocked the door to the most beautiful room Toni had ever seen. The suite was right out of a fairy tale. Everything in the room, including the furniture, was white.

In the middle of the room stood the bed. Two steps up, it was elevated to afford the most dramatic affect. In the center of the bed lay one, perfect, beautiful orchid. It was the only color in the room, and the sight was breathtaking.

"Keith, you remembered that the orchid is the national flower of my country. You think of everything." She said.

Keith was standing by the wet bar. "I'll fix us a glass of champagne. Why don't you go into the bathroom and try on your new negligee we bought?" he asked, smiling.

"Of course," she said, remembering the beautiful, filmy white negligee they had both selected at Saks Fifth Avenue in San Antonio. It had cost more money than she would have paid for a coat back home, but he had insisted.

"Nothing but the best for my wife," he had said.

* * *

When Toni came out of the bathroom, she was a dream walking. Her hair was still wispy wet from the shower, and her dark skin glowed through the film that was her negligee. Keith lay on the bed, completely naked, the effect of a hit of coke just starting to take hold.

"Oh." she said, embarrassed at seeing him naked for the first time. "I thought you'd have on your new pajamas."

"They're only in case of fire," he said, laughing at his own joke. "Come here."

Toni walked slowly to the side of the bed, her head slightly drooped due to her embarrassment.

"I fixed you a drink," Keith said.

"You know I don't drink." Came the reply.

"You do now. Come HERE!"

Toni didn't know what to do. This was not the charming, attractive man she'd grown to love over the months. She knew that a woman was supposed to obey her husband, but this was too much.

Panic began to fill her chest. She stepped up the steps and stood next to Keith, who had sat up on the side of the bed now, rubbing his erection and leering at her. He reached for the glass of champagne on the side table.

"Here, wife, have a drink. You're gonna' need it," he said as he smiled to himself.

She reached for the champagne, but he grabbed the glass before she could lift it.

"Let me help you," he said. He grabbed her hair, pulling her head back. "Open your mouth." As she did so, he poured the entire glass full of champagne into her mouth, some of it spilling out over her breasts and onto the top of her expensive negligee.

"I'm choking," said Toni, struggling and trying to get the bitter stuff down her throat. "Please wait."

"I can't wait much longer, Baby, I've been waiting for months to get at you, and tonight's the night."

He poured another glass of champagne. "Here comes number two," he said. This time Toni didn't open her mouth when he grabbed her hair. Instead, she clamped her lips shut and tried to catch her breath from the first encounter. This was not what your wedding night was supposed to be. This was not the Keith she knew and loved.

"I said to open your mouth, Bitch," Keith said, low and menacingly. He drew back his hand and hit her, not in the face, as she had expected, but right into the front of one of her breasts. The pain was excruciating.

"Wrestlers know where to hit so it won't show. You want some more, or do you want more champagne?"

Toni opened her mouth, grateful this time at the coolness of the fluid that ran down across her throbbing breast.

The room was starting to spin now, as the two drinks took effect. She wanted to lie down on the bed, but Keith was holding her up by the hair of her head.

"Take off your clothes, let me look at you," he ordered. "Quick!"

Toni reached down to lift the bottom of her gown over her head. Keith jerked her hair, forcing her upright again.

"I'll do it. Stand still," he said. She stood perfectly motionless, tears running down her face, while he pulled the gown up over the wet breasts and wetter face. Toni wanted to die with humiliation. Nothing had prepared her for this.

Keith picked her up in his arms and threw her across the bed, on top of the beautiful orchid. Thankfully, she felt as though she would pass out. She prayed she would. She watched as he stood over the side table, sniffing a line of cocaine from the tabletop.

"That will keep me up all night," he said, staring down at her.

The last thing she remembered as she blacked out was something entering her body with a sharp, tearing force.

* * *

The sunshine poured into the room as Toni opened her eyes. Quickly she remembered the horror of last night. She felt Keith next to her, and as she looked over, she stared straight into his eyes. The old Keith was back.

"Good morning, Mrs. Daniels," he said. "Time to get up. I have an interview at a radio station this morning, and I want to show off my beautiful wife. This will only take about an hour, and then we'll start gambling and having a good time."

Toni couldn't believe it. He was a different person. His eyes even looked different. Had the champagne made her dream last night? No, the pain was still there. Her breasts hurt, and she could barely walk when she got off the bed. It had really happened.

*   *   *

"Welcome to Sports Talk from KTUV" said the beautiful blonde with the bluest eyes he'd ever seen.

She was talking into the microphone when Toni and Keith entered the studio. She looked up, motioned for them to sit down and put on earphones so that she could interview them.

"This is Jane Maxwell and this morning we are pleased to have with us the newly wed Wild West wrestler, Keith Daniels and his lovely wife, Toni."

Why in the hell hadn't anyone told him that this gorgeous classy broad would be interviewing him? He had been told to contact a man by the name of Dan.

"We understand that you two were married only yesterday," Jane said.

"That's true, Jane," he answered, smiling at Toni. "My wife will be with me when we return next week for the "Wild Wrestling Wipeout at Caesar's. It'll be a night to remember. All the stars will be there." He said. Maybe he could take Toni back to the hotel and come back and ask this good looking broad to lunch.

"I understand that Omar Atlas is in the main event," said Jane. "Do you want to say anything about his match?" she asked.

"He's my wife's brother," replied Keith. "We're having a double main event and I'm meeting Cochise Whitedove in an Indian Strap Match." He said, anger beginning to show now. But Jane kept on.

"About Omar Atlas, he's so gorgeous. Would you like to tell our listeners some more about him?" she asked, determined to find out about the Latin star.

"Listen, Bitch," he exploded, furious that she had insisted on talking about Omar, "If you are that interested in the son-of-a-bitch, why don't you buy a ticket and go down and watch him? Maybe you'll get lucky."

"And that, ladies and gentlemen, concludes our show, and possibly our license," said Jane, trying to make light of Keith's foul mouth. Turning off the microphone, eyes blazing, Jane turned and said, "Take your foul mouth out of this radio station right now."

At that moment, the sound room door burst open and Dan, general manager of KTUV, came storming in. Having heard the entire conversation from the sound booth, he was furious.

"That's it, Pal. You've managed to scream profanities over our radio station and insult my sportscaster at the same time. I want you out of here now."

Toni looked at Keith's face. It was blank. "O.K., Man, I'm outta' here," he said. Then he turned, grabbed Toni by the arm so hard that she yelped in pain. Under his breath, where no one else could hear, he said,

"We're going back to the room. It's party time again."

*   *   *

29

Chicago. He'd always dreamed of some day coming here, but never in his wildest dreams did he believe it would be this soon, or under these conditions. Now he was here.

First, he'd see Lorenzo, get checked into a hotel, and then he'd go sightseeing. He had brought Toni's camera so that he could take back pictures of Chicago. Toni. His mood took a downward turn. He thought of her on her honeymoon with Keith. He felt revulsion and rage that he was absolutely unable to do anything about the situation. He had tried to warn Toni, but at 20, she was no match for Keith Daniels. His expensive gifts and bullshit had completely won her over.

Frances was in agreement with Omar. They had discussed the situation often. Max, on the other hand, was no help at all. What Keith wanted, Keith got. God, he was sick of this situation.

While I'm here, I'll talk to Lorenzo. I'll take him up on his offer, if it is still good. I can come here and make a name for myself and to hell with Wild West Wrestling. My debt is paid. And as for Toni, she has made her bed and she can lie in it. I've given her all my love and guidance and she has refused to listen. Time I started thinking about myself—my life.

* * *

"Lorenzo Petri, please," said Omar as he approached the receptionist on the top floor of "The Citadel," the building which housed

Hemisphere Championship Wrestling; the building owned lock, stock and barrel by Lorenzo Petri, the czar of professional wrestling in the United States.

Smiling warmly, the receptionist answered, "Yes, Mr. Atlas, Mr. Petri is expecting you. This way, please."

As she walked in front of him, Omar admired the long, slender legs, firm butt, and long, blonde hair on the woman. He hadn't been in America long enough to be used to blondes, and they still fascinated him.

"Hello, Omar," said Lorenzo, standing up and coming across the room to greet him. "Have a seat, and let's talk about your stay with us," he said. "Have you considered my offer yet? I told Max that I wanted you up here for a couple of weeks, but just tell me now that you're ready to join my team, and I'll start the publicity and get things rolling for you to join us permanently. What do you say?"

"I have been considering joining you, Lorenzo. Your offer is very attractive. I've called some of the boys in your territory and they tell me they are making ten to fifteen thousand a week here."

"Yes, and I'm planning to make you our new champion. We need a Hispanic champion and you fit the bill, which means souvenirs. You'll get one percent of all of your souvenirs we sell. You could easily make another hundred thousand a year on that. How about it?"

"It's a deal, Lorenzo, but I'll need until the first of the year to finish with Wild West Wrestling. They are working angles with me until then. I can give my notice when I go back."

"I'm afraid you are gonna' get some heat from them, Omar. I didn't mention this to you before, but I've been negotiating with them for a merger just so I could use you. Now that you have decided to join us, of course, I won't need to deal with the idiot savant and his father. Their reputations have reached me, and frankly, I don't need the headache. I assure you, you will be glad you chose to come here. Listen," said Lorenzo, "I don't want to rush you, but I need to be getting to the airport. I leave tonight for Germany, and I'll be gone for about a week.

When I get back, we'll get together with the booker and tell him we're gonna' switch the title from Lance Lawrence to you. Meanwhile, he has been instructed to feed you gibronis on television, and you'll get fast wins and build your reputation on the T.V. show. By the time I get back, we'll be ready to work an angle with you. Meantime, let me get my secretary in here to help you. She generally helps the new people here in town find their way around; she shows you the sights and makes you feel at home."

"Nancy," he flipped the intercom button, "can you come in here, please?"

*   *   *

"Nancy, this is Omar Atlas. Omar, this is Nancy Brown, my secretary and assistant."

Omar looked down at the small, petite blonde woman with the beautiful smile and the most gorgeous teeth he'd ever seen. Her green eyes looked squarely at him, and he knew he'd been evaluated in a brief second, and judging by her smile, he'd been approved.

"Nancy, please show Omar around the Citadel, then take him to dinner tonight at the company's expense. Show him Chicago and make him welcome. I'd love to go with you, but as you know, I'm leaving tonight for Germany."

*   *   *

Nancy took Omar through The Citadel. In the basement was a complete television studio with eight cameras and a crew of 16 people. There were boom mikes and an engineering room equipped with everything a television station used, including graphics. An audience of four hundred could watch the television tapings in the studio.

"This beats our mobile T.V. van at home," he said.

"Oh, we also have a mobile unit and a crew of eight who travel with the live shows."

On another floor, he saw Lorenzo's in-house travel agency. "Since we have forty wrestlers, ring crews, souvenir sales people, office people, medical people and seamstresses traveling, we do our own ticketing," said Nancy.

There was a photography studio, a tee-shirt factory, an advertising agency, a costume shop, and a public relations department, all on various floors. Payroll and Accounting, and Human Resources took up more floors. One entire floor was s print shop for printing the programs and monthly wrestling magazines. There was a staff of four reporters. Omar marveled at the efficiency of the operation. Lorenzo didn't miss a lick.

"We have a payroll of over three hundred people," said Nancy. "We send three seamstresses with the shows so that costumes may be made or mended on the spot; we send hair dressers, and we even send a doctor and nurse on the road with the boys to conduct periodic drug screening. The first time the doctors find drugs in your body, you pay for the rehabilitation out of your pay. The next time your test comes up "dirty", you are history. Lorenzo won't tolerate drug abuse, and he is particularly cautious since we had some bad publicity last year."

She looked at Omar's famous 20" arms. "You know," she said, "steroids are considered drugs, too."

"Don't worry about me, Nancy. I've never done steroids, and I never will."

*   *   *

"I'm leaving early, Madge, Lorenzo wants me to take Omar around town," Nancy said to the receptionist as she opened her desk to pick up her purse.

"God, how lucky can you get. If he'd ever ask me to do that, you can figure it would be for Igor the Missing Link and I could pull him by the chain on his neck clear through downtown Chicago," said Madge. "Just remember, Nancy, Lorenzo is strict about no dating the wrestlers."

"I haven't survived working her for four years by dating wrestlers," was the comeback. "I haven't fallen for any of them yet, and I won't start now. It sure won't hurt my feelings to have this guy beside me all evening, tho. Man, he even smells good. He really seems calm for a wrestler. Doesn't seem to be 'on' all the time, or ogling the girls. He looked me straight in the eye when we met. Didn't try to look down my blouse. I like that. It is unusual around here. Well, see you tomorrow, Madge," she said, as she turned to join Omar in the outer office.

* * *

Nancy took Omar to the Hilton, where all of the wrestlers stay when they are in town. He checked in and they went to his room so that he could change into some warmer clothes. Coming to Chicago from Corpus Christi in December is no small deal. The weather had been in the sixty's back home, and it was snowing outside now.

"Where to, Omar?" she asked when he was changed. "We can get a cab and go any place, and all the places you desire, courtesy of Lorenzo Petri. Where shall it be?"

He didn't hesitate. "to the Museum of Natural Arts, Mi amor," he said.

"How beautiful," she replied. What does 'Mi amor' mean?"

Omar hadn't even realized that he had called her "My love" until she asked. It just seemed so natural. She was so open and warm and beautiful that he hadn't planned to say it, it had just slipped out.

"It means, 'My love' in Spanish. I'm sorry. It just came out." He was embarrassed, and hoped he hadn't offended her.

"Please, it is beautiful, and I'm flattered," she said. Then, realizing that he was embarrassed, she turned quickly and pointed out the famous Waldorf Hotel.

Six hours later, their cab returned to the Hilton. By this time they were tired and cold. Neither wanted the day to end, however. They were both 'intoxicated' by the presence of someone new and wonderful. They sat in the back seat, looking at each other.

"Remember, Omar, we have a dinner date. Lorenzo will be upset if you don't take him up on it."

"I wouldn't miss it for the world," he said. "Where shall we go?"

"I know a little Italian restaurant just around the corner. We can leave the cab and walk from here." She said.

* * *

As they entered Luigi's, they were aware that all eyes were on them as they came through the door. They were a knock out couple and Omar was so proud. He was the picture of dark, brooding handsome; black eyes and hair, with dark olive skin and white teeth that looked even whiter in his dark skin. His massive shoulders filled the doorway when he entered. She was a contrast. Light blonde hair, light skin, and green eyes. Her mouth had a perpetual smile as though she had a joke with herself too precious to share with anyone. As he noticed people staring, Omar gently put his arm around her and ever so slightly, pulled her against his side. He noticed that she did not pull away. Rather, they stood, waiting for a table, two actors on a stage for all the world to see. Each basked in the excitement of being with the other. Not a word was spoken between the two; they were in complete harmony, completely at ease, and they didn't move until the maitre de asked them to follow him to the back of the room.

Omar couldn't tell you what he ate; nor could she. What they talked about wasn't important, they just talked. They ate and they drank Chianti wine. They had dessert and Cappuccino coffee. They touched hands, they touched souls. They had found each other.

"Are you ready to leave, Mi amor?"

"Yes, I am."

They walked, or rather ran, as it had started snowing again, back to the Waldorf. There were no unnecessary questions, they both knew the answer. Nancy went with him up the elevator to the eleventh floor without a word being spoken.

Inside the room, he took her gently in his strong arms and kissed her the way no man had kissed her before.

"Tu erres muey bonita, mi amor," he said. "Tu erres muey mi amor," over and over. He led her to the bedroom and sat her on the bed in the darkness.

Quickly he undressed; then he crossed the room and opened the curtains leading to the balcony. His magnificent body was silhouetted against the window. The night behind him was blue white and the snow was falling now, gathering on the railing, and creating a picture in her mind that Nancy would take with her into her old age.

The radio by the bed began to play. She never knew when he turned it on, but she heard Edye Gorme singing, Eesos Hombres" as his hands found her body.

While they made love, she saw only his big, black, velvet eyes on her, on her body, in her soul. His body was as firm as the palm of a hand. There was no give, and the muscles bulged with every move he made. She had never experienced lovemaking like this before, and she felt as though she might faint.

Again and again he reached for her in the night, each time more fulfilling than the time before.

As they made love the last time, the sun was coming up and the snow was silver and crystal on the balcony. Afterwards, he pulled her in to him with one motion of a big arm; her tired body fit the contour of his, and neither of them wanted the night to end.

*   *   *

30

Omar's eyes flew open and he was instantly alert. Years of training himself to be aware of everything around him at all times couldn't be erased in such a short while. He turned his head and saw Nancy, still asleep. One beautiful arm was draped over her eyes and she was oblivious to the world.

He closed his eyes once more, but his brain was ticking. He couldn't believe his good fortune. How could so much have happened to him in such a short period of time. He had it made. He had always known he would some day. Even back in Caracas he had known.

*   *   *

Caracas is the most beautiful city in the world. A fast-paced, metropolitan city of six million people, Caracas is nestled in a valley at the base of two sets of mountains. A wealthy petroleum industrial city, Caracas sits two hundred miles away from a jungle filled with aborigines, diamonds and gold. Orchids, bananas and mangoes hang from the trees. The "pretty people" live in luxury; sometimes bought with dope money.

He, however, hadn't been one of the "pretty people" of Caracas. His family, years back, had been the aristocratic Morales', but when President Olivares fell, so did his family. Their lands were confiscated, their property destroyed. The entire family had to run to the jungle to escape with their lives.

Years later, his Grandmother Morales had led the family back to Caracas. She started a small food vending business, first on a cart on the street, and then in a small building. She employed every member of her family, either as cooks, food handlers, or peddlers.

As the years went by, the family began to flourish. She had eight children to raise, Omar's mother Juanita being one of them. From the time they were small, they were on the streets, peddling the "arepas" their mamma made. The delicious fried hominy meal patties sold well, and within ten years the family was prospering, not like the famous Morales of before, but there was now a little restaurant, not just carts on the street.

By the time Omar's mother married, another dictator, President Perez was in the office and all was well. Juanita, like the others, worked in the store and her husband was a barber. Omar was born when they had been married a year, and within the next three years, Juanita and Toni were born, also.

But as is true with many Latin American countries, peaceful existence lasts a brief time. Within a few years, unrest would return, and to see soldiers fighting in the streets was not an unusual occurrence.

When Omar was eight years old, he was on his way to school, carefully watching over his two younger sisters. They were just passing through Simon Bolivar Park, when the first shot rang out. The park is in front of the House of Congress, so the children could see the large trucks as they sped up and stopped in front of the building. They heard the shots ring out, saw the guards drop, and watched, horrified, as the soldiers ran up the steps to the residence inside. More shots. The children stood, rooted to the spot. More shots.

"Andale, Hermanas," he said. "Vamoos buscar Papa." They ran for the barber shop to find their father. People were everywhere. Now the soldiers were spreading through the park, shouting at people, shooting at anything that moved. The children didn't dare stop, they knew that they could be shot. Their only thought was to get to the barber shop and tell Papa. If they could only make it out of the park they would be with Papa.

"Andale, andale, Hermanas," he screamed over his shoulder, telling them to hurry. He could see his father's barber shop through the trees. But wait, here came Papa out of the door.

"Omar! Maria! Toni," Papa screamed toward the park entrance. He knew that it was time for them to be coming to the shop. Omar watched in stunned silence, stopped dead in his tracks, his two sisters running into him from behind.

The three small children watched the big truck lumber by, saw a soldier lean out of the back with machine gun in hand, and seeing Papa, pointed it directly at him.

"Noooo," screamed Omar.

Time stood still. The truck was gone. His father was dead. There was no sound around him, he couldn't hear his sisters scream, he didn't see friends run toward his father's body. He saw only his father lying in the street, scissors still in his hand, apron over his clothes.

For as long as he would live, Omar would see this memory as if it had happened the day before.

There was no more childhood, no more carefree school days. Omar's mother was now the sole support of her little family. As in all revolutions, nobody wins, and this was no exception. The rebel soldiers seized the barber shop and grandma's restaurant, and a new president took reign of the country. Caracas had fallen again.

The Morales family started again. Latin Americans know the true meaning of "starting over." And over. Juanita, Omar's mother, began the twelve-hour days, which would be her trademark until the day she died. She was making arepas, and now it was Omar's turn to sell on the street. School was sporadic, at best, and now with two sisters to help support. Oh well, Mamma needed help.

By the time Omar was sixteen, his naturally large frame had developed until he looked almost like an adult. Day after day he stood in front of the Hotel Savoy selling his arepas in his cart, watching all of the "beautiful people" pass by.

On a particular day, he was there for the lunch hour, his best time of day for sales, when a long, black limousine pulled up and the chauffeur ran around to his side to let the passengers out. Omar expected to see the usual American with a lovely woman on his arm, or a general, complete with uniform and sword, there for some military program. But to his surprise, a young Venezuelan man, about his size, emerged from the back seat.

"My God," he said in Spanish, "How long has it been since I've had an arepa? Please give me one. Is it home made?"

"Yes, my mother made them this morning," Omar replied. "How do you know about arepas?" he asked before he thought.

"When I was younger, before I left Venezuela, I ate them all the time. Since then, I've been all around the world and haven't found them any place else to compare with these in Caracas."

Omar was proud; his mother would love to hear this tonight.

"Come, Manuel, come on," called the voice of the beautiful woman waiting on the steps for him to enter the hotel. "We'll be late."

"What is your name?" Manuel asked

"Omar Morales."

"We're staying here for a few days. I'm wrestling at the coliseum tomorrow night. I'll make you a deal. If you bring me two hot, steamy fresh arepas at eight o'clock in the morning for my breakfast, I'll have two ringside seats for you at tomorrow night's matches. How about it?"

Omar was ecstatic. He had never been to a wrestling match, but now all of a sudden, he realized that he had been talking to Manuel Munoz, the Caribbean Middleweight Wrestling Champion! He couldn't believe his luck.

For the past year, people had been telling Omar that he was so big he should be a wrestler, but he had no idea what wrestling was all about, and certainly never had the money for a ticket. Now, for the price of two of Mamma's arepas, he would be on the front row tonight!

*   *   *

The next morning at eight o'clock, Omar was in front of the Savoy, his arepa cart steaming in the sunlight. He hadn't thought to ask Manuel where he was to meet him for the trade. He knew he couldn't leave his cart in front of the hotel, and he couldn't' take it into the magnificent lobby.

Feeling stupid for not asking questions, he was standing there when suddenly, the bell captain came running down the long flight of steps.

"Are you the arepa boy?" he asked.

"Yes sir."

"Mr. Manuel Munoz wants you to bring two of them to his room. He says I'm to stay here and guard your cart. If you promise to hurry, I will, but I don't want my boss to catch me, so hurry!"

"I will, I promise. I'll be right back."

Omar turned and walked up the steps into the lobby of the hotel. He had never been inside before, and from the minute he stepped in the door, he had stepped into another world.

There was no roof in the lobby. He looked straight up, through treetops, which had been planted to look like the jungle, and saw the blue sky. Straight ahead of him was a bridge over a running stream of water. The bridge led into two restaurants and the swimming pool beyond. He turned around and headed back outside. The bell captain was behind his cart trying to explain to several tourists what an arepa was.

"Hey, I'm glad you're back." He said. "These people want to buy some arepas. How much are they?"

"They are two Bolivars apiece, and I haven't gone yet. What room will I find Manuel Munoz in?"

"He's in room 1209, and if you don't hurry and get back here, I'm going to park this cart in the lobby and forget it! said the bell captain, knowing full well that he wouldn't dare do such a thing. Then he'd have to deal with Manuel Munoz and he wasn't that stupid.

* * *

"Come in," said Manuel from the other side of the door in answer to the hurried knock.

Omar went into the suite, as the door had been left ajar for him. Manuel was there, fresh from a shower. It was obvious that he was preparing for tonight's match, because he had wrestling tights, boots, and several masks laid out on the bed.

"Ah, thank you so much," he said. "I have been looking forward to this since I got up this morning. Normally I don't eat until after the matches, like everyone else, but I knew if I ate early enough it wouldn't hurt."

"Why do you only eat once a day, Manuel?"

"For two reasons, my friend. First of all, if you eat right before you wrestle, your blood pressure will shoot up as you become more active. You can have a stroke. There have been several wrestlers who have died in the ring from such a simple thing as eating a meal before a match. You may also need surgery later."

31

Palacio de Los de Porte—Palace of the Sports —he'd never been inside before, and neither had his friend Eduardo.

As they handed the usher their tickets and followed him down front to ringside, they both looked at the crowds of people, mostly men, eating popcorn, drinking beer, and smoking. There was a blue haze of smoke already forming in the glare of the ring lights, and the smell of popcorn was everywhere.

"Eduardo," said Omar, "this is just like we saw in the movies."

"Do you see Manuel?" asked Eduardo. He knew that Manuel would be wearing a black and white mask, and he was looking for him. Eduardo had a very hard time believing the story that his friend had told him this afternoon. Up until he saw the tickets. Now he was a true believer. Now he wanted to meet Manuel.

"We are to wait at the dressing room door after the matches." Said Omar. "We won't see him until after he wrestles."

Both young men were excited, but very still. Each was caught up in his own thoughts, each was looking around, watching the crowds of people who looked like this was not the absolutely most exciting thing they had ever seen. People gathered in groups, discussing last week's matches, some were hurrying to the beer stands, because the first match was due to start and they didn't want to miss any of it.

The one thing they both noticed was that there were few women, and no children in the audience. Then they saw the sign that read, "No

Children under Twelve Allowed at these matches." This was a firm, fast rule. No children.

The lights dimmed, the music started, and the bell rang. The first wrestlers made their way down the aisle to the ring. Omar and Eduardo were completely enthralled. During the matches they screamed, they cheered, they jumped up and down. They were hooked.

By the time Manuel came to the ring, they were old veterans. They cheered the baby faces and booed the heels. They shouted words of encouragement to Manuel, and when he won his match, they were as proud as if they had done the deed themselves.

As he passed by them on his way back to the dressing room, they looked into the eyehole of his mask just in time to see one big, black eye wink at them.

Fifteen minutes after the last match, everyone had left the arena and the two boys made their way back to the dressing room door. They stood on the outside, but they could clearly hear the laughing of the men, the water running in the shower, and an occasional toilet flush. Finally, Manuel came to the door and, looking around to make sure there were no fans around, beckoned them to come in.

Inside the room were all of the wrestlers from the card tonight. Some were naked, some were partially dressed, some had half-filled beer bottles which they were gulping from.

"One of the hazards of the trade, Omar," said Manuel, "the drink. After a wrestling match when you are dehydrated, tired and hot, there never seems to be a water fountain around. There is always beer at the arenas."

Manuel took the two boys to each wrestler, one by one, and introduced them, explaining that he was interested in a possible wrestling career for Omar.

"Fantasma," he said to a young wrestler who was slamming his locker door shut. "Are you interested in trading some wrestling lessons for the best arepas you ever ate?"

"Sure, no problem. I'll tell you what, Omar, I'm going to be coming around here once a week for the next few months. You meet me at the downtown YMCA every Monday at eight o'clock in the morning and I'll work out with you and give you some pointers. Eduardo, you want to learn, too?"

"Oh, God yes!" came the answer. "I don't have any arepas, though."

"Don't worry, fella, I'll show you while I show Omar. Only one favor, please don't bring anyone else with you. I don't mind, but when you get too many guys together, no one learns, and my workouts are interrupted. With the two of you, though, we can all work together. I'll be honest with the both of you, though. It will be tough. I don't teach crybabies, and I don't teach guys who beat up on girls. Understood?"

"Understood."

"O.K., my friends, enough for tonight. We leave now for Maracai. We wrestle there tomorrow night. We'll see you next week."

As they left the building, the two boys felt as though they had been accepted into a secret club that most young men would die to join.

"That's it for me, Eduardo," said Omar. "I knew from the time I walked in the door here tonight, this is my future. No mater what it takes, no matter what I have to do, I'm going to become a professional wrestler. I'll work until I drop. He can't put too much on me, I'll ask for more. This is the way out for Mama, Toni, Maria and me. If it's the last thing I do, I'll go to America and send for them. I'll make big money, drive big cars, and have a big home for my family."

"Me, too," agreed Eduardo. "Maybe some day we can become tag team partners and wear matching tights like the Gomez brothers did tonight."

"And one more thing," said Omar.

"What?"

"I'm gonna' be the champion."

* * *

"First you run, then you wrestle," said Fantasma. For more than a month the two boys had been running up and down the steep hills which make up the streets of Caracas. Early in the morning, when the women were sweeping their sidewalks, they had sped past, painful at first, but now both boys were experiencing an almost euphoria each time they ran.

Where at first they had dreaded the early morning work out, they now looked for ward to it. Fantasma hadn't lied. He had been a strict teacher. They had started out running one mile, then two, now they were up to five miles each day. Their sprint always ended up back at the 'Y' where they joined Fantasma on Monday mornings for their routine workout.

He began by having them sit on the floor, facing each other, legs crossed. They grabbed each other's arms above the elbows. First one boy would pull as hard as he could, then the other. This not only stretched every muscle in each one's body, but also taught them the strength in another person's body. It also got them used to touching another man.

Jump rope, neck and back exercises, and light weights came next. Because of the boys' ages, the muscles came fast, and at the end of six months, both boys had gained over thirty pounds, ate continuously, and were lifting over three hundred pounds during their bench presses.

One Monday, much to the boys' surprise, Fantasma showed up at the 'Y' with Manuel.

"Oh, hi, guys," he said. "I've been hearing so much about your progress, I thought I would come down and see how you are doing."

Both boys were so impressed that Fantasma had even been discussing them that they were eager to show off their new skills.

"We are going to start ring maneuvers today," said Fantasma. "Omar, you stand in front of me." The boys, expectant and excited, stepped in front of the two men.

Suddenly, as if on cue, each wrestler reached down with his right hand, put it between the legs of the boy opposite him, and gripped his buttocks. The wrestler's left hand gripped the boy's right shoulder. S the wrestler moved forward, he raised the boy off the ground, tucking his head under his body, and threw him to the ground onto his back! They had just been body slammed for the first time.

Omar saw stars, and the impact forced all of the air out of his lungs. He stared up into the concerned face of Manuel.

"Are you O.K., Man?" Manuel asked.

"I'm fine," he lied. His head rolled to the left side to stare into the shocked face of Eduardo. Fantasma, like Manuel, was talking to the other boy.

"I'm fine, let's do it again."

No, we won't do it again until tomorrow. We just wanted you to see why you have been doing all the back exercises and all the running. The running will strengthen your lungs, and the back exercises will prevent you from receiving so many bad injuries. Always raise your head a little bit off of the floor, not where it can be seen, but enough so that the impact is on the top half of your back, not your head. Are you dizzy?" he asked.

"No, but please, I want to try the body slam again. I want to hurry. I want to start wrestling and make some money."

A knowing smile passed between the two seasoned grapplers.

"So you are hungry, huh?" Manuel said. "Well, if you know more than the teacher, so be it."

With that, Manuel and Fantasma both reached down, pulled the boys up by the arms, and once again body slammed them to the ground.

Over and over again.

By the time they had received eight body slams, the two boys were up and running, trying to make it to the bathroom, and throwing up all over the green mats on the YMCA floor.

"Lesson number one. Don't try to teach the teacher how to teach," laughed Manuel to Fantasma.

* * *

The next week, only Omar showed up at the 'Y'.

"What happened?" asked Fantasma.

"Eduardo has decided that he'd rather not wrestle. He doesn't like to throw up."

"You have just seen how we 'weed out' the serious from the not so serious potential wrestlers. Because you are here after your last lesson shows me that you are determined. That's what it takes, because your training has just begun. I will admit that is the worst part. After learning the body slam, the rest comes easier. Today we'll do the side and front headlock. Come here."

As Omar approached, Fantasma threw his right arm around the boy's neck, quickly pulled him into his right side, and grabbed his own fingers which were in an open fist position, thereby creating a "hook" with his fingers to prevent his opponent from escaping.

"Now," he said, "grab my hands with both of yours, spin your body to the left, and force my hands up over my head."

To Omar's amazement, when he did so, Fantasma immediately let go of the side head lock, allowed his arms to be raised above his head, and fell flat on his back on the floor, bringing Omar down on top of him, still holding onto his hands. A big grin spread over the grappler's face. You learn well, my friend, you learn well."

After practicing the side headlock and the front headlock for several hours until Fantasma felt that the boy had it perfected, they went through the weight routine, and met for a "strategy session" in the steam bath. They sat side by side, white towels around their waists, and sweat running down their large bodies.

"I'm proud of you, Omar," Fantasma said. "Just keep up the good work like you did today and you'll go far. I will be here for several more months, and will be able to help you a lot. When you get all of this down so that you look good, I'll get you booked into some small town and you can try your hand at an opponent. We always try to start someone out in a small town. That way, after you've made the big time, fewer people remember the times when you looked bad.

The first match I had," he continued, "I only wore one pair of tights, and the ring was very bad in that town. As I got thrown out of the ring, I hit a bad spot on the ring post, tore a hole in my tights, and "mooned" everyone in the audience. I was embarrassed to death. I thought I was a star and ended up being a clown. Now that I am on a big circuit and have become a star, I hope there were only twenty people in the audience who remember that night." He laughed.

"Do you really think I'm that good?" Omar asked. "I'll work until I drop. I've got the front headlock and side headlock, and one by one, I'll have all the holds learned. I can't wait. As soon as I learn everything, I'm going to America," he said confidently.

"Well, I have to tell you, Mi Amigo, that in America, every move you have learned here will have to be re-learned. Where we pull our opponent in to our right side, they pull in to the left side. Where we spin to the right, they spin to the left. When you first start to wrestle the Gringos, this can be confusing and scary."

"Why do they do that?" Omar asked.

"I guess because they are Gringos," laughed Fantasma.

32

The day began as usual: a five-mile run, work out with Fantasma, and the steam bath "strategy session." Today, for some reason, Fantasma didn't seem to be himself. He seemed preoccupied. For almost a year now, every single Monday, Omar had enjoyed the man's undivided attention. He was an apt pupil, learned well, and was naturally well coordinated despite his large size.

Now over two hundred and ten pounds, Omar was eager to please his teacher, and mistook his silence for disinterest.

Finally, Fantasma spoke. "Omar, I have some good news and some bad. You know I had always hoped to be there when you started your career. Well, I got word from my promoter this morning that next Sunday I leave for Madrid, Spain. That is a wonderful break for me, and I can't turn it down, but I will miss your first match. I have arranged for you to wrestle on Sunday night in Maracai. You will be in the opening match, fifteen-minute, one fall. Remember everything I have taught you and you will be fine."

Omar's heart raced, his head pounded. He had waited forever for this chance, and now he was afraid he would forget everything he had learned and embarrass not only himself, but this man who had been so generous with his time and knowledge.

"I know this is a bad time for me to leave you, Mi Amigo," he said, "but in this case, I have no choice. Spain is next, and then the United States. I will be waiting for you over there. Perhaps we will wrestle each other in Madison Square Garden some day" he said, trying to bring a smile to the stricken young man's face.

"I understand," said Omar. "I couldn't ask you to do more than you have already. If there is ever anything that I can do."

"I know," replied the man, "you've never asked me, but how do you think I got started? Someone helped me along the way, just as I'm helping you. That's why I will ask one favor. No matter how big you get, please always remember the young boys at the YMCA who need a helping hand."

* * *

The bus took three hours to get to Maracai. Toni had wanted to come, but Omar refused to let her. She understood that in Latin American countries women don't go to wrestling matches alone, and he didn't understand yet that the promoters made arrangements for family seating for the wrestlers.

This was his first match and he would be alone. He felt sorry for her, but promised her that she could go with him in the future.

The walk from the bus station to the arena was almost a mile. With no money, a taxi was out of the question, and since none of the wrestlers knew him, no one stopped to pick him up. He didn't care if he had to walk; he would have crawled on hands and knees to do this. He had absolutely no idea how much money he would be paid, or if he would be paid at all. It had never occurred to him that he was going to make more money tonight than he had ever seen at one time.

When he entered the building, Omar was surprised at how large it was. Dome shaped, it held 25,000 people, and it seemed to him that there wasn't an empty seat in the house. He walked through the audience, bag in hand. Everyone who saw him knew he would be on the card.

Slowly, he made his way through the crowd to the back of the arena where he had seen other wrestlers enter a door.

An older man, smoking a cigar was beside the door. He held in his hand the most beautiful eel skin wrestling bag that Omar had ever seen. It was brown and caught the reflection of the lights as it turned in the fat man's hand.

It must be so expensive he won't put it down. He thought.

Suddenly the man saw him. He put the cigar in his mouth, threw out his right hand and said, "You must be Omar Morales. I'm Jorge Batal, the promoter. Fantasma has told me so much about you that I feel like we've met. He didn't exaggerate your size; you look like Atlas, the Greek God who held up the world. From now on, your wrestling name will be 'Omar Atlas'. That's the way your name will appear on all the publicity" He said.

"I like that name," he replied. "I like it a lot. Thank you."

Omar could see inside the dressing room door. The men were dressing for their matches and working out with small weights to warm up before they hit the ring.

"Go on in, son, the others are already here. Meet me after the matches for your payoff. You will get a percentage of the gate. Oh yes, I almost forgot. This is for you. Last week Fantasma brought it here and asked me to give it to you."

It was the eel skin wrestling bag. Omar was stunned. As the promoter handed it to him, he said, "There is a card inside for you."

It said, "See you in America, Amigo."

*　　　*　　　*

33

Nancy stirred beside him, bringing him back from Caracas and the past.

"God Morning, Mi Amor," she whispered.

"Good Morning, Mi amor," he responded. He guessed he had awakened this way a thousand other mornings, with a thousand other women, but today was different. He smiled to himself at her Gringa pronunciation of "Mi Amor." It was beautiful. She was beautiful.

She suddenly sat bolt upright in bed. "Oh my God! It's nine o'clock and I haven't called work. Thank God Lorenzo is gone, but everyone will assume that they know what happened between us last night, because they know we left together. Lorenzo fires anyone in the office who dates a wrestler. What am I going to do?"

She looked at him with such terror in her eyes that he couldn't resist pulling her back down lying next to him, her head on his chest. Her warm body snuggled against him for warmth.

"My beautiful Rubia, My beautiful Rubia," he whispered into her hair, "don't worry, we can think of something. Don't panic. And don't stay this close to me, or we will never get you back to work," he laughed.

He felt her body melt into his and he squeezed her so hard that he heard the breath leave her body. Her leg raised over his hip, his erection penetrating her body as, once again, time stood still, the snow fell and the sky grew brighter outside.

* * *

The sounds of the shower could be heard in the bathroom when room service arrived. A steaming pot of coffee and a Danish for Nancy, bacon, eggs, toast, juice, coffee and fruit for Omar. He would eat this food, but after his daydreaming about home, he really would like an arepa this morning.

He could see Mamma making them now. She would be adding warm water to the salted hominy masa; she would knead them just to the right consistency, and then plop them into hot oil. They would be crispy on the outside, while the inside was heavy and delicious. He could smell them.

Omar picked up the telephone and called the Citadel. He asked for Madge, since she had seen the two of them leave together the day before.

"Madge, this is Omar Atlas. Please give me my bookings. When is the first night I work this week?" He heard the shuffle of papers.

"Your first shot is when we do television on Tuesday night," she replied. "You don't have to work until then, but please keep in touch. Lorenzo wants to arrange a meeting between you, Lance Lawrence, Lorenzo, and Paulie our booker."

He could feel the questions she wanted to ask. She was dying to find out what had happened and where Nancy was.

"I'm calling because I took a plane back home last night so I can bring some more of my things back. I'm in Corpus, but I'll see you Tuesday. Nancy helped me get a place yesterday and she's taking care of some things for me today. I'm getting ready to phone her now to see if she can take care of my deposits for me. These things have to be done and since I have no wife, I've asked Nancy to help me. Lorenzo has given her approval.

"Well, that explains why she didn't come to work or answer her telephone this morning. We were all very concerned about her, and have been trying to get her all morning. I guess she's taking care of things for you then," said Madge.

"I'm sure she is, she's a very professional lady," he said, smiling. As he put down the phone, he said softly, "liar."

Nancy was standing in the bathroom door. She had overheard the entire conversation.

"I am amazed at how well you came up with a solution for me. I owe you a big favor for that one," she said.

"And I intend to collect. Tonight," he answered. "Not only did I make an excuse for you this morning, but you may take the rest of the day off to have my telephone installed, also." They both laughed. "Let's go to your place, let you change clothes, and spend the day doing the things I told her you were doing. We'll come back here tonight so I can collect my debt." He pulled her up to him and kissed her very lightly on the lips.

"Omar," she said.

"Yes, Mi Amor?"

"What's a 'Rubia'?"

* * *

34

"How can it be that I don't look any differently?" pondered Toni, as Keith was dragging her through the airport. People still smiled at them and wished them all the happiness in the world.

In the airport, people had turned and stared when they recognized Keith. Of course, he didn't smile back, as he was now a "heel" on t.v. and had to live up to that reputation. He merely avoided eye contact with anyone, kept a firm hand on her arm, and went through the crowds, both when they boarded the plane in Vegas and while they waited in front of the airport in Corpus Christi to be picked up by Max and Frances. She, however, smiled at everyone; that was her nature. And they smiled back.

Funny, when she smiled at the fans on her way to Vegas she had been truly happy. Now, she lived a pretense by day, dreading the nights, and her only salvation were the nights that Keith snorted so much cocaine that he went directly to sleep.

As they waited on the curb in front of the airport, Keith looked both ways, standing on one foot and then the other.

"Hell, you ask the old man to do one fucking thing a day and he can't get it straight!"

"Please, Keith, your language, there are fans around," she ventured.

"Shut your lousy mouth, bitch!" Not only did his voice get louder and shriller, but he squeezed the arm he was holding until she yelped in pain. She saw several fans' mouths fly open and their hands come up to their mouths as they discussed what they had just seen.

Toni had chosen her pink suit to wear home because it had long sleeves, and even with her dark skin, the blue and green bruises were still visible from their last "party time" in the hotel room.

She prayed that she could count on Frances for help. She knew that she couldn't from Max. Her blood could be flowing and he would deny that his wonderful son had done anything. She loved Keith so much, and she wanted to believe that he would change. Maybe this was just his frustration at being unable to tend to business for a week while they were in Vegas.

"Here they come now. About fucking time!" he said, jerking her roughly down the curb and to the other side of the street for easier entry into his father's car. Grabbing the back door, he virtually threw Toni into the back seat.

"Go get the bags, Dad," he said as he climbed in beside her. "Nobody will recognize you."

Dutifully, Max lumbered out of the front seat, tipped the Red Cap, and put the bags in the trunk.

Inside the car there was only strained silence. Finally, Frances braved the silence and asked, "How was Vegas, kids? Did you have fun? Did you win any money?"

"Shit, are you writing a book?" he snapped back. "Make it a mystery and leave me out of it!"

Mortified, Toni replied, "Yes, we had a very good time. We didn't see any shows, but Keith enjoyed the gambling."

She couldn't bring herself to tell Frances that she had spent most of the time in the room waiting for him to return from the casinos. No matter what she said or did, he would find a way to have an argument with her and order her to the room. Much, much later he would return to either "party time", or "punish her" for something she had said, done, or wanted to do; or if she were lucky, snort cocaine until he passed out, fully dressed, on top of the bed.

"Why don't you two stay at the house with us until you can find some place for yourselves?" asked Frances, eager to have Toni back with her.

"Please, Keith, let's do that. Mama and I can look for a house while you and Dad work. It would be so much fun. Please."

"I couldn't care less where we live," was the reply. "I'm on the road so much I don't know where I am half the time now anyway. Just keep my clothes clean, my wrestling bag packed, and stay out of my way."

Thank you, God, she thought. At least in his parents' house he won't be so mean.

"Let's go into the den, Son, while the girls unpack. There are some things I need to discuss with you," said Max as they entered the large entryway. The women followed the maid up the stairs to the suite that Frances had fixed for the newlyweds, "just in case", and the men turned off into the den.

"A lot has happened during the past two weeks, Son. I've almost called you a couple of times, but I didn't want to disturb your honeymoon."

"Sure as hell wasn't much to disturb, if you really want to know," he answered.

Max really didn't want to know. If everything weren't perfect, he'd rather not get involved. That was the way he had survived 32 years of marriage with a woman he detested and 31 years with a son who loathed him. Now if the son had marital problems, that was his concern. Max would stay out of it. His motto: "See no evil, hear no evil, don't give a shit."

"Omar is in Chicago with Lorenzo," Max turned the conversation to safer grounds. "I'm hearing that Lorenzo is really after him. I can feel the merger coming on now. Omar owes me, and with his sister in the house, he won't dare leave. We're holding all the cards, Son."

"Do you even have a brain, old man? Don't you remember him leaving the reception, sneaking out the back door like a jewel thief in the night? May I remind you that we didn't even get a wedding card from the ass hole, and now you think he feels loyalty to you? I think he probably hates our guts. I know he does mine, and every time I think about it, I make his sister pay one more time."

Max didn't hear that, either.

"My informants tell me that there is a big meeting next week between Lance Lawrence, Lorenzo, Omar, and Lorenzo's booker," said Max. "You can't tell me that they aren't talking about a merger with Wild West Wrestling. I'll bet Omar calls me tonight to tell me."

"Listen, brain surgeon, if there was going to be a merger, don't you think they'd let me in on it? I'm the booker for Wild West."

"Don't get excited, I tell you," Max said. "I got a call from someone in their office today, and he said it looks real good for us. Lorenzo is in Germany now, but he is on his way back and he loves Omar."

"I'll tell you what, Dad. I'll call Omar up tomorrow. If he doesn't mention merger, I'll come out and ask him. If we were going to merge, we need to start making plans. We need bigger buildings, more publicity, more souvenirs; our business will triple when they come down here. Maybe I'll be able to get some better drugs," he said as he smiled knowingly at his father.

"Don't kid around about something like that, Son," said Max.

* * *

After dinner, Max, Frances, Keith and Toni sat around the fireplace. It really wasn't warm enough in December in Corpus Christi for a fire, but the women wanted one, so they had started one, as excited as a couple of little girls.

As Frances got up to go to the bar to mix another drink, she asked, "What are we going to do for Christmas? The girls will be home from school. Are we running any towns that day?"

"Jesus wouldn't want wrestling shows run on his birthday," said Max, looking up from an old rerun of a religious program. Even when the family sat down for a talk, the T.V. was showing a religious show or there was a tape in the VCR. Everyone wondered if Max didn't try to brainwash himself with the constant barrage of gospel. He had been a real "two fisted womanizer" in his day, and the abrupt change when his son had died had surprised everyone. Now he was so immersed in religion that he had actually lost touch with the real world. No one paid much attention to him, but it did get on everyone's nerves.

"Screw you, old man," said Keith. He glared at his father. "Thanksgiving, Christmas Day and New Years Day night are three of the biggest nights of professional wrestling. On those three nights, everyone has had about all of family they can stand. They need to get out. We're going to run one show on Christmas day, and two if we can get the buildings."

"But Keith," his mother said, "A lot of the boys are not going to want to work Christmas night. That means they have to drive all day and be away from their families. You have been working them 365 days a year for the past two years. I know they are tired. Why don't you give them that day off?"

"What the hell?" he roared as he jumped out of his chair. "Now I have to listen to you tell me how to run the business? Why don't you just keep that tennis racket going in one hand and a glass of booze in the other and keep the hell out of my business?" He had leaped across the room and was screaming in his mother's face by now.

"Max, are you going to let him talk tome like this?" Frances turned to Max in desperation.

"Now, now, you two, don't argue," Max said as he turned back to the rerun.

Suddenly Keith turned away from his mother and faced Toni. "Get up, Toni, we're going upstairs," he said in the soft voice that she feared so much.

"I want to stay down here with Mama for a little while and talk about Las Vegas, Keith."

He took two steps and was standing over Toni, still sitting in her chair. He grabbed her bruised arm and jerking her to her feet said, "I guess you didn't hear me."

Pushing ahead of him, Keith began talking in a low tone, beneath his breath, that only she could hear.

"That bitch! Trying to tell me what to do. And that ball-less wonder sitting there letting her do it. I'll show you how a wife should act." He pushed her ahead of him, up the stairs and through their bedroom door. He turned and locked the door.

"Please, Keith," she began to whimper, "Please."

"Time to do your wifely duty," he said. He threw her down on the bed and said in the same soft voice, "Take off your clothes."

Slowly she started to disrobe. Surely tonight would be different. *Not in his mother's house. Not tonight.*

God, she wished she had listened when Omar had tried to warn her. She had her chance and didn't take it. Now it was too late for her. She would never get away, and she knew it. She would be too humiliated to tell anyone about the things that went on between the two of them.

"Lie back," he said.

As she lay completely naked on the bed, she turned her face toward her husband. Through her tears, she saw him bend over the nightstand, she saw the cocaine on the mirror in little lines, and she knew the rest. She watched him open the nightstand, and as he turned and walked toward her, she saw his red cocaine-rimmed eyes, and she saw the belt in his hand.

*   *   *

Downstairs, Frances finished another drink and resumed staring woodenly into the t.v. They were watching another of Pastor Goodwin's video "Rules for Life" when she heard the first muffled scream. It sounded like a woman screaming with a hand held over her mouth. There it was again.

"My God, what was that?"

"I didn't hear a thing," Said Max.

35

Omar couldn't believe his good fortune. He had come to Chicago for two weeks, and Lorenzo was talking about him staying on, even becoming champion.

Things like this just don't happen. Not to him, anyway. Things had never come easy, he'd always had to work hard. This was a dream, and he wasn't going to let go of it. He'd call Max and explain. Surely he would understand. Although Max had never been good enough to work for Lorenzo, he had always dreamed of it. Surely he wouldn't expect Omar to pass it up.

Oh well, he has to understand. I'll call him. Let him tell Keith, he thought.

* * *

Max was sitting behind his big desk at the office when the telephone call came from Omar. The religious music was so loud that the secretary had closed the door in self-defense. Max had his eyes closed and his head resting on the back of his chair.

The intercom came on and Becky, the secretary, said, "Line one for you. It's Omar."

Max's eyes flew open. Here it was. The merger. Now all those doubting Thomases would believe him. Omar would never leave him, and Lorenzo has found that out. Here comes the offer, he thought as he picked up the phone and cradled it to his ear so as not to miss any of the music.

"Yes, Hi, Omar," the big man bellowed. How're they hangin', anyway?" He laughed at his own crude joke.

Max listened in silence, phone to his ear, the smile slowly falling off his face as awareness set in.

"I understand. Yes. I understand. We'll get a replacement. Yes. Well, God bless you. Yes, I'll tell her hello."

Max slowly replaced the receiver in its cradle, and sat back one more time. He thought about the call.

No merger. Staying there. Oh, God. Oh, God! Oh My God!

His eyes rolled up in his head, which jerked backward, striking the headrest of the office chair. His legs stiffened, throwing him backward and propelling him into the wall behind him with such force that he felt like he had received a whiplash. He slowly straightened his back, leaned forward, placed his head on the desk, and cried like a baby.

"What the hell are you telling me? Boy, there's a big fucking surprise. So Omar has decided to stay. Remember when I told you he had no loyalty? That Son-of-a-Bitch Mexican doesn't remember that he owes us for everything he is and ever will be, the bastard."

Alone in the house, the servants' night off, Keith had just dragged Toni to their room for another night of "party time," as he referred to countless hours of sexual torture for her. When the telephone rang, Toni prayed that it would be Frances or Max saying that they would be home early, and that Keith would change his mind.

She wouldn't even care if it were Brenda. They thought that she was too stupid to know that when Keith got calls from the "office secretary" and would leave quickly saying that he had to do some paperwork, it was usually Brenda with another orgy for him to attend. She would welcome a night away from him.

When Toni heard Omar's name mentioned, she got excited. Maybe he was coming home! She would swallow her pride and go to him. He had never deserted her before and wouldn't now. Maria was on her way to the United States for a visit. The last time she had called she said she would be here this week. Then the calls had stopped. She believed her older sister, though. She would come this week. She feared that Keith had been intercepting her calls. Toni had left calls all over Chicago for Omar. She couldn't find him, either. But now, was he coming home?

"Screw that ass hole," said Keith as he threw the telephone receiver across the room, tearing it out of the wall. "Well, I guess you are proud of that son-of-a-bitch you call brother," he said as he came toward her. He's staying in Chicago. Mr. Big Shot. Forgot all about his 'baby sister' in Corpus Christi. I guess you know how much he cares about you," He said as he came closer.

"Please, Keith, don't say those things. He does love me, but I'm your wife now, and I belong with you, not with him."

"You bitch! How dare you argue with me," he screamed at her. He covered the length of the room in two strides and drew back his hand to slap her across the face. Quickly he remembered. Not wanting his parents to know that he beat Toni, he dropped the arm. Not that he gave a shit what the bitch and the ball-less wonder thought, but he sure didn't want the other wrestlers to know. He remembered what had happened to a wrestler when the boys found out he had been beating his wife. They beat him to death in the ring every time he had a match until he finally left the territory. He really didn't want trouble like that. They might really hurt him. The worst beating he ever saw was delivered to a wife beater.

Ray Rivera, "Wild Man Jack" not only beat his wife, but bragged about it in the dressing room. That night he was in a battle royal in the main event. Twelve wrestlers in the ring at one time. The winner is the man who stays in the ring after everyone else has been thrown out over the top rope. Well, of the twelve men, twelve had blades stashed under the tape on their hands. Before the first man went out over the top rope, the wrestlers were dancing around Ray, each man with a blade. Zip! One would hit his shoulder. Zap! One would pull his blade up Ray's leg. He screamed in pain, but they wouldn't let him out of the ring. Zing! A cut over one eye. The audience couldn't figure out why Ray was bleeding. He looked like a sieve, was screaming like a banshee, and no one had said a word. Finally, when the tenth man went over the top rope, they all picked Ray up, dripping blood from over fifty superficial cuts. As they threw him over the top rope, someone said in his ear, "This is for Rita. Next time will be worse."

As Ray hit the floor on the outside of the ring, he realized that a "Z" had been cut the entire length of one of his buttocks with a dull blade. He never hit Rita again.

Keith's frustration was complete. He wanted the championship title. He wanted Chicago. He wanted the classy broads that Omar seemed to get. He was sick of Toni. Hell, he'd only married her to get even with Omar. To show him he had more control over his sister than Omar did. His only pleasure out of her was seeing how much pain and humiliation she could handle. He was so mad he could scarcely breathe.

Jolted back to reality, he looked at his wife.

"Come here, bitch."

36

Omar and Nancy had a great day. After a leisurely brunch at the hotel, they went to Nancy's apartment for her to change clothes.

"Welcome to my home," she said as she unlocked the door and stood aside for him to enter.

The beautiful, neat, homey apartment impressed Omar. The large, bright living room was beautiful with comfortable, overstuffed furniture and a large fireplace. Simplicity and taste were the theme.

The kitchen was white and immaculate and warm. All of this appealed to the wrestler. As his basic nature was to be immaculately clean and his personality was quiet, he felt completely at home, even though this was his first time there.

He knew it would not be the last.

"What do you think?" she asked.

"The colors are warm and invite me to stay."

"I invite you to stay," she said, as she walked up to him to be encircled in his arms once again.

"You'd better not do that, Mi Amor, or we'll be here all day instead of taking care of business. You have to be able to say you have accomplished something today. Remember your excuse," he laughed, gently pushing her away.

"You're right. Why don't you start a fire in the fireplace, and I'll get into some fresh clothes. Then we'll start our "errands". After all, you have to get into your apartment when you get back from Corpus Christi," she laughed.

Omar bent down and began making a fire. She went into the bedroom where she deliberately hadn't asked him. Nancy knew that if he touched her once, they would not leave the apartment. Her face burned at the thought. She stood in front of her closet and suddenly couldn't remember why she was there.

Oh, yes. Fresh clothes, she thought. Feeling like a teenager dressing for her first date, Nancy couldn't understand it. She had been out with men before, even though never with one of the wrestlers. Nancy had always honored Lorenzo's No fraternizing rule, because she had a wonderful job which she loved and which paid her far more than any place else she could work.

Lorenzo paid well; he paid for efficiency, professionalism, and most of all, he paid well for confidentiality.

Over the years, she had become familiar with every facet of the wrestling promotion; she was Lorenzo's right hand and was "smart to the business," as they say.

Nancy could still remember when she had first come to work at HCW. She had been hired after many interviews, reference checks, and a drug screen. She felt as though she was being hired to run the United States.

When Nancy had question why all the investigation, Lorenzo had told her, "You'll understand later."

After she was hired, others told her that Lorenzo didn't trust easily, and didn't bond with anyone. A real "loner," Lorenzo had come up the hard way.

He had started in the business as a "gibroni," or novice, at age twenty-one. He was big. 250 pounds of dark brooding man who took everything seriously. Two years after he was hired by HCW, the promoter, old Barney McBride, had decided he wanted to retire. Being childless, he decided to sell to one of "the boys" who worked for him. Not having a family had been to Lorenzo's advantage. He had no one to support, and had saved a lot of money for just such an occasion. When the promotion came up for sale, he bought it at a fraction of its worth.

From day one, Lorenzo was obsessed with making a go of the business. He immediately involved himself with every aspect, from wrestling to television promotion to public relations/publicity. Now, at forty-two he was recognized as the czar of professional wrestling.

Nancy took the challenge of her co-workers who had told her that he didn't bond well. She would create the bond that is so necessary for any efficiently run organization. There has to be a commitment by the secretary and the respect from the boss.

From the first it was evident that this relationship existed, although for the first few months, from time to time she would approach someone talking to Lorenzo, and world hear the words, "kay fabe," either from Lorenzo or the other person. Then they would immediately begin talking about something else. When she asked Lorenzo about this, he would reply, "You'll find out later."

One day she entered Lorenzo's office with coffee. One for Mighty Kong, the huge three hundred pound grappler who was just coming on board, and one for her boss.

She heard Kong say, "You know, Lorenzo, I am good at getting juice. In fact, I'll use the condom in the mouth if you want." Both men heard the coffee cups rattle in their saucers as Nancy closed the door behind her.

"Kay fabe," Lorenzo said to Kong, and they began discussing the territory, the pay, and other things that she was aware of. Nancy pretended that she hadn't heard anything, sat the cups down, excused herself, and left the room. She was fuming. She either worked here and was Lorenzo's right hand, or she was an outsider, a "mark," and she intended to find out what "kay fabe" meant, and she would find it out today.

Busying herself around the office with one eye on the clock, Nancy waited until Kong stopped by her desk to thank her for the coffee. He was on his way out, wearing burlap pants and coat and a heavy fur cape flowing behind him as he went.

Quickly she looked at her telephone/intercom. She looked at the buttons that signified whether or not Lorenzo was on the phone. He wasn't.

Before anyone else could go in his office, she opened his door. Lorenzo looked up from his morning mail as she walked across the office, which seemed like five miles to the frightened young woman. Her stomach was churning; she had never "demanded" anything from this man before. She knew he was no pushover, but she resented the way she was being treated.

Sitting down in one of the large chairs in front of his desk, she sat back, took a breath, looked into his smiling face and began.

"Are you happy with my work?"

"Yes." Still smiling.

"Do you trust me?"

"Yes." Still smiling.

"What does 'kay fabe' mean?"

The smile stayed, but the eyes flickered once, then settled on her. He looked into her eyes long enough to make a point. This was serious.

"Since you can't wait until I feel it is time for you to know, and you are so 'huffy', I'll tell you. I have more confidence in you than anyone else who works for me, including Paulie and Steve, so I'll tell you now. Don't make me sorry!"

Instantly she wished she had never started this conversation. Why couldn't she have waited? She was thrilled to hear how much he trusted her but she certainly didn't miss the drift of what he was saying. She knew this was serious.

"Only very few people in any wrestling company are 'smart' to the business; the promoter, the booker, the wrestlers, and whoever else the promoter feels it is absolutely necessary to tell. This business is entertainment, no different from any other form of entertainment, only more violent. It is a world of illusion. Fans don't want to know how we make something happen, and if we tell them we take away the illusion.

When two people who are 'smart' are talking about very secret things and someone comes up who is not 'smart', you say, 'kay fabe.' This is international. The wrestlers in Germany and France and the Latin American countries will stop when you speak the words. Now you know. Now I will stop 'kay fabe' around you. Do I need to say what would happen if you told something you heard in this office, Nancy?" His eyes were no longer soft and smiling. They looked at her so hard that she physically winced from fear. She knew this man was powerful, and she knew that she would never tell.

"What we were talking about today is an illusion. A wrestler is going to get hurt in the ring. We may want to give him a vacation or we may want to book him some place else for several weeks. Whatever, we need to have him gone, but keep up interest in him for his return. Right before the match where he is going to get 'injured', he will draw blood out of his own arm with a needle, squirt it into a condom, put the condom in his mouth and hold it closed with his front teeth. At the appropriate time, he is 'injured'. Just as he hits the mat, he will release the condom from his teeth, push up with his tongue, and blood will flow all over the place."

"Oh, my God!" said Nancy. "How gross."

That maneuver is done only by the bravest of men," he answered, "and then not too often."

* * *

Still standing in front of her mirror, Nancy snapped out of her reverie. Enough of the past. The future was what counted. Omar was waiting for her in the living room, so she'd better hurry.

Quickly she selected a lime green pants outfit. Hooking the hanger on the door knob, she checked her makeup. Thank God she had taken it with her last night. After the shower this morning at the hotel she had very carefully applied fresh makeup. Since her hair was naturally curly, she never bothered with hot rollers or curling irons. She quickly put on filmy hose, slipped into the pants suit and lime green shoes to match and then stepped back to look into one of the mirrored doors which lined one side of her bedroom. She liked what she saw.

Grabbing her short sheared beaver jacket, she was ready to go. Oh yes, one quick squirt of Chanel and she was out the door.

"Mi Amor, you are muey bonita," he said when he saw her. "You are very beautiful," he translated before she could ask.

Swiftly he covered the area that separated them and took her jacket.

"Con permiso," he said. Again he translated. "With your permission." He held out her jacket and when she backed into it she also backed into his open arms.

He folded his arms across her breasts, pulled her into him and said, "Your hair smells as lovely as the rest of your body." He held her for a moment only, and suddenly pushed her gently away. Embarrassed at his emotions, he led her to the door before things became more serious.

Outside, as Omar bent to lock the door, Nancy asked, "Where did you learn such beautiful English, Omar? Did you go to college?"

He laughed at the thought. "No, Mi Amor, I wasn't that lucky. Are you sure you want to know?"

"Of course."

"When I first came here, I met this beautiful bilingual gringa" he began.

"That's enough. I understand," she said, surprised at the instant jealousy that had sprung up at the thought of him being with another woman.

"Get hold of yourself, girl," she told herself. "You have just met this man. Don't blow the deal before you ever get started. I know these Latin men. Act the least bit possessive and they are history."

He smiled. "You wanted to know."

"Now I know."

37

Lorenzo came pushing through the swinging doors headed to his office. Everyone was rushing either toward him or along behind in his wake. His magnetism was powerful.

"Call Paulie, call Omar, call Lance and set up a meeting at eleven o'clock" he said to everyone and no one, confident that his orders would be carried out. Easing himself into the large comfortable desk chair, the day had now begun at HCW.

Everyone evaporated but Nancy. She held her ground at the door. Bringing his messages and correspondence to him, she turned her attention to the silver coffee maker beside him and handed over a cup of his special blend.

"Thanks. That's one thing I couldn't find in Germany. A good cup of coffee. Anything I need to know, Nancy?" he asked.

"No, not really," was her reply. "Paulie is still hovering like a chicken hawk," she laughed. "A couple of the boys got hurt in a car wreck and I sent cards in your name, notified Paulie, and notified Public Relations. But, all in all, its been very quiet. Do you want me to take notes at your eleven o'clock meeting?"

"Yes, in case we need to look up any details."

She returned to her desk outside his door to wait. She enjoyed these meetings. You never knew what you would hear, from business to gossip, and she was interested in both.

At eleven o'clock sharp, the four men were sitting comfortably in Lorenzo's office. Omar was nervous and ill at ease. Lorenzo and Rick were talking and Paulie was trying to see his reflection in the large plate glass window behind the desk.

"Gentlemen, I think we have a plan," Lorenzo announced and all four men looked at him. "Lance, you want some time off, right?"

"Yes, Lorenzo, I've got a couple of movie deals I'd like to look into."

Lorenzo nodded. "O,K., we've got Omar here. He's been setting record ticket sales with Brown Velvet. I've been watching some tapes and they look good." He looked at Omar. "We'll let you finish with Velvet any way Max wants. You come here and we'll work you up with an angle and within a couple of months, we'll pass the title on to you. You'll also get one percent of the novelties. How does that sound to the two of you?"

"Great," Lance said.

Omar just nodded his head, grateful that Lorenzo wanted him enough to cut him in on the novelties. That was unusual.

Paulie spoke up. "Omar, you and I had better get together and go over a few things. We have to make some decisions."

Lorenzo looked up quickly and said sharply to Paulie, "No meetings are necessary. The decisions are made. Understand, Paulie?"

"Yes, Lorenzo," he answered, pouting and slumping down in his chair. Too bad, he thought, Omar's gorgeous.

Lance turned to Omar. "Do you do much flying in the ring? I know most of the Hispanic guys do. Maybe we could figure something out.

"Yes," Omar said. I really like the acrobatics. And the fans do, too."

Paulie rallied and came up with an idea. They would have Omar win each week and build up his reputation and following of fans. Then he would request a championship match and win by throwing Lance over the top rope.

No title can change hands that way, so the following week should be a sell out. The two men would wrestle a good, exciting, evenly fought match. Suddenly, a wrestler whom Omar had recently defeated would do a "run in" from the back of the room and hit him over the head. That would give the promoter another good show the following week.

By now they would be advertising that the match would have to be held in Madison Square Garden because of so many requests for tickets. In the final week, the crowd would be so "hyped up" they would pay any price. But they would get a show for their money.

Omar and Lance would wrestle fast and furious until they both looked half dead. They would both juice themselves and blood and sweat would flow. The match would run overtime and it would be the match to end all matches.

And so the deal was set and it went according to plan. Omar defeated one man after another. Lance continued to wrestle and win. Occasionally, on the television show Omar would make comments about, "When I'm champion," etc.

On the T.V. show one week, Omar did a pleading request to the wrestling commissioner for a championship match. Next week there was a whole segment on the "signing of contracts" between Lance and Omar.

Right on schedule, the first show went on. Over the top rope, no title change. Second show, the Hawaiian hit Omar over the head. Announcements in the paper. Madison Square Garden. Right on track.

* * *

By eight o'clock on Saturday night, the Garden was jammed to capacity, plus some. Lorenzo and the boys were overjoyed. Their share of the "purse" increased with every ticket sold.

The opening match came and went. Some people were still running around talking to friends and getting popcorn and didn't pay much attention. Besides, the fans all know the opening match is where the new wrestlers start.

The semi-final match used an old fake finish. Near the end, the baby face had been working over the heel, had him on the mat and started to get up after the second count, and as he rose, the man on the mat reached up, grabbed his opponent's trunks, and they fell almost to his thighs.

The fans loved it; the arena rats loved it, and so did the wrestlers. Naturally, that match was all over with a no win. The audience was howling with laughter.

Lorenzo called an intermission so that everyone could settle down and not be distracted from the main event.

The sound of music brought the fans back to their seats. The announcer entered the ring. Lance Lawrence started down the aisle. He had bleached hair tied in long braids with beads. He came to the ring in a turquoise satin robe trimmed with fluffy marabou feathers. Matching trunks and boots completed his ensemble. Noted for his beautiful ring wear, some of his robes cost two or three thousand dollars.

Omar came down the aisle in a deep purple robe covered with fifty white satin roses with long, green winding stems. As he entered the ring, he walked to the center, held his huge arms straight out, and as he slowly turned in a circle, the ring lights went out and the white roses lit up. The audience went wild.

As the lights went on again, Greg Lamont announced that this was to be a championship match. Lance held the belt high above his head as he paraded completely around the ring. It was big, heavy and beautiful. Greg announced that the belt had been made twenty years ago and had over one hundred and twenty carats of diamonds and rubies on it. In fact, it had been made five years ago in Mexico and had over one hundred and twenty carats of cubic zirconiums and red glass on it. As the ring lights hit the face of this beautiful tooled leather belt, the reflection danced on the walls of the arena and into the eyes of the bedazzled spectators.

Everything went as planned. Both grapplers put everything they had into the match. During the first fall, Omar juiced himself and at the beginning of the second fall, Lance did the same thing after Omar caused a distraction in one corner. Both men looked as if they would collapse.

The match had been going on for fifty-five minutes. The referee said under his breath, "O.K., boys, let's 'take it home', meaning, "let's finish the match."

To the audience, it seemed that every move took more energy than the men had. They were slippery from blood and appeared to be moving in slow motion. As each man was thrown to the mat, he would give forth a long, low groan.

Finally, both men bounced off the rope, running toward each other as if propelled to the center of the ring. And as if by accident, slammed full force into each other, hitting both chests and heads. They immediately fell backward onto the mat, face up, and their backs flat on the mat. The referee ran and slid down beside them on his stomach.

"One," he began to count them both out, "Two," he continued. Each man struggled, raised his head, and tried to turn over onto his opponent, then fell back down.

"Seven," the referee said. The fans were standing in their seats, each screaming the name of his own favorite grappler.

"Eight," the referee slapped the mat with his open hand. Omar seemed to revive; suddenly, he got upon his arm and side, and in one last, desperate move, threw himself over Lance's still body.

With Lance on his back, the referee started over. Now he would count the champion out.

"One, two, three," the referee said. The whole place went wild with excitement. Lance Lawrence had been champion for twelve years. And tonight he had been defeated! He had put up a good fight, but had lost. The referee had both men on their feet by now and they shook hands and walked to their corners, hanging, gasping over the ropes. Lance stepped between the second and third rope and made his way to the dressing room with applause ringing in his ears and blood dripping in his eyes.

Omar rallied, held the belt over his head, and trotted around the ring. He had done it he was tired and bleeding, but he had done it.

At last the fans were beginning to calm down, so he took the belt and left the ring and trotted his way back to the dressing room with fans reaching out to touch him, talking to him and the security guards closing in around him.

Lorenzo would be happy. This had been a good production. The fans must be pleased with the show, thoroughly screamed out and worn out. After one of these spectaculars was staged and was over, you could almost feel the exhaustion when the ring lights went out. The people filed out, almost silently from the arena, leaving behind empty popcorn boxes, spilled drinks, cigarette butts, beer and soft drink cups, and echoes of the night.

Small boys ran around and jumped into the ring to strike wrestling poses until the ring crew moved them out to begin dismantling the ring, ready for tomorrow's show in another town.

Back in the dressing room, everything was as usual. The men dressing, the arena rats waiting for their men for the night's fun. To the wrestlers, it's just one more night, one more show, and one more woman.

To three men, however, tonight was different. Lance Lawrence was free to go make his movies, Omar Atlas was one step closer to Madison Square Garden, and Keith Daniels didn't even know that the belt had changed hands.

38

The gold plaque on the wide mahogany door read "Paul T. Swain, Booker."

The secretary in the waiting room was reading a magazine as Keith swaggered toward her. "Hi, Gorgeous. I'm Keith Daniels, and I have an appointment with Paulie for three o'clock. Is he in?"

She glanced up at him over the top of her magazine. "So you are. I was just reading about your wedding last month. Boy, that must have been something. Congratulations."

"Thanks," he replied.

"Yes, Mr. Swain is in and is expecting you. Just one tip, though, nobody calls him "Paulie" unless they know him real well."

"Thanks, Doll. I'll remember that." He chuckled as he started past her to the private door. *She obviously doesn't know about their night on the town last time he was in Corpus.*

Paulie's office was very impressive, to say the least. A long oak desk sat up on a platform, so Paulie had the advantage of looking down from his seat. Black leather furniture filled the ample room. A large, comfortable looking couch, chair and low coffee table gave the impression that many important decisions were made in this room, but in comfort.

Damn, you could live here, Keith thought.

"Hi, Paulie," he said as he crossed the room to the massive desk.

"Congratulations, Man," replied Paulie. They discussed the wedding for awhile and then Keith got down to business.

"Paulie, I'm here to see what it'll take for me to get a chance at Lance Lawrence. Do you or Lorenzo have the final say?"

"I'll have you know that I have the final say on all bookings! Everything goes through me. Don't forget that. Ever!" Paulie was furious to think there was someone on this planet who didn't realize how important he was.

"The only way you can get lance is work, work and more work. And you would have to 'show me what you've got', if you know what I mean." Paulie couldn't believe that this hick from Texas hadn't heard that Omar had already taken the championship belt from Lance, but he wasn't about to tell the dumb schmuck.

"Well, yes, I think I do." Keith had heard rumors about Paulie controlling who got to wrestle in Madison Square Garden. He would play along so far and then deck this wormy son-of-a-bitch!

Paulie rose from his chair and started around the desk. Keith was sitting on the big chair facing him. Paulie walked straight over to him, ran his hands over the younger man's shoulders, and slowly made a complete circle around Keith. As he was walking, he kept up a constant conversation about wrestling, bookings, how important the booker was, how he was only one step below the promoter.

Keith was extremely uncomfortable. He instinctively felt revulsion at this man. But he didn't say a word all during the soliloquy of self-importance.

Paulie mistook Keith's silence. Pleased, he said, "Why don't you come back here tonight after work and we can go over the details. I think I can really help you out."

Anxious to leave as quickly as possible, Keith eagerly agreed. Seven thirty was decided upon and he shook Paulie's hand and left.

Downstairs, as he hailed a cab, Keith thought, What a sick bastard he is. Even so, he knew he would be back.

* * *

Promptly at seven-thirty, Keith returned to the office building. This time, though, there were no people. Not even the security guard was there. His footsteps echoed as he walked to the elevator and pushed the button to what he hoped would be one step closer to Madison Square Garden and the championship.

"Come on in," Paulie answered Keith's knock, his voice coming from the bathroom. "I'll be right out. Fix yourself a drink. Everything's on the bar."

Keith looked around the room again. Where the bookcase had been this afternoon, was now a completely supplied bar, as the wall had turned around to expose a long, mirror-backed bar. Every liquor imaginable, ice cubes, soda, and the largest silver bowl of cocaine Keith had ever seen. He headed straight for the bowl. He knew that tonight he would need all the help he could get.

By the time he heard the bathroom door open, he was flying high. Out stepped Paulie.

"Here I am," he said in a low voice with his eyes closed halfway into what he assumed was a sexy look.

Keith stared through "coke" red eyes. He wasn't quite sure what would come next, but he didn't think he was going to like it.

* * *

39

When Toni came downstairs, Frances was sitting at the breakfast table. Wearing her newest white Catalina tennis outfit, she had her usual breakfast going of coffee and cigarettes. By the looks of the ashtray in front of her, she had either been here a long time, or was unusually nervous this morning. Her head was down and she was engrossed in the morning newspaper.

"Good morning, Mamma," said Toni in barely a whisper as she walked, with great difficulty, into the breakfast room. The early morning sun shown through the tinted, etched glass windowpanes, creating a kaleidoscope effect on walls, table linens, and occupants alike.

"Good morning, Toni." Frances didn't look up from her paper. "Is Keith up yet? He's had a couple of telephone calls already."

"No, Mamma," came the answer, barely above a whisper.

"What's wrong with your voice this morning?" asked Frances as she folded the newspaper and put it on the table next to her. "Are you coming down with a cold?" She looked at the girl with concern. Something wasn't right.

"Yes, Mamma, I have a cold." Again the whisper. "May I have some coffee, please? It will make my throat feel better."

Frances reached for the pot next to her and stood up to pour a cup for Toni. As she did, Toni reached to her right to retrieve a napkin. Her robe fell open as she did so and revealed her entire right breast. It was black. There were yellow splotches on it, and it was swollen twice the size of the left one.

"My God!" screamed Frances. "What has happened to you?"

Toni's head bent down over her coffee. "Nothing."

As Frances stood there looking down at the shining black hair of this girl she loved so much, she reached out and touched her head. Toni screamed in pain. Frances' hand came away bloody. A chill started at her ankles. It moved up her legs, her stomach, her heart, and her face. She was suddenly very cold. She was shaking. The hair at the nape of her neck began to rise, and then the ringing began in her ears that grew to the pitch of the afterburner of a jet aircraft. She wanted to run. Her knees gave out and she had to sit. Toni never raised her head, just sat there, mortified, and wishing to die.

Frances regained her composure, but she knew. Now she knew. "Stand up, please," France said.

Toni stood.

"Look at me, please."

The eyes that looked into Frances' eyes reminded her of the wounded puppy they had put to sleep many years before. He had been Keith's dog, and had been mysteriously injured so badly that they'd had to put him to sleep.

Under Toni's eyes were dark shadows. Her chin began to quiver and she tried to keep from crying.

"Please, Toni, let me help you. What happened to your breast?" she asked again. She waited. She wanted to scream because Toni really didn't have to tell her. She knew.

"Nothing's wrong, Mamma. It's just the reflection from the windows. Please believe me, I'm O.K."

Frances stood up, walked around the table and stood in front of Toni. She very gently reached down and untied the sash of her robe. She opened it and saw her daughter in law totally naked, totally exposed, and totally bruised from breast to public area.

"My God! Turn around, please," Frances said, having to force the voice from her throat. Toni, the whipped puppy that she had become, dutifully turned around for the woman to view her backside. Both of her beautifully formed hips were bruised and green, and the right hip still bore the perfect imprint of the letter "D", which was raised up on the back of the couple's matching silver hair brushes, a wedding gift from Max and Frances.

Now the tears came. First Toni and then Frances. Quickly Frances covered Toni's nakedness, both to ease the girl's embarrassment and to cover her son's crime.

"Please, Mamma, please don't tell Keith. He'll punish me more and I can't stand any more. Please."

Frances slumped down into her chair. She couldn't bear it. She looked at this wonderful girl and she knew hate like she'd never hated before. She hated Max. She hated Keith. She hated herself for allowing this to happen. She'd sold out years ago when she'd agreed to stay. She hated her empty God damned life filled with tennis and booze and devoid of love from either her husband or her son. She even hated her two daughters who had managed to escape from this hellhole she called home.

The one ray of sunshine in all of her miserable existence had been Toni. Frances had poured all of the love she had into this girl. How could she have been so blind all this time not to know that the miserable low-life she called her son was torturing her?

Everything fell into place now. The long sleeves Toni wore in the summer, the muffled screams, which only Frances seemed to hear, the fear of being alone in the house. God, it wasn't fear of being alone, it was fear of being alone with him!

Frances wasn't even aware of leaving her chair. Grabbing her tennis racket which was leaning against the side of the table, she ran up the stairs two at a time, her feet barely touching the carpet as she ran. She burst through the door of his bedroom to find Keith, sitting red eyed and naked on the side of the bed, sheets rumpled and bloody, with one hand in the night stand searching for cocaine.

He heard the shriek before he saw his mother. Then all he saw was a streak of white coming toward him just as she hit him square in the face with her tennis racket.

"I've known for years that you were an evil devil, but I never knew before how bad you were. I'm sorry I brought you into this world, but so help me, God, you'll pay for this one. You'll pay for what you've done to Toni."

The impact of the tennis racket had knocked him backward into the headboard. He saw white flashes behind his eyes, and as he began to focus, he could see only his mother's face, close to him, red and ugly, and it looked as though it would explode with fury.

She swung again, but this time the tennis racket ricocheted off the headboard, cracking her on the shoulder. She screamed and fell to the floor.

Quickly seizing his opportunity, Keith jumped off the bed and onto her prone form. Hysterical, she was almost hyperventilating. Heaving and gasping, she tried to get up, but he easily subdued her and turned her over onto her back, her hands up over her head.

"You stinking bitch," he said into her face, "This is all your fault. For years I've heard you blame me for everything. I've watched you stand with your drink in your hand and tell everyone how you could easily have been a model. Shit, woman, you're a skinny rag. Look at yourself. You call yourself a mother? Where were you when I played Little League? Not there. Where were you when I played my school football games? Not there. Where were you when I started wrestling? Not there. You made every game and every play any of the others were in, but not me. You've never been there for me in my life and you've always wished it had been me killed in Japan instead of Gregg. I hate you. And now you have the nerve to be mad at ME because of something I did to Toni?

Just who is that bitch, anyway? I only married her to get back at Omar. I wanted her because she was a virgin and because she was his sister. Man, I don't even get turned on when I look at her, just like my dad doesn't get turned on by you. The only pleasure she gives me is when I'm hurting her. I like to see how much she can take. I hate her as much as I hate her brother, and it isn't going to stop, so you do whatever you want to, Bitch."

Heaving with anger, he jumped off of his mother, backed up and leaned against the dresser.

"So you hate me?" she said as she got up. "Well, I'll let you tell it to the police. I've already called them and they are on their way here now."

He didn't believe her for one minute. Stepping away from the dresser, he grabbed Frances by the arm and slung her toward the open door.

"Get the fuck out of here and send that Venezuelan bitch in here to me," he said. His eyes were burning as he stood in the center of the room. He was still naked and held a silver hairbrush in one hand, pounding it into the palm of the other. His eyes moved from his mother, focused on the door, and he smiled.

Standing there, eyes wide with fear, tears of pain, humiliation and rejection running down her face, was Toni. Frances turned, grabbed the girl and together they made their way back down stairs.

40

"No, officer, I don't know what you are talking about. It must have been a practical joke. No one in this household has fights. We are all God fearing Christians who server the Lord. You're welcome to come in and look around, though," said Max, a look of shock and bewilderment on his face.

The two officers had been escorted to the Sun Room, so named because one complete wall was glass, allowing a magnificent view. Max, ever the showman, had decided to greet the lawmen in this room, because it was so sunny and not ominous or threatening in any way. Other rooms in the mansion were so large and they weren't as friendly as this one. He wanted absolutely no suspicion in anyone's mind that his family was not functioning properly.

"We'll just look around, then," said one of Corpus Christi's finest. "How many people live here?"

"We have four, plus four servants," replied Max. Frances hadn't spoken a word. Instead, she sat with her arm around Toni, now dressed in long black pants and a long sleeved red silk blouse.

Max had returned home just in time to see Frances come flying out of Keith's bedroom door, and had been quickly brought up to date by her regarding today's happening. The only thing he understood in the whole scenario was that Frances had called the police.

"What?" he screamed at her. "Have you lost your stupid mind? All we need is some publicity like this now and not only won't we have any crowds at the shows, Lorenzo won't let Keith wrestle for him. You know how he is about bad publicity."

"That's all you care about?" Frances screamed. "Your son is a maniac pervert who tortures his wife and all you can think about is business?" she shrieked.

"Shut up for now," he had said, "and get her dressed and back down here. We have to get rid of the police, and then, if you keep your stupid mouth shut while they're here, I promise we'll handle this as soon as they leave," Max said.

Frances had stayed with Toni in her suite while she put on some clothes. Keith got dressed and followed his father downstairs, silent and sullen.

"Do you have any idea who could have made a complaint like this about you, Keith?" one of the officers was speaking. He was one of the police who regularly work off-duty hours providing security at the wrestling matches, and was paid by Keith and Max after the shows.

Keith, standing by the fireplace with a cup of coffee in his hand, laughed and said, "Hell, you know how the arena rats are, Ernie. Could have been any one of them trying to get back at me. They want me to party with them like I used to, but look at my wife. If you had her at home waiting, would you be playing around?"

"Absolutely not," agreed Ernie, looking at Toni, noticing with his practiced eye that she didn't appear to be the happiest person he had ever seen. Dull eyes looked back at him. He thought he noticed Frances shiver.

Ernie stood up from the squat he had affected to write on his clipboard, and put his pencil back in his pocket.

"Sorry for the inconvenience," he said. "Guess that's all part of being a celebrity. No privacy."

"We appreciate your coming out, anyway," said Max as he stood up and began to walk to the big double doors leading into the foyer. "See you Thursday night at the matches."

"Good night," said Ernie as he walked toward his partner. "Guess this wraps it up here, Tom," he said as they walked out the door.

Out on the sidewalk, Ernie took out his car keys as the two of them walked toward the squad car.

"If that ass hole didn't beat his wife up, I'll kiss your ass on Chaparral Street at high noon. That son-of-a-bitch is a wife beater if I ever saw one. Could you believe that crap about 'coming home to his wife?' Guess he doesn't think we know about the orgies at the house that he used to rent. I heard the reason he didn't ever take the Mrs. There to live was because he still goes over there for sex and drugs."

"I've been hearing rumors that he's a closet fag," said Tom.

"I wouldn't be a bit surprised."

*   *   *

As soon as the door closed after the two policemen, Max turned to Frances.

"You must have still been drunk from last night to pull a stunt like that, Frances," he said.

"I'm not drunk, I wasn't drunk, and you know it. You told me we would handle this problem if I kept my mouth shut to the police. I did and now it's up to you to do it. Your son is abusing his wife in every way possible," said Frances. "You've got to do something about it and tonight. I can't let her go back upstairs with him again."

"Now, Mom," Keith began as he walked over to where she sat. Squatting down in front of Frances where she sat next to Toni, he began his act.

"Now, Mom, you know I didn't mean all those things I said. I just get so mad sometimes that I don't know what to do. You jumped me before I got out of bed, shouting those awful things at me. I couldn't hurt my baby like that."

He stood up, walked over to the bar and fixed his mother a double on the rocks.

"Here, Mom, help you calm down."

Toni looked at Keith, squatted in front of her, smiling at his mother as though he thought she was the most wonderful thing since ice cream. He felt her looking at him and as his mother gratefully gulped her drink, he slowly turned his head, ever so slightly so that he could see Toni. Her eyes were riveted to his. The smile went out of his, and in its place she saw evil like she had never seen before. He was willing her to open her mouth. She knew if she did, he would surely kill her. She started to chill.

"Oh baby," came the syrupy voice of her husband. Let me fix you something that will warm you up."

Keith knew that Toni didn't drink. "Let me fix you something sweet for the sweet," he said. Once again he went behind the bar, into the refrigerator, and fixed his wife a White Russian. Two shots of milk, one shot of Kahlua, one shot of gin.

"Tastes just like chocolate milk," he said.

Toni tried the drink. It did taste good she had to admit. Later when he asked her, she consented to another. This time, he doubled up on the gin. When he took it to Toni, he also took another gin and tonic to Frances.

"I don't know what got into me, Mom, I think I need help. And Toni, I don't want to lose you, Baby, you mean the world to me. It is the cocaine. It makes me do bad things. Please, Baby, please give me one more chance," he begged.

"See, I told you it would be O.K.," said Max as he stood up to turn on Brother Watson and his Happiness Hour on the TV.

Toni's head started to spin. She hadn't had breakfast, and he had given her two stiff drinks. She wanted to believe him, she loved him so much, but she couldn't forget the conversation she had heard upstairs. He hated her. He hates his mother. He wanted to make Toni hurt. And his mother didn't have any idea of what all he had really done to her. Toni prayed that no one would ever know.

Keith sat down on the long couch between Toni and his mother. Divide and conquer, he thought to himself. Very carefully, he took Toni by the shoulder and drew her over against him.

"How could I have done this to you? You are so good and so pure. I must have been crazy. Please say you'll forgive me and we can start over just like all this never happened. You know I love you, Toni."

"Well, you two lovebirds need to work it out," said Max. "I'm going down to the office. You coming, Keith?"

That's right, stupid, thought Frances, Just like everything is O.K. God, I hate you!

"I can't leave Toni like this, Dad, I'm going to see that she's O.K., and then call a marriage counselor. Nothing matters to me except my beautiful wife. Not the business, nothing."

"Fine, Son, I'll see you when I get home." And he was out the door.

Toni was thrilled. Keith did love her. He was going to call someone, get some help. Maybe it would work after all.

Frances looked at Keith and couldn't hide the hatred that she felt, the revulsion at her own son. She was starting to feel the five drinks she had indulged herself with. She had two while she was waiting for the police; no, maybe it was three. Anyway, she had needed them this morning. Slightly light-headed now, she looked up at her son.

"Can I get you another shot, Mom?"

"I guess one more wouldn't hurt."

*　　　*　　　*

Three drinks later, Frances, Keith and Toni were all talking together. They had left the couch and the Sunroom and had decided to go outside and enjoy lunch on the patio by the pool.

"Lets all go in for a swim later," Keith suggested. It sounded fine to the intoxicated women. "Let's put our suits on now, we'll eat, and then swim this afternoon. That way I can work on my tan," he said. "Toni, let me help you put your suit on in the bath house," he suggested.

Fear gripped her. Through the fog of the White Russians, came a warning from her brain. NO!

She tried to say no, but the words wouldn't come. She saw Frances get up and walk into the women's dressing room to put on one of the many bikinis she had stored there. Since she had kept herself a size five her entire life, a bikini was nothing new to her.

"Stay here, Baby, I'll run up to the room and get one of your suits and help you put it on. The cool water will feel good to your bruises." He jumped up and disappeared into the house.

Toni lay back in the tanning chair to wait for him. She fell asleep, so it seemed like only a second before he was back. Frances had put on her black and white suit, and was in the middle of the pool, floating on a clear float that was complete with headrest and snack tray. She had a tall gin and tonic in the stand, sunglasses on her eyes, and was snoring like a lumberjack.

"Get up, Baby, and I'll help you with your suit."

"No, I can do it," she tried to fight him off, but couldn't lift her arms.

"Come on, I'll help you," he said, lifting her out of the chair and carrying her like a baby into the women's dressing cabana.

Toni felt like she was blind; they had gone from noonday sunshine into the blackness of the cabana. The cabana, cold from the air conditioning, was like stepping into midnight.

Keith switched on the light. Her eyes snapped shut involuntarily. Slowly she forced them to open and she looked around. She could see their reflection in the mirrors along one wall. He stood holding her cradled in his arms just as though she were a child. Carefully, he put her down and she stood on her two feet. Then her knees buckled.

"Whoa," he said, "Better let me help you." He laid her back in one of the huge wicker chairs. The cushion embraced her as she lay against the back.

Gently, lovingly, Keith removed her blouse and lacks, her shoes and hose, then her brassiere. She lay naked, exposed, and completely at his mercy.

As light as a feather, Keith cupped his hands around the swollen, bruised breast of his wife. "Poor baby," he said, "I'm so sorry. He gently began to rub the sore breast. He slowly leaned down and kissed it. Then he kissed the other breast. Then he kissed Toni's mouth.

"Please believe me, I do love you," he whispered as his mouth moved downward to kiss more bruises.

*   *   *

When Toni and Keith finally came out of the cabana, Frances was out of the water and sitting, wrapped in a towel, on a white deck chair. She hadn't stopped drinking, Keith noticed.

"Where are the damn servants when you need them?" she asked.

"I gave them the day off when I went inside a minute ago," said Keith.

"What? Why? Why would you do that?" Frances demanded.

"Because this has all been embarrassing and I don't want any tales told out of school. You know how people like to talk. I plan to call a counselor and I don't want it spread all over the world and I don't want to read about it in the National Tattle Tale next week," he said.

He really does mean it, thought Toni. Maybe this is what he needed. Maybe I should have told before. In the cabana was the first time since they'd been married that he had been gentle with her. He had told her just to lie back and enjoy. And after the first few minutes of fear, she had enjoyed. And now to hear him say he was going to counseling. Her heart fluttered. Her bruises miraculously didn't hurt as much now, and she was alive again. She also couldn't remember when he had gone this long without cocaine since they had been married.

All afternoon the three of them stayed outside, Keith and Toni in the pool and Frances in the shade under an umbrella.

Keith was as attentive to his mother all day, also. He carried drink after drink to her. She switched from gin and tonic to straight gin and never knew it. By five o'clock she couldn't stand up. By then, Toni was floating on the water, White Russians making her relaxed and calm. She was happy again. She was in love again. The horror that was her marriage was pushed to the back of her mind by one afternoon of tenderness and six White Russians.

The telephone rang, but although it was right beside her, Frances couldn't answer it. Through the fog of her brain, she barely heard Keith answering Max's questions from the other end.

"Yes, Dad, everything's fine. Mom's her usual self, passed out again. Toni and I are swimming and having a fine time. Yes, I'll take good care of her. You can count on that."

41

"C'mon over here, Baby," Keith said after he put the phone down in the cradle. Toni could hear him, but she couldn't raise her head to reply. Her first day of drinking would prove to be her last, and she was not doing well now.

"Paddle over here to me," he said with a smile on his face. It was lost on Toni. She couldn't even see his face. Finally, he gave up, jumped in the water and swam to her float.

Coming up to the side he said, "Hang on, Baby, I'll pull you to the side." Now Toni was getting motion sick.

"I don't feel so good," she said. "I need to lie down."

"Sure, Baby," he replied, "I'm gonna' take care of you."

In two strokes, Keith had Toni, float and all, over to the side of the large pool. She lay back, motionless, while he pulled himself out of the water.

Reaching down, he grabbed one of her arms and pulled her straight up and into his arms. He held her against him for a minute, then reached down and picked her up in his arms, just like he had when he had carried her into the cabana. Remembering what had happened to her there, she mumbled, "I wanna' go back to the cabana."

"I'm gonna' take you some place better."

Then she blacked out.

When Toni came to, she was in her own bed, naked and alone. She could hear Keith in the bathroom softly whistling. Turning her head to one side she could see into the open drawer of the nightstand. There they were. The cocaine and the tape that Keith had used over her mouth sometimes. Fear came up like bile into her mouth. But no, hadn't he said it would be different now? And hadn't he stayed off of cocaine all day? She had to believe him. He was her husband and he loved her.

The whistling became louder as Keith came into the room. He was naked and sober. Even in her drunken stupor she could tell by his eyes that he hadn't been doing drugs.

"How do you feel, Wife?" The chill h it her. The eyes were bad again. He was the old Keith again. She tried to move, but couldn't.

"How about them White Russians? They're killers, aren't they? They're gonna' be tonight." He threw his head back and laughed at this own joke.

As Keith walked toward the bed his eyes darted to the nightstand.

"Have you touched anything in there?" he asked. "You're real familiar with everything in that drawer."

She didn't know whether it was the fear or the whiskey, but she felt so sick she couldn't raise her head off the bed.

"Let's see now," he said as he sat on the side of the bed. "Why don't you open the drawer wider for your husband?"

Toni couldn't raise her arm, so he picked her arm up, directed her hand toward the drawer and made her open it, revealing more of the contents inside.

"Tell you what, Baby, why don't you just reach in there and get yourself some 'stuff'? You're gonna' like it. Too bad you've had all that booze, it won't go too well with cocaine. Oh well, we'll see."

Toni lay there, frozen, unable to defend herself, too sick to scream and too drunk to move. Keith took out the zipper bag of cocaine and took out a pinch of white powder. He turned to Toni, eyes blazing, and roughly grabbed her shoulder, turning her over on her side facing him.

Now she knew what he was going to do. Only this time, instead of smearing the coke on his body, he held it pinched between his fingers.

"No," she screamed at the top of her lungs. "Mamma."

"Scream your brains out, bitch, she's too drunk to hear you and I gave the servants the day off, remember? I also told Dad that I'd be down later, so he'll wait at the office."

"Do it easy or do it hard, but you're gonna' do it, bitch," he said between clenched teeth. He grabbed her hair, pulled her head back and dropped the entire pinch of cocaine in one nostril.

Fire made its way up into her sinus cavities and she couldn't catch her breath. She saw colored lights behind her eyes, and had she not been choking, would have felt euphoria. Quickly he funneled cocaine into the other nostril. Again the lights, the choking, she still couldn't breathe.

Gratefully, she could finally catch her breath but she still couldn't raise her head. He had finally let go of her hair.

"You ever heard of 'rough sex', bitch?" he asked. "That's what I'm gonna' tell them happened to you."

Those were the last words she ever heard. He filled her nostrils once again with cocaine and the last thing she ever saw was the blue pillow as he lowered it over her face.

*   *   *

It was 10 PM when Max's car pulled into one of the garages behind the mansion. He could see that no lights were on in the house, but there were lights on in one of the cabanas and around the pool.

God damn it, I've told her to put the lights out before she goes to bed.

He lumbered out of the car, made his way up the stone sidewalk that led to the pool area, and came around the side of the patio.

"Frances," he screamed, "For Christ sake, get up. You look indecent out here sprawled all over a chair in a bikini. For God's sake, woman, act your age."

Her eyes snapped open as if the brain inside was physically forcing them. It was she against the gin, and the gin was about to win.

"Where's Toni?" she asked, fear smashing into her with sudden impact. Her eyes flew open now.

"I don't know. I just got home," he said, "What happened after I left?"

"Well, we had a few drinks and then decided to come outside. Keith was courting her all over again. He was so charming. I wish I could believe him,F but Max, you didn't see that girl's body. She was covered with bruises. One time just could not have done that much damage. I think he's been abusing her since the day they got married.

"Nonsense, he's a big man. He probably accidentally bruises her when they are playing around," he said, a picture of his son in his mind.

"Don't be so stupid. He's not as big as you are, and to get her breast completely black, you'd have to do more than accidentally hurt someone. It was black, I tell you.

"Where are they now?" he asked.

"I don't know. He fed me drinks all afternoon. I should have known better, but they seemed so happy. She was even drinking White Russians. He told me again that he was going to call a counselor. I hope he means it, Max, but I don't believe him at all.

"You never do give him a break," Max started. Then he stopped.

They both heard it at the same time. "Noooo, Noooo"

"What in hell was that?" asked Max. "It sounded like it was coming from the house."

They both ran, Max with his bad knees, Frances reeling from drink. They made it up the stairs together, following the wailing sound. They both stopped outside Keith's bedroom door.

Max quickly turned the doorknob and threw the door open. There, inside, Frances' worst nightmare had come true.

Totally naked, Keith stood next to the bed where the body of Toni lay, white powder around her mouth, in her nose, all over her naked body.

Keith's head was down, his hands were at his side, and he was repeating over and over, "Noooo, Nooo–"

Frances knew the girl was dead, and she knew that Keith had killed her.

"What happened, Son?" asked Max. "Tell me what happened."

"We came up here to be alone, Dad. Toni had been drinking White Russians all day and we were both feeling pretty good. I had promised to go to counseling and start all over, and I hadn't touched cocaine all day. Mom will back me up on that." He looked at Frances. She was suddenly very sober.

"She said she wanted to do some coke, and I said, 'You shouldn't, you've been drinking'. Anyway, she did, and we started to make love. She wanted me to get rough. You know, she liked that, Dad, she really did."

Frances wanted to vomit. She knew that Toni had never done cocaine in her life, except when Keith had forced her to.

"She kept shoving cocaine everywhere, and finally she got too much up her nose and couldn't catch her breath. I tried to help but I couldn't. Nothing worked."

"Why didn't you call the servants?" Max asked.

"He gave them the day off today," said Frances, "We'd better call the police."

"No way do you call the police," said Max. "My son isn't going to be investigated. Call Doctor Jenkins, the wrestling doctor. He'll sign the papers we need."

*   *   *

42

When the plane sat down in Corpus Christi at ten o'clock that Friday morning, Omar and Nancy were the first to deplane. Neither said a word. Omar was lost in thought, remembering when he had met Toni here at this same airport a lifetime ago. He had come here to tell her hello and now he was here to tell her goodbye.

As they walked across the airport, making their way to the baggage pickup, Omar glanced at the front door. He couldn't believe his eyes. Standing there was Lorraine Black, now Women's Wrestling Champion, waiting to escort the two of them to the cars waiting outside. Lorraine walked up, without a word, and hugged Omar. Then she turned to Nancy and not knowing the woman but seeing that she was there with Omar, she hugged her, also.

She said, "There are a lot more of us outside, but because of the crowds, the rest are in their cars.

After picking up their luggage, the three made their way out the front door. There at the curb, lined up bumper to bumper, were the big cars of the wrestlers from Wild West Wrestling. Inside, all patiently waiting were Cochise and Marilyn, Glen Massey, Cowboy Nelson, and Gorilla Lopez. Keith was very noticeably absent.

The trunk of the new Cadillac swung open, Lorraine tossed the luggage in, and Omar and Nancy climbed in with Cochise and Marilyn. The whole operation had taken place with the split second timing of a wrestling promotion, with no fanfare, no notice, and in good taste.

After introducing Nancy to Cochise and Marilyn, Omar asked where they were going. He hoped it was not to Max and Frances' house. He never wanted to see any of those people again in his life. The sorriest day of his life was when he left his sister with them. They had offered her sanctuary and gave her betrayal.

"We're going to the funeral home first," said Cochise, "and then after the funeral, you two can stay with Marilyn and me for as long as you want."

"Thank you, Cochise," said Omar, "but the minute the funeral is over, we'll be leaving. This town holds no good memories for me, and I have told Lorenzo to book me tomorrow night in Houston. I have to keep busy to keep my mind off of everything. I'm afraid I'm really having a hard time, Amigo."

Nancy slipped her hand into his, and noticed that he did not return her show of affection. His hand was like stone. Not moving.

"We'll help you in any way we can, Omar. Just say the word."

"Can you tell me when she got hooked on drugs, or why, or anything? I can't get a word out of Max or Frances, and of course, Keith is enjoying keeping me in the dark."

A quick look passed between the lovers in the front seat.

"We have heard stories, Omar, but you know how this business is. You really can't go by what you hear. We never saw a mark on Toni, and she kept so to herself that we didn't really think anything was wrong," said Marilyn. "She stayed in the house with Frances so much and she never came to the matches. They were getting ready to buy a new home and everything. She had so much to live for."

"The thing I can't understand," Omar continued, "is why she would kill herself now. She's been through two revolutions, poverty, coming over here scared to death, and she wanted Keith so much that she defied me for the first time in her life. To give up now that she had everything that she wanted didn't make sense.

"Sometimes it's better not to delve into things in the past," said Cochise, trying to console the big man. "Nothing will change now, and the more you try to make sense of it, the worse it will probably be."

"I know," answered Omar.

The foursome drove in silence the rest of the way to the funeral home.

He wasn't sure he could make this ordeal. He'd buried his father and his mother had died while he was in the United States. Now he had to bury his baby sister. It was too much. Maria had flown in from Venezuela. What would he tell her? She didn't know about drugs. She only knew that her baby sister, the one she had raised since childhood—was dead.

As they pulled up in front of Shady Grove Funeral Home, he saw Maria standing outside. He jumped out of the car before it even stopped rolling.

"Maria, Maria," he cried. She turned, running, and grabbed him like she would never let him go. They were both crying now, openly, unashamed. Embarrassed, Cochise, Marilyn, and Nancy walked ahead, into the quiet foyer of Shady Grove.

Soft music was playing, the harps of Venezuelan music crying for Toni. Candles were in banks along one wall of the hallway.

"She's in room four," said Maria in English so that all could understand.

Omar had known fear before. He had been afraid when he saw the soldiers drive up and take aim at his father. He had been afraid when he stepped on the ship taking him to America. He had been afraid when he watched Toni become the bride of Keith Daniels. But none of those fears could touch the fear he felt as he approached the body of his beloved baby sister, Toni.

She lay on a white satin cushion and wore a white satin, high-necked gown with lace encircling her beautiful long neck. Her black hair cascaded down onto both her shoulders. In Toni's beautiful, long fingered hands she held a white bible and rosary, and placed beside her face was one, beautiful, perfect orchid. Frances had remembered.

As he gazed down, he took the last final look at the person who meant the most to him in the entire world, and he knew that he would never be the same again. He would go on, but he would never be the same. He looked up into the faces of his friends, all gathered around, and saw reflected in the candle light, raw, open grief. They cried, not for Toni, but for him.

In the cool, hushed funeral chapel, Omar asked Nancy to join him in the family section of the pews. She, Maria and he waited. At exactly two o'clock, when the funeral was to begin, the side door was suddenly opened, and the sun shone in. A flurry of movement, and he saw that Keith, Frances, Max, and the two daughters had entered the building. They all made their way up to the front where Toni lay surrounded by flowers.

Frances, completely in black, with black hat and veil, stood silently looking down at her daughter in law. To everyone's amazement, she suddenly leaned down, bent over Toni's face, and whispered into her ear. No one heard, and no one tried to hear. It was between the two of them.

Next came Max, all 255 pounds of him, lumbering up to the casket on old football-injured knees.

He had a bible in his hand, and tears were streaming down his once handsome face. "My daughter, my daughter," he said, loud enough for the congregation to hear, "We could have helped you."

Then came Keith. Unshaven, gray wrinkled suit, no tie, he was the picture of despair. He hung onto the side of the casket, he cried, he beat his chest and screamed, "Why didn't you tell me? I loved you so." He bent down, plucked a flower from one of the baskets and rammed it into his coat pocket just before his legs went out from under him. His two sisters helped him back to a chair next to the door.

The music began. The service was conducted in Spanish and in English. The priest told everyone what they already knew about Toni, and then invited them to the interment at the Shady Grove Cemetery.

Omar and Maria, Max and Frances stood at the door as everyone filed out. All of the wrestlers hugged the four of them, and went quietly to their cars to wait in line for the procession to the cemetery. Within twenty minutes, everything was ready to finalize the goodbye.

First the hearse pulled out carrying Toni's body. Then the limousine followed carrying Omar, Nancy and Maria. The third automobile carried Max and Frances. The wrestlers followed.

In their grief, no one noticed Keith sneak out the back door of the funeral chapel, climb into Brenda's car, and hand her one long stemmed American Beauty Rose.

43

Nancy lay in bed, looking out the window and wondering about Omar. She couldn't get him off her mind or out of her heart. It had been four days since the funeral. She could still feel the sinking sensation she had felt at how unresponsive he had been to her touch.

The ride home was quiet, cold and long. Lost in his own suffering, he hardly acknowledged that she existed. He didn't even get out of the car and walk her to the door. She had stepped out onto the curb and his only words had been, "Goodbye, Nancy." She had played it over and over in her mind until she could scream. Was it goodbye for the night, a few days, or forever? Wanting to give him time, she hadn't called. She had hoped he would call her.

Nancy looked at the alarm clock next to her bed. Three o'clock and she had to get up at six thirty and get ready for work. How could she possibly face the day? Her eyes were swollen and her nose red. Makeup can only do so much.

I've got to call him. I can't keep doing this. I'll lose my job. Quickly, before she lost her nerve, she reached for the phone. Her hand lay immobile. After a minute of doubt, she dialed his number, held her breath and prayed silently that he would answer.

"Hello"

A pause, and then, "Omar? This is Nancy. Are you asleep? Are you all right? Can we talk? " When she did start talking, she babbled on as if she was afraid he would hang up if he had a chance.

"Nancy," he began, "I'm all right. I was asleep, but not now. What do you want?" He was so quiet and business-like, it was as though he had slapped her. This was not her Omar. This was a stranger.

"I don't want anything. I was worried because I haven't heard from you."

"I'm O.K., but could we talk tomorrow?"

Her heart was heavy. Somewhere, deep inside of her, she felt a door shutting. She was very afraid of this conversation. She wanted to stop it and didn't know how.

"Shall we meet at 'Mandy's Place' around six thirty?" she asked timidly.

"Not 'Mandy's,'" he replied, "Too many of the guys would be there. Meet me at the Italian Gardens down the block. You know where that is. Good night, Nancy."

"Good night, Omar. See you tomorrow."

It was over. She knew it. He didn't even have to show up. But she knew he would.

How will I be able to sit there and listen? She thought. But nothing more could be done tonight. She turned over in bed and cried again until the alarm clock rang to begin the long day ahead of her.

*   *   *

Nancy was already seated in the back booth of the Italian Gardens. It was usually a great place to go. Green and white umbrellas were on white tables for outdoor eating. From the patio you could see downtown and yet feel the country because of all the plants and trees strategically placed.

But this evening was not festive for her. In a way, she just wanted to get it over with. Maybe she would end it herself. Save him the trouble, and at least she could walk away with some pride left. There's a lot to be said for pride. No one was going to laugh at her. It had probably been just one more roll in the hay for him.

She looked up from her wine and saw him coming straight toward her. Damn him, she thought. Damn him to hell. I love him and I'll sit here and die by inches, I know it. But, if there's only one small chance that he loves me, I'll take it.

"Hi," she said.

"Hi," he smiled sadly and slid into the booth across from her.

Here it comes, she thought, this is it.

"Nancy," he began, "I know I've hurt you these last few days and I'm sorry for that. You're a wonderful woman and we've had a great time together."

Oh, God, no, she cried inside.

"I will never forget you. But, right now it's not fair to ask you to be around me. I am filled with guilt and bitterness and hate. I would destroy you in no time. You need someone to love you and to take care of you. Right now, I have no love, no passion, and no tenderness. I must use all my energy to get through each day. I can forget only for awhile. Only in the ring."

He reached across the table and took both of her hands in his. It was the only time he had touched her.

"I don't know how long it will take. I have no right to ask you to wait. I'm not really sure that I want you to. Can you understand? I have to go through this alone and I don't know who I'll be after I come through it. I'm so sorry you got mixed up with me." His head fell forward slightly and they sat there in silence, holding hands.

"Omar, look at me," Nancy said. He slowly raised his eyes to hers. Large tears ran silently down her cheeks and were lost.

"I don't regret one minute we spent together. And I thank you for all of it. I understand your sorrow over Toni. Totally. But you were a good brother and she made her own choices. Some day you will get over this. You'll never forget her, but in time, you'll remember the good times, too. I love you with all my heart. I always will. If the day comes and you still want me, you know where I am. But please, don't come 'home' until you're sure it is for good. I can't go through this again. If you hurt me again, I will hate you then as much as I love you now. Thank you for telling me the truth. I know how hard this must have been for you."

His eyes softened and he started to say something. Nancy stopped him by putting her finger to his lips.

"Shhh," she said, "Please don't say anything more." Sliding slowly out of the booth, she let go of his hands. "While I still have a shred of dignity left, I'm going through that door. Goodbye, Mi Amor," she said, walking away quickly.

"Goodbye, Mi Amor," he whispered.

* * *

Nancy's life had finally gotten back on track. She had stopped crying most nights. If she knew Omar was to be in the office, Kelly or one of the other girls would take her place. Even Lorenzo knew she was having a hard time. At first, the girls had questioned the red eyes and Nancy told them everything, holding nothing back. By telling the story herself, the usual office rumors didn't fly as fast or last as long.

Several times during the first few weeks, men asked her out and the girls wanted her to double date with them. But she turned them all down. Most of the time the lonely young woman went straight home or to a movie alone and then home to her empty apartment. The tears may be gone, but the memories were as fresh and as painful as a paper cut. So, she went on with her life and job. She could keep busy during the day and keep her mind from whirling and turning. The entire company was caught up in the big match at Madison Square Garden, but she knew she would not attend. She knew who was in the main event. The day of the match as she sat at her desk, Kelly walked by on her way to the publicity department.

"Hey, Nancy, some of the girls who aren't going to the match tonight are going to get together at Dominique's for drinks. Please say you'll come." Nancy was delighted. She wouldn't have to think about Omar tonight, wondering how he was, how he looked,–.So, to Kelly's surprise, Nancy had said 'yes' and now five excited young women sat at Dominique's, drinks in hand, scoping out the men. Several sat around the bar, eyeing the women, dancing and talking. Nancy began to think she should have done this a long time ago. She hadn't laughed like this for weeks and weeks. She and the others danced again and again.

By eleven o'clock, several men sat at their table and everyone had 'coupled off". Stan, Nancy's companion was well built, somewhat older and had "old world charm". His three-piece business suit and white shirt gave the overall impression of a successful businessman. In every other way he was the exact opposite of Omar. Gray hair and light blue eyes, his face reflected his kind disposition. Because of this, she was totally at ease with him. The four glasses of wine helped. As they all laughed and talked, Stan whispered in her ear and lightly kissed her neck. She leaned into him and whispered back.

The two of them rose and made their way to the dance floor to join the other dancers in a rhumba. After only a few minutes, the other couples cleared the floor to watch them dance. They moved as one. Each felt the music the same way, in the same rhythm. Stan was a strong lead and Nancy followed his every move. Side steps, twirls, even the head movements looked professional.

When it was over, everyone applauded as they made their way back to their table. Hot, tired and exhilarated, they were proud and pleased at their own performance. Neither could explain it; it was as if they had been dancing together all of their lives. Again and again they moved to the dance floor and danced each piece of music, regardless of the tempo.

Finally, almost closing time, Stan whispered in her ear. "Shall we go?" They both knew what he meant.

"Yes," she answered, leaning against his chest. She wanted to leave before the club turned up the lights to signify the closing for the night. Nothing spoils an illusion as quickly as bright lights or close inspection.

When they reached her apartment, she invited him in. Over coffee, they got more acquainted. She found him to be very warm and caring. Maybe this could work out, she thought. As they sat on the couch in front of the fireplace, he kissed her. As she tried to work up enthusiasm and passion, Omar's face was there. His smell. The memory of his arms. She couldn't do it. She backed away from Stan, gently, not wanting to hurt his feelings or to lead him on.

"I'd better say good night," she smiled. "Tomorrow will be here soon." He got the point. Being the gentleman that he was, he quickly said good night and promised to call soon. As he left, Nancy burst into tears and ran for the shower.

Why, why can't I put him behind me? she cried. But she knew why. She loved him. When she could finally pull herself together, she slept, dreaming erotic dreams and rolling and tossing.

She awoke with a buzzing noise in her head. She looked at the clock. The alarm hadn't gone off, it was only five thirty. What could it be? As her head cleared a little, she realized it was the doorbell ringing.

Who can that be? She was caught up in the fear everyone everywhere has who has ever been awakened in the middle of the night.

Grabbing her robe as she ran, she called, "Who is it?" No answer.

Finally, she threw caution to the wind and opened the door. "I said, 'who is it?"

She did not need to ask again. There he was, the maker of her dreams, the center of her life, her heart. Omar had come back.

44

Madison Square Garden. The top, The Roman Coliseum. Every wrestler dreams of working in "The Garden." The show is bigger, the crowds large, the pay the top.

Tonight's championship match had been sold out for two months and Lorenzo had spared no expense. The pyrotechnics alone would be ten thousand dollars extra. More stage hands, ushers and security had been purchased. Tonight would be the wrestling match of the decade.

Paulie, the booker of all times, had not been unaware of the situation between Keith and Omar. The death of Toni had been the talk of the wrestling world for months. Everyone had skirted around saying what they all feared to be true. Toni's death had been no accident. No one knew how Max had managed to pull the cover up of the century, but he had. The death went down officially as a suicide; everyone knew in his/her mind who the guilty party was. Everyone knew that Frances had left Max and entered a mental hospital where she was currently under heavy sedation, even after all this time. Max continued to run wrestling in his Texas territory. But Keith, after his first encounter with Paulie "one on one" was actually expecting big favors from Paulie, and Paulie was going to give him one. At a price that Keith would never forget. Paulie would make Keith Champion, and Keith would be under personal contract to Paulie "for the duration". It had made Keith's skin crawl at the thought of being under Paulie's control for the rest of his career, but he believed he could "handle the little fag" when the time came. Even though he hadn't managed it on the first occasion.

At first, Omar wouldn't consider giving the belt to Keith. He swore to himself and Nancy that he would never let it happen. He had other things in mind for Keith. But after several months, it had become perfectly clear to Omar that Keith and Max would prevent any personal confrontation between the two of them at any cost.

So, at last Omar had decided that if he were ever to get his revenge on Keith, it would be in the ring, in front of thousands of people. Losing his belt would be worth it Lorenzo had promised a rematch and regaining the title. Omar didn't plan to ever have a rematch. This would be no regular wrestling match.

He signed the contract.

For weeks now, Keith and Omar had been making T.V. promos, promising to annihilate each other when the met in the ring. The fans believed what they saw, mainly because they had been literally bombarded with the television and radio "spots" over the last few weeks. Lorenzo had purchased the spots not only in New York City, but also in every small town in a two hundred-mile radius. Wrestling fans will easily drive two hundred miles to see a spectacular if it is hyped hard enough, and they want to see the match.

*   *   *

Keith left his car and walked up the ramp in the back of the building. Fans were standing on both sides, held back by the security guards. Two stagehands came running, one on each side of him, eager to carry his wrestling bag or his small suitcase.

"Keep your hands off my shit!" he screamed at them as they tried to take the bags. The fans, quiet until now, immediately started to boo and make catcalls at him.

"Screw You!" he said, throwing his head back and slipping into his "ring strut." Someone threw a cup of beer on his Brooks Brothers suit. Before the two ushers could get out of the way, Keith had thrown down his suitcases; he managed to knock the legs out from under one man, and he threw the other man to the ground in an attempt to get over him. Keith realized that Security would nab the fan immediately, so he fumbled with the two fallen men just long enough to enable Security to do their job. He spun around and ran over to the place where the beer-thrower lay prone, face down on the ground between two police who were calling the paddy wagon.

"Not so tough now, are ya', scum bucket?" Keith said, as he jumped high in the air, bent his right knee under him, and landed full force on top of the helpless man. The force of Keith's knee hitting the small of the back directly over his kidney caused so much pain that the man passed completely out. Fans screamed and surged toward Keith. Enraged that this man would injure someone lying totally helpless on the ground, they wanted Keith.

"Get out of here, Man," said one of the security police, "I can't promise that we can hold them back any longer. You realize you're gonna' get sued." It was a statement rather than a question.

Keith started to run. He was glad that the two ushers had taken his suitcase inside. He bolted through the back door into the darkness of the stage area. The ushers were standing guard over his suitcases.

"I told you not to touch my shit!" he screamed.

*   *   *

Back stage was alive with people. Technicians were testing the fog machine and pyrotechs were assembling the fireworks. The hairdressers, makeup artists and dressmakers were all running to and fro, each with his own destination, his own tasks.

Lorenzo looked up from his clipboard and came over when he saw Keith. Holding out his hand he said, "Glad to meet you at last. Paulie has been telling me about you." Lorenzo smiled and looked through Keith's eyes, straight into his brain. He smiled again.

Keith's face burned. He wondered what Paulie had been telling Lorenzo. He'd better not be saying much, or he'd kill the little dwarf bastard!

"I understand you had some trouble outside," Lorenzo said.

"Yeah, you'd better take care of that for me," responded Keith. "Maybe you should call your lawyer."

Lorenzo's eyes clouded over and Keith couldn't tell what he was thinking.

"We'll talk about that later," the promoter said.

Lorenzo led Keith down a long, narrow hall. There were two dressing rooms. As they passed the first, the door opened and Keith could see into the large, well lit room, lockers on every wall, and long wooden changing benches down the center of the room. He saw eight men, tonight's baby faces. Some were playing cards, some were undressing, and one was shaving his legs and body in keeping with the tradition of baby faces shaving their entire bodies. Baby faces are smooth, heels are hairy.

Then his eyes focused on one lone figure against the wall. Omar sat alone, away from the rest, completely ready for the ring. Staring into space, oblivious of all the other men, he sat grieving and silent. The usual horseplay between the men was not present out of respect for Omar and his sorrow. Where once their friend had been a laughing, loving person, he was now sad, dejected, and lonely for the little sister who had been with him through political revolutions, poverty, good times and bad.

Toni had never known that he was finally the champion. For that he would be eternally sorry. For leaving her with Keith he would be eternally guilty. Slowly his sad eyes turned and focused on the two figures in the doorway. They stopped on Keith. They stared. They didn't blink, and they were still burning in the empty space as Keith walked away. Toni had been dead one month.

Lorenzo, suddenly realizing his poor manners, turned back to Keith and said, "I was sorry to hear about your wife's death."

"Oh well, the show must go on."

Lorenzo shivered. *Man, that's cold*, he thought.

* * *

The heels' dressing room was a replica of the baby faces'. *Shit, I must be the last guy here*, Keith thought to himself. He could hear the showers running in the next room. No one spoke to him first, the newcomer. In his inexperience, he didn't know that he should speak first out of respect. He knew nothing of respect.

Some of the men were in the showers, he could see wrestling bags opened, contents spilled out around them, towels tossed casually on benches, and saw lockers with padlocks on them, testimony to the fact that the clothing and valuables of the men were inside.

This sure as hell isn't like back home, he thought. *Those ass wipes would be around me like stink on shit by now.*

Selecting a locker, Keith threw the small suitcase inside and threw his wrestling bag on a bench. He'd shave and shower before the matches. He gathered up his gear and headed toward the noise of the showers.

The lavatories were lined up on one wall, ten of them, complete with mirrors and makeup lights. The heels were in various stages of readiness, from total nakedness to dressed for the ring and jumping rope.

Keith found an empty lavatory and, spreading his shaving gear over the top, proceeded to lather his face. *You assholes don't speak to me tonight, but tomorrow you'll all treat me with respect when I'm the new champion*, he thought. Lost in thought, his hand slipped and he cut his chin and dropped his razor.

"Ring time two minutes," came the voice of a stagehand outside the door.

This is it, Loser, he smiled to himself as he imagined Omar's face tonight when he lost the title. *This is what makes it all worthwhile.*

Opening the door to the long hallway, he very carefully stepped out, glancing toward the baby faces' dressing room door, not wanting to face Omar alone.

The way he looked at me, no telling what he's liable to do.

Quickly walking the long hallway, Keith emerged behind the stage. Baby faces would exit on one side, heels on another.

"Hold it, Keith," called Lorenzo from the stage where he was overseeing the activities. "Wait until you hear your name before you go through the door. Watch the T.V. monitor."

Keith saw it then. An 18" screen T.V. monitor had been strategically placed so that the wrestlers could see what was happening in the arena before they entered.

Pretty fancy, he thought. *I'll have to call Dad and tell him to start doing this back home.* He watched, fascinated, and saw what the T.V. audience would see and hear when the show aired on television.

"Ladies and Gentlemen, the main event of the evening, one fall, sixty minute time limit match for the HCW Heavyweight Championship of the World."

He watched on the monitor as the stage lit up all at once. Fireworks had been placed strategically on frames, and at the precise moment, everything happened at once.

The announcer said, "The Challenger, from Corpus Christi, Texas, weighing in at two hundred and twenty-five pounds, Keith Daniels."

Immediately the fireworks went off and created the American flag in lights. So bright it hurt your eyes, the flag was made up of over two thousand cartridges and not one dud. There was Old Glory, "stars and stripes" ablaze, made from fireworks.

From the center of the fifty two stars, a dais was raised, and a country western singer, dressed completely in red; boots, pants, shirts and guitar, began singing, "The Eyes of Texas." The fans cheered and stomped, some for the flag, some for the singer.

Back stage, a cue card was placed over the picture. The monitor said, "Enter" and Keith went through the door.

Suddenly bathed in light from the spotlight, he flicked his wrist at the audience, tossed his head back, started his strut, and slowly made his way up the fifty-foot aisle toward the ring.

The cheers turned to boos. Catcalls and hisses; Keith was so easy to hate.

He hoped he looked good. He'd oiled his body and doubled up on steroids to try to bulk up for this match. He couldn't figure it. He'd been getting steroid shots from his old man since he was nineteen and had little to show for it. Cowboy Nelson takes them six months and doubles his size. Keith had never cared to acknowledge the fact that for steroids to build muscle, you have to work out, also.

*   *   *

He was in the ring now. He found his corner and turned the direction of the baby faces' entrance.

"Now Ladies and Gentlemen, our champion from Caracas, Venezuela, weighing in a two hundred sixty pounds, Omar Atlas.

Again the fireworks, only this time they formed the Venezuelan flag; three wide horizontal stripes; yellow, blue and red, with a rainbow of seven stars in the center of the flag. As they began to burn down, the dais raised once again, this time to bring a Venezuelan singer in white tuxedo, singing "Alma Llanera."

When the song was over, the crowd was on their feet, stomping and cheering. Then from the dressing room door ran the champion, Omar Atlas.

The roar of the crowd was deafening. He ran past the people who were trying to touch the champion, dressed entirely in black and magnificent with the jeweled belt around his waist. As was his usual style, he grabbed the top rope and vaulted over into the ring.

No one knew as they watched this star with the dazzling smile, glittering eyes and smooth brown skin, how he suffered. The smile was frozen on his lips, and he was conscious of only one feeling: burning, tearing hate.

As he automatically went to his corner to remove the belt, he said to himself, *this is for you, Toni, tonight is for you.*

They met in the center of the ring. The brothers-in-law. Eyes sought eyes, hands clasped each other's hands. All the years of waiting were over for Keith. Tonight he'd be champion. And Omar would know he'd been screwed.

All the months of hating were over for Omar. Tonight he'd beat Keith within an inch of his life. And the fans would never know. They'd think it was part of the match. He'd been waiting for months to get his hands on this maricon, and now he was ready.

Heads bent, fingers entwined, they met in the age-old stance. Omar turned Keith's hands backward and applied pressure. It felt to Keith like his elbows would snap backward, and his wrists would break. Facing each other, Omar's eyes burned into Keith.

Deliberately, quietly, the challenger asked, "Know how Toni got hooked on coke? I did it." And then he laughed.

What? What was this pervert saying about Toni? He relaxed his grip a little, and Keith broke the hold.

Releasing one hand, Keith moved around behind Omar, pulled his arm up behind him, and stood behind him and whispered, "I put coke on my body and made her lick it off. She hated it for awhile, but after a few beatings, she decided she loved it. Hell, after awhile, she was begging for it."

Omar was shocked into action. Adrenaline flowed so fast his ears rang and he couldn't hear the filth that was pouring out of this animal's mouth. He didn't want to hear.

Pushing with all his might, Omar backed into the ropes, reached behind him, grabbed Keith, not by the neck as he was supposed to do, but rather by the hair on the back of his head. He dragged Keith over his shoulder and dropped him to the mat at his feet. It was a move appreciated by all except Keith, who lost a handful of hair.

Shrieking with indignation and pain, foam coming from both corners of his mouth now, Keith chopped Omar in the neck, and when Omar fell, Keith fell on top, talking all the way.

"Man, I h ad to force it up her nose—she'd choke and choke, but when I finally got her hooked, she'd come up begging for more. One time I made her…"

Omar lost it then. All the years of discipline went down the drain. He knew that he was going to kill this man and didn't care what the consequences were.

He had spent hours trying to figure out how his little sister Toni, the kindest, most gentle soul he had ever known could have turned into a cokehead. Now he knew. This piece of human scum had done it. He had killed Toni. Omar's world turned red as the reality of his sister's death rushed up to his brain, exploding behind his eyes.

No one saw it coming.

They saw Omar on his back on the mat with Keith smiling and talking into his ear, and then suddenly, Omar was up. He had Keith by the hair, running him into a turnbuckle, a ring post, and then he pulled him, still by the hair, out of the ring and into a corner post. Running around the outside of the ring, pulling Keith into the fence that surrounded the ring, finally he pulled him upright and punched him squarely in the face. He dragged the now unconscious man through the ropes and into the center of the ring.

The savagery of the attack held everyone motionless.

Omar was not in Madison Square Garden entertaining a crowd of people who had paid money to see him; he was in the center of the universe and he had the devil by the hair.

This would be his revenge for his father, this would be his revenge for his sister, and this would be the revenge for his lost childhood and all the nieces and nephews he would never have now because of this maricon faggot he held in his hands.

The crowd knew something was wrong. Blood poured from Keith's face and head and the referee was standing, speechless, motionless, frozen in time and space, unable to stop this terrible thing from happening. Another referee came running, hoping to stop the madness.

Omar stooped down, and in one motion, picked up the limp form. He walked around the inside of the ring with Keith held at arm's length straight over Omar's head, as he selected the place where he would throw this unconscious monster. The third row. He would splatter Keith over three rows of chairs. If he were still alive, he'd jump down, drag him back, and throw him again. Omar stepped back and took aim. People were running to get out of the way. They knew what was coming.

"This is for you, Toni, mi hermana," he screamed.

A hand was on his shoulder. A voice from the past whispered in his ear, "No, Omar, he's not worth it. No, mi amigo, put him down." It was Fantasma.

Still holding the limp body over his head, Omar turned and saw his mentor. "I told you we'd meet in America one day," his teacher said. "I start here next week, so I came down to see your match. Don't throw it all away for this piece of trash. Toni wouldn't want this. Put him down, my friend."

No one stirred. No one spoke. Time stood still. Omar looked into the face of his teacher, the man to whom he owed everything. An eternity later, Omar made his decision. He lowered his arms and dropped Keith over the top rope straight down onto the concrete below.

The bell rang and rang. The wrestling commissioner and Paulie came from the dressing room and conferred with the referee. Omar stood, head bowed, and then Fantasma led him, with crowds applauding as they passed, back to the dressing room.

Two ushers helped Keith to his feet, but his legs buckled under him when he tried to walk. One under each arm, they were halfway back to the dressing room when the referee announced:

"Ladies and gentlemen, the wrestling commissioner has decided that due to the severity of the attack on Keith Daniels by Omar Atlas, the championship will be awarded to Keith Daniels."

The crowd broke through the barriers and tried to pull Keith from the ushers' arms. Security came and held them back while the ushers dragged Keith, toes down, through the dressing room door. Paulie waited on the other side, smiling.

Such was the making of the new champion.

45

There had been no party to celebrate Keith's championship. No wrestler wanted to celebrate an unearned victory with someone as unpopular as Keith. He was the champion, but he had crossed the boundary of decency. A lot can be forgiven in the wrestling world—a lot can't.

Back in his hotel room where he had been unceremoniously dumped by two of Lorenzo's men after he'd been patched up at the hospital last night, Keith took the championship belt out of its felt-lined carrying case.

The beating had been worth it. The abuse by Paulie had been worth it. Because Madison Square Garden had been a sell out, he had carried away one of the largest purses ever won by a wrestler, and because Omar was so popular, Lorenzo and announced a rematch in one month. Hell, that meant that he'd have to deal with Paulie again.

Now that Keith was the champion, he knew that every woman he met would want him. Now he really had it made. He would use them all. They were all just like his mother. No good. She wasn't even there when he won the championship. Well, screw her! He didn't need her. Didn't last night prove that? He didn't need anyone.

Keith had a 10:10 flight back from New York and would be home by 3:30 AM. Tomorrow he'd see the old man and go to the office.

I guess they'll have some big party then.

The snow fell in sheets, driven by a hard wind from the north. Few people were standing on the streets of New York City in a snowstorm after dark. Keith was. Cold to the bone, he pulled his collar up to protect his neck.

Well, it took some doing, he thought, standing on the curb as he hailed a taxi. *Even with the old man pushing. The guys hated me because I never had to "do any jobs". Not me. Not my face. Let the gibronis do that shit.* Their scars were on the outside; his were on the inside.

He remembered what he had done with the booker to get the championship and how devastated he had been when he realized that he'd actually enjoyed it. The other guys could never find out. It would kill him. He had paid a high price for this match. Maybe too high. But it was done, no turning back now.

A cab pulled up and he got in for the ride to the airport. Immediately the cabby recognized him.

"Ain't you Keith Daniels? Man, I saw you last night. Can I have your autograph for the old lady?"

"Yeah." Keith signed the paper the cabby handed back to him.

"Got the shit beat out of you, didn't you?" the cabby laughed as he drove away.

* * *

Keith boarded the plane quickly. He eyed the stewardesses, wishing he wasn't hurting in every bone in his body. He sat down next to the window in the first class section. Shortly after the plane took off, the little blonde he had been watching came over.

"Would you like a drink, Mr. Daniels?" she asked sweetly. "We are so glad to have you on board."

"Yeah, thanks," he replied, giving her what he considered his hardest, sexiest look. Later, when she brought his scotch and water, he took a long, deep swallow, put his head back and shut his eyes.

Here's to all those ass holes who didn't want me to win. I can't wait to see them crawl. Now they'll have to admit I'm the toughest son-of-a-bitch in the ring. At least to my face!

A big, satisfied smile started slowly across his mouth and suddenly froze in terror.

There was a loud roar and the plane dropped for what seemed like miles. Finally, it pulled up level again, but the roar continued. The liquor in his belly turned to acid.

"What the hell?" he screamed as he looked out the window. The whole plane was shaking as though it would break apart and the sky had turned orange. Flames crept over the wing. There was a loud explosion and his whole world turned dark red. Time stood still and the silence was so loud it was deafening.

Nothing mattered now. Not the championship, not the money or the women, not tomorrow, just right now. His hands gripped the arms of his seat. His eyes were riveted to the fire outside the window.

The last thing he ever heard was the silence being broken by a God-awful sound starting in his soul and ending on his lips.

"M—o—t—h—e—r"

The end

About the Author

Charlotte Mijares was part owner and promoter of Southwest Championship Wrestling out of San Antonio, Texas and was one of only four women promoters in the business during the years 1970–1984.

In her capacity as Editor/Writer for the wrestling magazine which was sold at all of the live shows, she wrote all of the articles and worked with the printers in the layouts of the magazine.

Since her marriage to Omar Atlas in 1984, Charlotte has retired from the wrestling world. She and her husband still live in San Antonio, where she has started working on her next novel.